IT'S IN HER KISS

RACHEL LACEY

COPYRIGHT

1

Julia Vega closed her umbrella and ducked inside the brick building in front of her. She pulled the door shut behind herself, scuffing her wet boots against the mat as she glanced around to get her bearings. A directory on the wall showed that the production office she was looking for was on the second floor.

She entered the stairwell, grimacing as she caught a glimpse of her reflection in the window. The weather had really done a number on her hair. Luckily, she'd arrived early enough for today's audition that she should have time to polish her appearance before they called her back. A tingly feeling took hold in her stomach at the thought.

Jules had been performing on Broadway for eight years now, so the audition process was a familiar—albeit nerve-racking—experience for her. Today's audition was more stressful than usual for several reasons, most notably because she was auditioning for the lead.

This role, if she landed it, would be a dream come true, the culmination of a lifetime of training, the chance to step out of the chorus line and into the spotlight. She wanted it so badly, she could taste it, a hint of something sweet on her tongue, teasing her with the flavor of success. Or maybe that was just the lozenge she'd finished on the walk over.

On the second floor, she approached the receptionist, a woman about her mother's age with gorgeous silver hair and a friendly smile. Jules returned it with one of her own. "Hi, I'm Julia Vega for the four forty-five audition."

The receptionist glanced at her computer as she tapped several keys. "Ah, there you are. You're all set, Julia. There's a restroom at the end of the hall if you need to freshen up."

"Thanks so much," Jules told her gratefully as she headed down the hall. Once she'd closed herself inside the restroom, she peeled off her damp jacket and tucked it into her bag before pulling out her toiletry case. She spritzed her hair with a polishing serum, smoothing away the frizz that had resulted from her fifteen-minute walk in the drizzling rain. Then she reapplied her lipstick, painting her lips a shiny plum.

After repacking her bag, she surveyed herself in the mirror. She ran her hands over her blouse—almost a perfect match with her lipstick—making sure it was tucked neatly into her black slacks. Sucking in a deep breath, she made her way back to the waiting room. It was empty except for the receptionist and one other woman, who was probably waiting to audition for the same role. Jules sat across from her. She set her bag on the chair beside her and pulled out her water bottle and the tin of Grether's Pastilles she never auditioned without.

"Lozenge?" she asked the woman across from her, holding out the tin.

"Thanks, but I've got it covered," she answered, holding up an identical tin with a smile. She was about Jules's age—

late twenties or early thirties—with long, curly brown hair and a strikingly pretty face.

"Great minds," Jules joked as she popped a lozenge into her mouth. Nerves made her throat dry, and that was the kiss of death for an auditioning actress. "I'm Julia Vega...Jules."

"Sophie Rindell," the brunette answered.

"Are you reading for Bianca?" Jules asked. It was one of her more annoying habits, or so she'd been told. She felt compelled to make idle conversation in waiting rooms like this one. She couldn't help it. Apparently, nerves also made her chatty.

Sophie didn't seem to mind, though. "I am. You too?"

Jules nodded. "I don't know about you, but I'm really excited about this one. I don't get many chances to audition for a lead." *It's in Her Kiss* was an off-Broadway play, a brand-new production right here in Brooklyn, walking distance from her apartment.

"Same," Sophie said, leaning forward in her seat as her leg bounced with restless energy. "And a queer lead at that. It almost feels too good to be true."

"Yes, it's amazing," Jules agreed as her stomach gave a funny swoop. She embraced roles that challenged her as a performer, but playing a woman coming to terms with her sexuality hit uncomfortably close to home for Jules. Just being here was more of a statement than she'd ever made on the subject, as the casting team had expressed a preference for LGBTQ actors to audition for this role.

"Sophie?" the receptionist called. "They're ready for you."

Sophie sprang to her feet.

"Good luck," Jules said as Sophie gathered her things and stepped through the door into the audition room.

Jules pressed a hand against her stomach to calm the flutter of nerves there. Alone in the waiting room, she took the opportunity to run through the scene and the song they'd asked her to prepare. Her phone chimed with an incoming text message. She swiped it from her bag, revealing her mother's name on the screen.

Good luck! Can't wait to hear how it goes.

Thanks, Mami, she replied. *I'll call you later and let you know.*

Jules turned her phone to silent and sucked in another deep breath. No one else had entered the waiting room. She was probably the last audition of the day, which might work in her favor if she left the team with a positive impression, or the opposite if she didn't. Her agent had told her she should hear if she'd gotten a callback as early as tonight.

Jules ran through a few scales to warm up her vocal cords and crunched through what remained of her lozenge. The door opened, and Sophie reentered the waiting room.

"How did it go?" Jules asked.

"Really well, I think," Sophie said, a triumphant look in her eyes that Jules knew well, the look of an actress who had just nailed an audition.

"I'm so glad," Jules told her.

"Thanks." Sophie shrugged into her coat and headed for the exit. "Well...bye. And good luck."

"Thank you." Jules tapped her fingers against her thighs as the door closed, leaving her alone in the waiting room. It wasn't ideal, going in right after another actress had just wowed the casting team. Her stomach tightened uncomfortably, and her throat was dry again. She reached for another lozenge.

"Julia?" the receptionist called. "They're ready for you."

Jules grabbed her bag and lurched to her feet as that

cold, tingly sensation spread from her stomach through her whole body. She went through the door beside the receptionist desk and found herself in a large, white-walled room. A row of people sat facing her. Jules recognized the director, a petite woman named Kari Wong. She'd worked briefly with her before. Kari's black hair was pulled back in a neat ponytail, glasses perched on her nose as she gave Jules a nod in greeting.

"Hello," Jules said, clasping her hands loosely in front of herself. "I'm Julia Vega. It's an honor to be here today."

After brief introductions, the casting director, a man named Frederick Beck, spoke. "You can start with the scene where Bianca speaks to her friend, Melissa. Liz will read for Melissa." He gestured to the assistant seated beside him.

Jules nodded, sucking in another breath as she got into character. "I'm ready."

"You look sad today, Bianca. Is something wrong?" Liz read.

"No, it's...well, I've had something on my mind," Jules said.

"It's Trevor, isn't it?"

Jules gave a weak laugh, raking a hand through her hair as she let Bianca's discomfort become her own. "Yeah...Trevor."

"I knew it!" Liz said triumphantly. "You like him."

Jules let her eyes linger on Liz, giving her a veiled look of longing as Bianca wrestled with her secret feelings for her friend. "I like him, but I'm not sure I want to date him."

They finished the scene, and then Jules performed an upbeat song that would be part of a group musical number. She'd rehearsed it dozens of times, and yet, with the casting team watching, she flubbed the lyrics, beginning to repeat the first verse instead of moving into the second. Hopefully, it wasn't a fatal mistake, but it definitely wasn't the impression she'd wanted to make.

When she'd finished singing, the playwright, a short-haired woman named Maggie Tate, lifted a hand to get Jules's attention. "One last thing," she said. "As you know, *It's in Her Kiss* is a coming out story. I'd like to know how you feel about that responsibility, and are you comfortable kissing a woman onstage?"

Jules blinked like a deer in headlights. "Yes, of course," she blurted, hoping the team hadn't seen her momentary panic. She'd never kissed anyone onstage before, and she'd never kissed a woman, period. She'd thought about it, though. Lately, she'd thought about it kind of a *lot*, and *oh God*, she wasn't sure how she felt about her first time being onstage. But none of that mattered if she didn't do something to salvage this audition. "I really relate to what Bianca's going through, and I would consider it an honor to portray her journey onstage."

"Thank you," the casting director said. "We'll be in touch."

Jules thanked everyone for their time, gathered her things, and left. She didn't feel nearly as confident as Sophie had looked as she made her way back through the waiting room, and she wasn't at all sure she'd handled the question about Bianca's sexuality well. Jules jogged down the stairs, bursting with restless energy. Maybe she should change and go to the gym, anything to keep from sitting around her apartment waiting for the phone to ring.

The first thing she noticed as she stepped outside was that the rain had stopped, and thank goodness for that. The second thing was Sophie Rindell walking out of the coffee shop next door.

"Post-audition caffeination?" Jules called with a wave.

Sophie glanced over her shoulder, pausing so Jules could catch up to her. "Something like that. How did your audition go?"

Jules put on her jacket, sweeping her hair out from beneath the collar. "Good, I think."

"I'm glad," Sophie said.

They stared at each other for a few seconds of awkward silence. Making idle conversation in the waiting room was one thing, but Jules didn't make a habit of hanging out with her competition after the audition. Something told her Sophie didn't either.

"Which way are you headed?" Jules asked, halfway hoping they were going in different directions, an easy way to say goodbye.

Sophie gestured to the left. "I don't live too far from here, near Prospect Park."

"Oh yeah? We're practically neighbors." Jules fell into step beside her.

"You audition a lot?" Sophie asked.

"Every chance I get," Jules told her with a laugh.

"Same." Sophie gave her a thoughtful look. "You look vaguely familiar to me. Maybe we've crossed paths before."

"It's possible," Jules agreed. They fell into an easy conversation as they walked, discovering that they'd auditioned for several of the same productions, although maybe not at the same time, and Jules found herself glad for Sophie's company after all. It was always fun to chat with someone else who understood the crazy whirlwind of the theater life.

"Hey, I'm actually meeting a few friends for a drink on my way home," Sophie said. "Want to join us? There's a new gay bar on Seventh that we wanted to check out, if that's your scene."

"Dragonfly?" Jules asked hesitantly. She didn't know much about gay bars, but she did know this one.

"That's the place," Sophie confirmed with a nod. "Have you been?"

"I have, although maybe not for the same reason as you. I adopted two kittens from the owner."

"Really?"

"Yeah. Josie runs a kitten rescue, in addition to owning the bar. And sure, I'll join you guys for a drink," Jules said, making a snap decision. Going out for a drink sounded like the perfect distraction while she waited for her phone to ring. Plus, it would be nice to see Josie and update her about the kittens.

They made a left onto Seventh and walked several blocks to Dragonfly, its lavender logo reflected on the wet sidewalk. Jules hadn't been here in a few months. Hopefully, Josie was working tonight. She followed Sophie through the door, pausing just inside while Sophie looked for her friends. Soft jazz music played over the sound system, and the white fairy lights that usually spanned the ceiling had been accented tonight with purple and orange in honor of Halloween, which was just a few days away.

A pair of women waved from a table along the back wall, and Jules and Sophie made their way over to them.

"Hey, ladies," Sophie said warmly, giving each of her friends a quick hug before turning toward Jules. "This is Jules. We met at the audition, and she stopped by for a drink. Jules, this is Gia and Kit." She gestured across the table at her friends as she introduced them. They waved at Jules, their expressions open and friendly.

Jules dragged an empty stool to their table and sat beside Sophie. "Nice to meet you guys. Do you act as well?"

"Nope," Gia told her. "I'm a financial analyst, but I love to live vicariously through Sophie."

As it turned out, neither of Sophie's friends were actors, which was somewhat unexpected. Not that *all* of Jules's friends were part of the theater world, but certainly most of them were. They both seemed nice, though, and Jules was glad she'd decided to come. The four of them chatted through a round of drinks, the alcohol helping to keep the conversation flowing.

"So, you guys auditioned for the same role today?" Kit asked, eyebrows lifted as she sipped from her drink.

"Yep," Sophie told her.

"And, according to my agent, we should hear about callbacks tonight," Jules added.

Sophie straightened on her stool. "Really?"

She nodded. "Yes."

"Ooh," Gia said, looking delighted. "This could get interesting."

Jules glanced at Sophie. "Yes, it could."

"Jules?"

She turned to see Josie standing beside their table. Tonight, Josie's ever-changing hair was streaked with pink and purple, a perfect match for her personality. Jules beamed at her. "I was hoping to see you tonight." She turned toward Sophie and her friends, remembering that this was their first time visiting Dragonfly. "This is Josie Swanson. She owns the bar and runs a kitten rescue in her spare time. I adopted two kittens from her this spring."

"My theater kittens," Josie said happily.

"Yes," Jules confirmed. "I named them Phantom and Pippin."

"The other two are Blanche and Hamilton," Josie told them. "My girlfriend adopted them."

"That's freaking adorable," Sophie said as awwws went around the table.

Jules pulled out her phone, scrolling through her photo roll until she found pictures of her cats.

"I assume Phantom is the black one?" Sophie asked, leaning in for a closer look.

"How did you guess?" Jules turned her head, and their eyes met. Sophie's were warm and brown, crinkled with laughter. She smelled nice too, like spiced vanilla.

"They've gotten so big," Josie said, looking over Jules's shoulder at a photo of Pippin and Phantom curled up together in her bed.

"They sure have," Jules agreed. "They look like cats now, but still act like kittens. Thank goodness they take most of it out on each other instead of me."

"The reason I always recommend that people adopt two," Josie said.

"If I ever get my own place, I'd love to have a cat," Sophie said, sounding a bit wistful.

"You should follow Josie's YouTube channel," Jules told her. "She posts super cute videos of all her foster kittens. That's how I got my kitten fix until I was ready to adopt."

"And generally, all of my kittens are adoptable," Josie added.

"I'll check it out." Sophie reached into the back pocket of her jeans, pulling out her cell phone, which was ringing. If the wide-eyed look on her face was any indication, her agent was calling. "I need to take this. I'll be right back."

Phone in hand, she rushed out the front door. Jules sipped her drink, swallowing her disappointment that Sophie might have gotten a callback instead of her. Of course, it was possible for them both to be called back for the second round, but it wasn't very likely, especially after

Jules had let her nerves get the better of her during her audition.

"I'm so glad you came in tonight," Josie said, drawing Jules out of her thoughts. "I had been meaning to catch up with you and see how the kittens were doing. It's so good to see them. And you, of course."

"Would you like to come see them sometime?" Jules asked. "I mean, you and Eve could totally stop by and visit them if you'd like."

"Please." Josie clasped her hands in front of herself dramatically. "We would love that."

"Yeah, definitely. You've got my number. Just give me a call, and we'll figure something out."

"Oh, we are totally going to take you up on that," Josie said before heading back to the bar with a wave.

Jules was halfway through her second drink and a lively conversation with Gia and Kit when Sophie came back inside. Her cheeks were pink from the night air...or her mood. Jules couldn't be sure which, but Sophie was rushing toward their table with a visible excitement that seemed to hint at the latter.

She hopped onto her stool and lifted her glass, casting Jules a slightly apologetic glance. "You guys, I did it. I got a callback for *It's in Her Kiss.*"

The table erupted in cheers and whoops, glasses being clinked in celebration. Jules joined in, tapping her glass against Sophie's, happy for her despite the sting of disappointment in her belly. Her phone, poised on the edge of the table, remained silent. "Congratulations," she told Sophie earnestly.

"Thank you," Sophie said. "You may still get a call too, you know."

"Aw, aren't you guys being good sports," Kit teased. "No catfights at our table!"

"This is part of the job," Jules told her with a shrug. "I've auditioned with friends before...not that Sophie and I are friends, exactly, but you know what I mean."

"Yep," Sophie agreed. "And it's not like this means I've got the part either. But, hot *damn*, it feels good to still be in the game. I want this one so bad, you guys."

Jules studied her for a moment in silence. Yeah, she got that feeling about Sophie. There was a hunger about her when it came to this role, or maybe that hunger reflected her attitude toward her career in general. Jules didn't know her well enough to say. As much as Sophie wanted this role, as much as *Jules* wanted this role, there were probably a dozen other women across the Manhattan area tonight just as eager, just as sure they were the perfect Bianca.

Jules exhaled slowly. She felt it in her bones, the feeling that this was *the one*. If only her phone would ring...

SOPHIE LIFTED her drink and took a hearty sip in an attempt to ground herself, because she had the crazy urge to dance on the bar, and she wasn't even drunk. Not on alcohol anyway. She was pumped up on adrenaline, almost giddy with it. She'd actually gotten a callback for *It's in Her Kiss*.

Not only was this a lead role, it was a *queer* lead role. The role of a lifetime.

She'd been at this for over ten years now, a decade of endless auditions that had netted her a decent résumé of supporting roles on and off Broadway, as well as a handful of walk-on parts in television and commercials. But she didn't want to be Dancer #3 this time. She wanted to be the star.

Maybe even more importantly, she needed the paycheck this role would provide. It had been over a year since Sophie had landed an acting job, and she was sick to death of waitressing to make ends meet. If you could consider sleeping on her friends' sofa making ends meet. Her parents sure didn't. Once upon a time, they'd been fully supportive of her Broadway dreams, but lately, they thought it was time for her to accept that it hadn't worked out and get a real job. Her bank account seemed to agree with them.

But Sophie wasn't ready to admit defeat. She just needed her big break. And maybe it had come with *It's in Her Kiss.*

"What's that?" Gia asked, pointing to Jules's drink. "It's pretty."

"It's called a Midnight in Manhattan," Jules told her, tucking a strand of honey-brown hair behind her ear. "It's similar to a mojito, but with lemon instead of lime juice. It's one of the house drinks. Josie convinced me to try one, and now I'm hooked."

"Oh, that's the one with the myth attached," Kit said. "I'm too superstitious to risk it."

"A myth?" Sophie leaned closer to Jules, peering into her glass.

"If you drink one at midnight, supposedly you'll fall in love before the end of the year," Jules told her. "But I've been drinking them for months now, and no such luck."

"You want to fall in love?" Kit gave her a skeptical look. "Girl, I've been there and done that, and it sucks. Trust me."

"I'm in no hurry, but I'm certainly not opposed to the idea," Jules said, taking another sip.

"Any prospects?" Sophie asked. Yeah, she was fishing. Now that she wasn't preoccupied with waiting for a callback, she wouldn't mind asking Jules out, if she could just figure out whether or not Jules was straight.

"Not at the moment." Jules shrugged. "I dated a guy for a few months over the summer, but things fizzled pretty quickly after that. So like I said, I'm not in any hurry. You should try the drink, though. It's good."

Kit threw her hands out in front of her. "No way. Not taking any chances."

"Me either," Sophie confirmed as she lifted her whiskey sour.

Jules pressed a hand against her heart, drawing Sophie's attention to the plunging neckline on her blouse and the cross pendant glinting there. "So many skeptics at this table."

"I haven't sworn off love forever," Sophie told her. "I'm just not at a place in my life right now where I have much room for it."

"Fair enough," Jules said, glancing at Sophie. Her eyes were a deep brown, highlighted by thick eyeliner and a shimmery eyeshadow that sparkled under the bar's track lighting. And her hair...well, she looked like she'd walked out of a shampoo commercial. It was long and wavy, with golden highlights in her natural brown. Combined with her charismatic personality, it was no wonder she was an actress. If Sophie ever got the chance to see her on stage, she was certain she wouldn't be able to take her eyes off her.

Right now, she'd settle for Jules's number. She'd mentioned a boyfriend, but that didn't mean she wasn't bi or pan. Surely she wouldn't have auditioned as Bianca today if she wasn't at least curious, would she? Usually, Sophie had excellent gaydar, but she couldn't quite make up her mind about Jules.

On the table between them, Jules's phone began to ring.

The name Pierce showed on the screen, and she let out a little gasp. "My agent," she said breathlessly, grabbing her phone and rushing for the door as Sophie had done earlier.

"What are the chances?" Sophie muttered, reaching for her drink.

"Does this mean you've both made it to round two?" Gia asked, looking delighted.

"Maybe. We'll see," Sophie said as she drained her glass. She walked to the bar for a refill. By the time she'd made it back to their table, Jules had reentered Dragonfly with an unmistakable bounce in her step.

Sophie caught her eye with an inquiring lift of her eyebrow. "Good news for you too?"

"Yes," Jules confirmed. "And my agent says that unofficially, there are only two of us in contention for the role."

"Oh wow." Sophie gulped. "So, it's between you and me?"

"Sounds that way."

They stared at each other for a beat of loaded silence before Sophie lifted her chin with a smile, putting her attraction aside for now because Jules was the competition. "Better bring your A game on Friday, Vega."

Jules met her gaze, amusement sparkling in her eyes. "I'm not worried."

"You should be." Sophie lifted her glass, tapping it against Jules's. "May the best woman win."

2

Sophie buzzed around the apartment on Friday morning, too restless to sit still. She dressed in her go-to outfit for a dancing audition: stretchy jeans that felt more like leggings, paired with a snug-fitting black top and jazz shoes. She put her hair in a ponytail and styled big, loose curls into it. After polishing her makeup, she went into the living room to warm up.

Thankfully, Nathan and Anthony were both working at the moment. Yes, she lived with men, and they were great roommates, except for the fact that Sophie didn't actually have a room. She slept on the pull-out couch. Since all three of them were Broadway performers with unreliable incomes, it had been a mutually beneficial situation.

But she was dying a little bit week by week, having no true space of her own. No privacy. Her clothes and belongings limited to an armoire in the corner. The waterproof vibrator that she occasionally brought into the shower with her was the only action she'd seen in over a year. How could she date when she lived like this?

The role in *It's in Her Kiss* would provide her with a

steady paycheck for the next few months, enough that she might be able to upgrade her living situation. It wouldn't allow her to afford her own apartment, but maybe she could upgrade to a roommate arrangement where she'd at least have her own bedroom. And hopefully, this role would be a steppingstone to more reliable work.

In the living room, she stretched and warmed up her muscles. Luckily, since the audition was here in Brooklyn, she could walk there, which would make it a lot easier to keep herself warm on the way. She put on the music her agent, Estelle, had sent and ran through the dance routine several times before adding her vocals, rehearsing until she'd worked out all her nerves.

She drank the rest of her tea and chased it with a Grether's Pastille while she packed up. After a quick trip to the bathroom, she was on her way. As she jogged down the stairs to the street, she wrapped a thick scarf around her neck to keep her vocal cords warm.

Thirty minutes later, she entered the waiting room where she'd met Jules earlier that week. Today, there were a handful of other women in the room, all rehearsing the same dance routine Sophie herself had spent the last two days perfecting.

Unofficially, there are only two of us in contention for the role.

Who were these other women? Had Jules's agent been mistaken? Or was something else going on? Sophie checked in with the receptionist and took a seat along the back wall, one foot tapping restlessly as she hummed the song under her breath.

One by one, the other women were called, until Sophie was the last person in the waiting room. Why wasn't Jules here? An uncomfortable feeling took hold in the pit of Sophie's stomach. Something wasn't right.

As soon as she stepped into the audition room, her fear came to fruition.

"Sophie Rindell," the casting director called out, announcing her, "performing for a role in the ensemble."

And there it was. She hadn't been called back to audition as Bianca at all. Now she was fighting for a position in the ensemble, one of the nameless dancers who would support the main cast. This was something her agent should have communicated to her but hadn't, and it wasn't the first time Estelle had let her down.

Sophie pushed past her disappointment, plastering a bright smile on her face as the music began to play. She could roll with the punches with the best of them, and she gave her all to this performance, laying every ounce of her talent on that black-tiled floor.

Afterward, she thanked the casting team for the opportunity, gathered her bag, and left. Like she'd done on Wednesday, she headed next door for a coffee. Today, though, she had to be at work in an hour, ready for a long afternoon of waiting tables for demanding tourists.

Where was Jules? Had she actually gotten a callback for Bianca? Probably. It didn't seem likely that both of their agents would have screwed up. Sophie scuffed her foot against the dusty floor as she poured cream into her coffee. *Dammit.* She'd worked so hard for this. She shouldn't be disappointed, not when she still had a chance at being cast in the production.

But still, as she left the coffee shop, she felt an all too familiar bitterness rising up inside her. After ten years, she couldn't believe she was still clutching at the fringes of her dream, that success kept slipping through her fingertips.

She stomped on a leaf on the sidewalk, producing a satisfying crunch.

The truly ridiculous thing was that if she hadn't initially been up for the role of Bianca, Sophie would be *so freaking thrilled* that she'd received a callback at all. So what if she was a member of the ensemble? At least she'd be on stage. Yes, it was off-Broadway, but the Sapphire Theater had a reputation for housing quality productions, and the production company was renowned as well.

It's in Her Kiss had all the markings of a critically acclaimed new production, and Sophie would be lucky to be associated with it in any capacity. If only they'd seen her potential as Bianca...

She took an overenthusiastic sip of her coffee, scorching her tongue in the process. Hot coffee seared its way down her esophagus, burning through her disappointment. She hated feeling like this. Lately, it had been happening more and more often, and frankly, it scared her. If she let herself get consumed by bitterness, it would ruin her joy for performing.

She went home, changed, and headed to work at the diner. As was her usual audition protocol, she did her best to put it out of her mind. It was out of her hands now. In all likelihood, she would never hear another word about *It's in Her Kiss*. That had been the theme of her year, anyway.

When her phone rang with a call from Estelle the following Monday, Sophie wasn't sure whether that meant good news, or if her agent was merely calling about a new audition. Either way, she answered with bated breath.

"Congratulations," Estelle announced. "You've been cast as a member of the ensemble in *It's in Her Kiss*."

"Really?" Sophie found herself grinning despite her earlier frustration about the audition misunderstanding.

"Yes," Estelle told her. "And they've also selected you as the understudy for the two female leads—Bianca and Melissa."

"No way," Sophie breathed, a ripple of excitement spreading through her. An understudy was a step up from the ensemble. It meant she might get a chance to play the lead, a chance to prove herself in a way that might open more doors for her in the future. And it also came with a much nicer paycheck than she would have received for the ensemble alone.

"Rehearsals will begin next week, with previews opening just after the new year," Estelle told her.

Sophie did a little happy dance in the privacy of her living room. She'd landed her first acting gig in over a year, and while it wasn't the role she'd wanted, it was still better than she'd expected to receive.

It wasn't until after she'd gotten off the call that she thought to wonder who had been cast as Bianca. Had the role gone to Jules? Had Sophie been cast as her understudy?

JULES PULLED leggings and her favorite fleece-lined hoodie over her leotard, muscles comfortably sore after her hour-long dance lesson. She gulped what remained of her bottle of water as she packed her bag to head home, noticing a voicemail on her phone. A shiver slid down her spine. It was probably her mom. After all, she called every day, and Jules hadn't talked to her yet today.

But when she checked the call log and saw her agent's name there, that shiver turned into a full-out tingle, coursing through her system to land in a nervous ball of energy lodged in her stomach. Unlike her first audition for

It's in Her Kiss, she felt like she'd nailed her callback. Did she dare hope? Not bothering to listen to the message, she pressed the icon next to Pierce's name and dialed.

"Hello, Julia," he answered, his standard greeting. Somehow, he'd never managed to embrace her nickname. His tone gave nothing away, but it never did.

"Hi, Pierce. You called?"

"I did," he confirmed. "I was hoping to congratulate the new Bianca Scott in person."

"What?" Her voice sounded embarrassingly like a squeak, and she pressed her free hand against her lips. Her knees went soft, and she dropped onto the bench behind her.

"You heard me," Pierce said, sounding genuinely pleased, which was a lot, coming from him. "You got the part."

"Oh," she whispered as happy tears welled in her eyes. "Wow."

"Can I take you to lunch to go over all the details?" he asked.

"Yeah...yes, that would be great." She gave her head a shake, still waiting for it to sink in. She'd done it. She'd landed her first leading role. Her fingers clenched around the phone.

"How about Flora at one?"

"Perfect. I'll see you there. Thanks again, Pierce."

"My pleasure," he said.

She stood as she ended the call and twirled in the changing room, glad she was the only one in here at the moment. As much as she wanted to shout her news from the rooftops—and call her mom—she also wanted a few minutes to savor it for herself, to walk home with a secret smile on her face and a spring in her step.

So that's what she did, daydreaming her way home as she envisioned herself up on stage with the spotlight in her eyes, basking in applause from the crowd, taking a bow during curtain call. For the first time, she'd be the one out front. It was more than a dream come true. This was a pinnacle moment in her life, the reason she'd left her family in Miami and moved to New York. It was the realization of their hopes and dreams for her, and okay, it was starting to sink in now.

She felt herself smiling as she climbed the stairs to her apartment and let herself in. Pippin trotted out from behind the red-patterned curtain she'd strung across the room, hiding her bed from sight. It provided as much privacy as she could hope for in a studio apartment. He meowed as he reached her, twining his gray-striped body around her legs.

"Hey, Pepito," she said as she knelt to rub him, one of her many nicknames for him. Pippin was her affectionate cat. His brother, Phantom, lifted his head from where he slept on the couch. Phantom was less vocal about his affections, but he was a total goofball, often sleeping in the most ridiculous positions and making meme-able faces, which had made him the star of Jules's Instagram feed.

She turned on the espresso machine to make café Cubano, although surely the last thing she needed right now was caffeine. Her hands shook as she poured ground espresso and water into the machine.

Bianca Scott.

Fresh tears pricked her eyes. She went into the bathroom for a quick shower while the machine heated up. She'd make her coffee, and then she'd call her mom. Her mom would tell her grandma and her brothers, and before Jules knew it, her whole family would have booked tickets to New York to see her on opening night.

Opening night. *This is really happening.* Jules dressed and returned to the kitchen. She brewed her coffee on autopilot as her brain spun through visions of herself on stage, performing the piano solo she'd learned for her callback audition. With a happy sigh, she lifted her cup and inhaled the rich aroma. It wasn't as good as her grandma's, but Jules hadn't found anywhere in Manhattan to get a better cup of Cuban coffee than her own.

She blew on it and sipped, letting the sharp flavor zap away the haze in her brain. Then she sat on the couch next to Phantom, picked up her phone, and dialed.

"I did it. I got the part," she blurted the moment she heard the call connect.

On the other end of the line, her mom let out a shriek more reminiscent of a teenager than a woman in her fifties. "Oh my goodness, baby, I am so proud of you! I just knew it. I knew in my heart this was the one for you."

"I had a good feeling about it too, but if I had a penny for every time I've felt that way over the years..."

"It's your time," Paula said. "Oh honey, I just can't believe it. Hang on, let me get your *abuela*." There was a pause, and Jules heard her mom call, "Mami, get in here! She got the part." Another pause. "Yes, she's on the phone right now."

Jules smiled, picturing them together on the floral-printed couch in the house where she'd grown up. There was a rustling sound, and then her grandmother's voice came on the line.

"Julia, I am so proud," her grandma said, her voice gruff with emotion. "I can't wait to see you up on that stage, shining like a star. *Mi estrella*."

"Thank you," Jules said, pressing a hand against her heart.

"You've worked so hard for this." It was her mom again. "All those years of training and classes and auditions."

"I'm going to need to add piano lessons back into the mix," Jules told her. "I have a solo near the end of the second act where I'll play the piano on stage."

"My baby girl, Broadway star. Oh, *mija*, your father would have been so proud."

"Papi will be there in spirit." Jules's throat tightened. She'd lost her father five years ago after a long struggle with kidney disease, and she still missed him so much, it took her breath away in moments like this, when she realized he wouldn't be able to see her realize her dream.

"He'll be watching over you every night," her mother said.

"I know." Tears rolled over Jules's cheeks, the same tears she heard in her mother's voice. Right now, she would have given anything to have her mom and grandma there with her, to give them both a huge hug, to spend a girls' afternoon together, celebrating her good news. She loved living in New York and had the most supportive family ever, but sometimes, she missed them so much, it hurt.

"Tell me more about your role," Paula said in her ear, shifting them back onto less emotional ground.

"Well, it's a brand-new production, written by a woman, which is amazing. I play Bianca, who's an actress herself, trying to balance her personal and professional life. And ultimately...it's a coming out story."

"Coming out of what?" her mom asked, completely oblivious.

Jules sat straighter on her couch, stomach clenching as if she was the one coming out. "Coming out of the closet. I'll be kissing a woman on stage."

"Oh my," her mother said with a laugh.

Jules's cheeks heated. She'd be kissing a woman on stage, night after night. What would that be like? Would it help Jules figure out her own sexuality, or would it make her even more confused? Was this role a sign that it was finally time for her to face this part of herself she'd been avoiding for so long?

"Does it bother you?" she asked her mom cautiously. Her parents had always supported her and her brothers unconditionally, had encouraged them to follow their hearts and their dreams, but they were a traditional Catholic family, after all.

"Of course not," her mother answered. "It's not like it means you're gay. I think it's very brave of you to play a role like this."

"Right." Jules slumped against the couch. How would her mom react when and if she did come out to her? The thought felt more terrifying—and real—than ever before.

"Oh, sweetie, I can't believe we're talking about your first starring role on Broadway." Her mom had choked up again.

"Well, it's off-Broadway, but yeah, I know."

"Remind me what the difference is?" Paula asked.

"The theaters are smaller," Jules told her. "Anything with fewer than five hundred seats is considered off-Broadway. I won't be eligible for a Tony. I mean, not that I would have been nominated anyway, but Broadway is a requirement for that. The theater where I'll be performing is in Brooklyn, not too far from my apartment, actually. It's the perfect start for me, Mami. Off-Broadway can be a great place for unknown actors to showcase themselves."

"This is your big break," her mom agreed.

"I sure hope so," she whispered. "I still can't quite believe it's really happening."

"Well, I can. You deserve this. In fact, it's been a long time coming."

By the time Jules hung up the phone, she was ready to take on the world. A conversation with her mom—and her grandma—tended to have that effect on her. Lunch with Pierce further bolstered her mood, especially the contract he'd brought for her to sign.

Back at her apartment, she thumbed through the paperwork, curious to see who else had been cast in the production, if she knew any of the other performers. A woman named Micki Fredriksson would be playing Melissa, the other female lead. And *oh*. Sophie Rindell had been cast as both Jules's and Micki's understudy.

Well, that was certainly a happy surprise.

3

J ules stepped through the Sapphire Theater's back door as she'd been instructed in the information packet she'd received last week. Instead of using a separate rehearsal space, since the Sapphire was currently closed to the public while it underwent renovations, they would get to rehearse right here on the stage where they'd be performing.

This morning, she would meet the rest of the cast and the production team for the first time, and that afternoon, they would do their first full read through of the script together. Jules had done this enough times to be familiar and comfortable with the process, but she'd never done it as the lead.

That part was new and exciting, although also slightly terrifying. Jules walked down the back hallway, following the sound of voices past several offices, a kitchen, and a conference room. She rounded the corner and found herself standing in the eaves of the stage. From here, she could see a semicircle of chairs arranged at the center of the stage and several people already standing around talking.

Let's do this.

She stepped onto the stage. Several heads swiveled in her direction. She spotted Kari Wong, the director, and headed over to say hello. She'd first met Kari when she had a walk-on role in a play Kari had directed a few years ago.

"Julia," Kari said warmly as she approached, extending a hand. She was a petite woman, several inches shorter than Jules, which gave her the rare sensation of feeling tall. Today, Kari was dressed in all black, her dark hair pulled back in her usual no-nonsense ponytail. "Welcome. I'm so thrilled to have you on board with us for *It's in Her Kiss.*"

"It is an absolute honor to be here," Jules said, clasping her hand. "And please, call me Jules."

"You got it." Kari motioned for Jules to follow her as she introduced her to the stage manager, musical director, and choreographer, as well as their assistants. Jules had met the choreographer, Simon Frampton, briefly during auditions, and he greeted her enthusiastically.

"We'll get started as soon as everyone's here," Kari told her.

"I'll start introducing myself around," Jules said, turning toward the cluster of actors in the center of the stage.

"Hi," one of the women said as Jules approached.

"Hi," she responded. "I'm Julia Vega, but please call me Jules."

"Oh," another woman said. "You're playing Bianca."

"Yes." And just like that, everyone was staring at Jules. Well, this was new.

She studied each face carefully as she was introduced, repeating the person's name as she shook their hand to commit it to memory. An acting coach had taught her this technique years ago, showing her how to note a distinctive facial feature or other unique characteristic as she repeated their name, and it really worked. People were endlessly impressed when she showed up on the second day of rehearsal and remembered their names.

Truthfully, she hadn't prepared herself for the extra attention she was receiving as Bianca, and now she felt the pressure to impress more than ever. The last thing she wanted was to be a disappointment in her first starring role.

"I'm Micki Fredriksson." A woman with a blonde pixie haircut stood in front of her. "I'm playing Melissa."

"Hi Micki. I'm Julia Vega, but please call me Jules." *Micki pixie.* Jules was so focused on committing Micki's name to memory that it took her a moment to realize what Micki had said. She was playing Melissa. This was the woman Jules would be kissing every night on stage.

"Excited to work with you," Micki said. "I guess we'll get to know each other pretty well, won't we?" With a wink and a wave over her shoulder, she walked away. Strutted was more like it.

That was...odd. Jules frowned as she turned to introduce herself to another group of actors. She was deep in conversation with a man named Amir when a familiar face entered her line of vision. Sophie stepped onto the stage wearing jeans, a black jacket, and a confident smile, her brown hair hanging loose and curly over her shoulders.

"Excuse me," Jules told Amir. "I see someone I need to say hello to. I can't wait to read with you later." Amir would be playing Trevor, Bianca's wannabe love interest.

"Sure, yeah. Great meeting you." He turned to the woman beside him.

Jules ducked out of the group to intercept Sophie as she crossed the stage. "Hey, stranger."

"Hi," Sophie said, glancing around the stage, distracted.

"I was excited to see your name on the casting list," Jules told her.

"Congrats on landing Bianca," Sophie said, polite but distant, not at all the way she'd been the day they met, when she'd invited Jules for drinks after their audition.

"Thank you. I still can't quite believe it."

"I bet it'll feel a lot more real after today," Sophie said.

"Probably," Jules agreed. "Anyway, I'm glad we'll get to work together."

"Mm," Sophie said with a nod, but she didn't look very glad. If anything, she looked...annoyed was the first word that came to mind. Was she still upset that she hadn't gotten the part of Bianca? Surely she wouldn't hold that against Jules. This was just part of the business. Neither she or Sophie had any control over it, and it wasn't like this meant Jules was a superior actress. She'd just been a better fit for Kari's vision for the production.

"Well, I'm sure I'll see you around," Sophie said. "Congrats again."

And she walked off, leaving Jules standing there, somewhat baffled and definitely irritated. *What the hell, Sophie?*

SOPHIE LET her pissy mood spoil her first morning of rehearsals, and as she returned to the stage after lunch, she felt terrible about it. She'd had a shitty start to her day, first sleeping through her alarm and then getting hassled by some asshole on her way to the theater. When she walked in and saw everyone fawning over Jules, for a minute, all she could think was...*that could have been me.*

But she'd given herself an attitude adjustment during her lunch break, and as she sat in one of the chairs onstage to read through the script for the first time, excitement burned away what remained of her earlier bitterness. The initial read through was always a thrill, and while Sophie didn't have any lines to read today, she would be paying close attention as Jules's and Micki's understudy.

She sat between fellow ensemble members Elena and Tabitha, across the circle from Jules, who had obviously already done her homework. She barely looked at her script as she read and sang. She had a pretty voice, much richer than Sophie had anticipated. With her Pantene commercial hair and shimmery green sweater, she certainly looked the part of the star.

As they reached the pinnacle scene at the end of the first act, Jules blew Micki a kiss across the circle, a substitute for what would be their onstage kiss, drawing laughter from the cast. The rest of the read through went smoothly, and when it was over, everyone had smiles on their faces. The actors all seemed to share a good rapport, with the possible exception of Micki, who was a bit of a drama queen.

Kari Wong promised to be a solid director, casually tossing out suggestions that had already sharpened their performances. Their stage manager, Andrew Marshall, also seemed competent and easy to work with. If this was any indication of the rest of rehearsals, Sophie was in for one of the better experiences of her theater career.

As everyone stood to gather their things and head out for the evening, Jules asked, "Anyone want to grab a drink?"

Almost immediately, she'd gathered the whole group of actors, except Elena, who had to get home to her kids. Sophie loved going out for drinks with her castmates, and it would be a good chance for them all to get to know each other better. Plus, she probably owed Jules an apology for the way she'd acted earlier.

"I noticed a pub next door, although I have no idea if it's any good," Amir offered.

"It's very good," Andrew told him as he headed for the door. "I wish I could join you guys, but I've got to get home to the family. Have a good time, and great job today, everyone. I'm looking forward to working with you all."

Sophie followed the group out the back door, and together, they walked to the pub. They were seated at a big table in the back, because, as it turned out, they were hungry as well as thirsty after a long day of rehearsals. Several people had already crowded around Jules. Between her charming smile, matching personality, and status as the lead, she had quickly become everyone's favorite.

Sophie took a seat at the other end of the table, between Amir and Tabitha. They chatted through burgers and beers, sharing plenty of laughs.

"Seems like a great group," Tabitha commented as she drained her beer.

"It does," Sophie agreed.

"Sometimes it's nice not having any stars around," she said with a conspiratorial grin. "No big heads causing drama. It's refreshing."

Sophie snickered. She'd worked with her share of divas, of all genders. "Tell me about it."

Several hours—and even more beers—later, Sophie made her way outside, hoping her roommates would have already retired to their room for the night by the time she made it home. It was past nine, and they often watched TV in bed together to give her some privacy in the living room. Sleeping on the couch was really an unglamorous life.

A hand tugged at Sophie's jacket, and she turned to find Jules behind her on the sidewalk.

"Didn't see you much today," Jules said, her eyes searching Sophie's.

"It was a busy day," Sophie replied, fighting the urge to take a step back, putting a little distance between her and Jules, because standing this close to her, Sophie could see the golden flecks in her brown eyes and smell the floral scent of her perfume. The wind blew a lock of Jules's hair over Sophie's arm, and even through her jacket, she shivered at the contact. She'd hoped her attraction would have faded since the day they met, but apparently, it hadn't.

"I just thought I picked up on a funny vibe from you today," Jules persisted, falling into step beside Sophie as they walked away from the pub. "You aren't upset about me playing Bianca, are you?"

"No." Sophie blew out a breath, shaking her head. "I'm sorry for giving you that impression. I was in a bad mood this morning, but it didn't have anything to do with you."

"You sure about that?" Jules asked.

Sophie sighed, fighting a smile. "Okay, maybe I was feeling a little sorry for myself when I walked in this morning, imagining what it would have been like if I'd gotten to play Bianca, but that was petty of me."

"You can't help how you feel," Jules said.

"I'm happy for you, Jules. Truly."

"Thanks," Jules said, looking relieved. "I'm glad we'll be working together."

"Me too," Sophie told her.

"So...friends?"

"Yep," Sophie agreed, glad they'd cleared the air between them. "How did you feel about today's rehearsal?"

"I thought it went really well," Jules said. "You?"

"Same."

"It's a lot of extra pressure, playing the lead," Jules said, frowning slightly.

"I bet. Are you nervous, you know, about the kiss?" she couldn't help asking.

"No," Jules answered, maybe a little too quickly. They walked for a few more steps in silence. "Maybe a little. I've never actually kissed anyone onstage before."

"I haven't either," Sophie said.

They lapsed into silence again. Jules's lips were pressed together in a firm line, an indication she might be more nervous about the kiss than she'd admitted.

"Have you kissed a woman before?" Sophie asked impulsively.

"No." Jules looked over, and their gazes locked. "Have you?"

Sophie laughed. "I *only* kiss women. I figured you already knew that about me."

Jules rolled her eyes. "Well, yes, I thought so, but I didn't want to make assumptions. Better to just ask, in my experience."

"Oh, it definitely is," Sophie agreed. She always preferred to be direct, especially about her sexuality. And maybe it was the beer talking, or more likely her interest in Jules, but she was feeling especially direct—and nosy— tonight. "Have you thought about it?"

"Thought about what?" Jules asked, slowing to a stop as they waited for the crosswalk ahead to change.

"Kissing a woman."

Jules's gaze fell to her hands, which were clasped loosely in front of herself. "No."

And there it was, the answer Sophie had been looking for since they met. Jules wasn't into women. Sophie tried not to read too much into it, because she knew Kari had wanted to cast a queer actress in the role of Bianca, but maybe she knew something Sophie didn't. Either way, Sophie needed to kill this crush right now, before it made things between her and Jules any more awkward than they already were.

"I think I'm more nervous about my piano solo than the kiss," Jules said. "I mean, I've been dreaming about a role like this my whole life, and now that I've got it, I'm terrified of screwing up. And I just want to absorb every moment in case I never get this opportunity again."

"Something tells me you will," Sophie told her.

"Hopefully, we both will," Jules said with a small smile in her direction. "I get the feeling you've been working at this as long and hard as I have."

"Maybe longer and harder," Sophie said.

"Oh yeah?" Jules said. "Try me."

"Moved to the city when I was eighteen, and I've been auditioning ever since," Sophie told her.

"And how old are you now?"

"Twenty-nine."

"I guess it depends on how we define 'working,'" Jules said thoughtfully. "I moved here at fourteen to attend LaGuardia High School. You know it, right?"

"I do." It was the performing arts high school where *Fame* was set, and it was ridiculously hard to get into, not to mention expensive, because you had to be a New York City resident to attend. "How did you pull that off, residency-wise?"

"My mom moved to Manhattan with me when I was in eighth grade to establish residency, while my dad stayed with my brothers in Miami. She lived here with me until I turned eighteen, and then she went back home. My dad was starting to struggle with kidney disease, so he needed her more than I did at that point."

"That's very dedicated," Sophie said.

"I've never wanted anything but to be a Broadway actress," Jules told her. "And my parents have always been really supportive."

"That's great," Sophie told her, feeling a twinge of jealousy. She wished her parents had been that dedicated to her dream or had enough money to send her to a fancy performing arts high school. "Sorry about your dad's kidney disease, though."

"Thanks." Jules's expression turned brittle. "He passed away five years ago."

"Oh, shit. I'm so sorry." Now Sophie felt like an ass, feeling sorry for herself about where she went to high school when she had two loving parents at home.

"Thanks." Jules blinked rapidly. "Kills me a little bit that he won't be here to see me in this show."

"Oh, Jules." She turned and wrapped an arm around her shoulders, just for a quick squeeze, since they really didn't know each other well enough for hugs.

"Anyway," Jules said, waving her hands in front of her face as she warded off tears. "My parents wanted me to go to college, so I got a degree in Theater Arts. I didn't actually start auditioning until I was twenty-two, and I'm thirty now, so if you count years we've been actually auditioning, you have been at this longer than I have."

"I think it's safe to say we've both worked our asses off," Sophie said.

"Yes," Jules agreed, smile back in place.

"I'm this way," Sophie said, gesturing toward Carroll Street to her right.

"Okay, well, I'll see you tomorrow, then."

"Bright and early," Sophie confirmed.

"Actually, I'm not on the roster until after lunch," Jules

said. "I think Kari wanted to focus on some of the group numbers first. I may come in early to watch, though."

"Nah, sleep in while you can," Sophie said.

"We'll see. I guess you could say I'm overzealous, but I've always loved trying to absorb every bit of a production that I can."

"Nothing wrong with that. Night, Jules." With a wave, Sophie crossed the street, headed toward her apartment. Exhaustion crept in as she walked those last blocks. It had been a *long* day. She was excited about the production, though, despite her conflicted feelings for Jules. They'd shared an insightful walk home together.

Hopefully, the inconvenient attraction would pass, since it was obviously one-sided. On that note, Sophie pulled up her Tinder app as she walked and started swiping through photos. She didn't have time or space in her life for a relationship at the moment, but a one-night stand to reset her system? Yeah, she could fit that in. In fact, it had just become a priority.

4

Jules sat about ten rows back from the stage, watching the ensemble rehearse. Every director had their own style, and Kari seemed to prefer to get the choreography down first. Jules wasn't part of the first musical number, so she didn't have to be here this morning, but there was always something to learn by observing. That wisdom had been drilled into her in high school, and she'd never forgotten it.

It's in Her Kiss wasn't a dance show at heart. It was more about the music and the drama, but even so, there was a fair amount of choreography involved. Jules loved watching Simon, the choreographer, as he worked, the way he tirelessly adjusted the actors to get the results he wanted. Occasionally, Kari jumped in with her own input, while Andrew, the stage manager, made notes on his tablet and moved stage props for the performers.

Jules had studied every aspect of theater in college, from set design to directing, and she was fascinated by all of it. Basically, the theater was her happy place, and she couldn't see herself ever working anywhere else.

After a few minutes, though, her focus shifted to one dancer in particular. Sophie was magnetic that way. Jules's attention always seemed drawn to her when she was in the room, and she hadn't liked it a bit when Sophie pulled away from her yesterday. Hopefully, they'd sorted things out last night, because Jules really hoped they would be friends, at least until *It's in Her Kiss* wrapped.

When the group on stage broke for lunch, Jules stood, gathering her purse and jacket, so she could join them.

"Miss Vega?"

She turned to see an employee of the theater standing in the aisle. "Yes?"

"I'm Sarah," she said brightly. "And I wanted to let you know your dressing room is ready for you."

"Really?" Jules couldn't fight the grin she felt spreading across her face. Andrew had apologized yesterday that the theater was in the process of being repainted as part of its ongoing renovations and the dressing rooms had been inaccessible. But the part Jules couldn't quite wrap her head around was that she would have her own dressing room.

That had never happened before. And it was so friggin' exciting.

She followed Sarah down a flight of stairs into one of the theater's basement levels, where the dressing rooms were located, tucked away beneath the stage. Sarah showed her to a room at the end of the hall. A white piece of paper had been taped to the door with JULIA VEGA printed in big block letters across it. And she was totally going to geek out and take silly selfies in front of it as soon as she was alone.

"See this stairwell?" Sarah asked, gesturing to the door across from Jules's dressing room.

She nodded.

"If you go up those stairs, you'll be in the hallway to stage left. Would you like me to show you?"

"No, that's okay," Jules told her. "I'll go back up that way and see where it comes out."

Sarah opened the door to the dressing room, indicating for Jules to follow her inside. It wasn't one of the fanciest dressing rooms Jules had ever seen. This was a smaller theater, after all, and nothing about it was particularly fancy. But to her, it was perfection. There was a large sofa to her right and the dressing table to her left, facing a mirror ringed with bulbs where she'd sit each night to do her makeup.

"The bathroom is through there." Sarah pointed to a door on the far wall. "And you have a mini fridge and a microwave here." She pointed again. "It's stocked with water and a few basic snacks, but if there's anything in particular you'd like, let us know, and we'll do our best to accommodate you."

"I'm sure whatever's in there is fine," Jules said, nearly overcome with the urge to jump around and completely lose her cool, because...bucket list!

"Okay. Just let me know if you need anything," Sarah said as she backed out of the room.

"Thanks so much, Sarah." Jules stood there for a moment, taking it all in. She whisper-squealed her excitement, and then she snapped a quick selfie to send her mom. Almost immediately, her phone rang.

"Tell me all about it," Paula said in lieu of hello.

"Wait. Let me FaceTime you instead, and then I can show it to you," Jules told her mom. "Hang on." She ended the call and dialed her through FaceTime, smiling when her mom's face appeared on the screen. "Hey."

"Oh! I see your makeup table," her mom said, peering

intently at the screen.

"Can you believe it?" Jules panned her phone around the dressing room, letting her mom see the whole space. "Oh, and they said there were snacks in the fridge. Let's see what I've got." She crouched, opening the door to the mini fridge. Inside, she found a sampling of fruit, yogurt cups, and crackers, although she wasn't sure why those were in the fridge.

"I can't wait to see it in person," Paula said. "We've already booked our flights for the first night of previews. Your brothers are just staying for the weekend, but your grandma and I will be there almost a week. And yes, we're seeing the show every night."

"Aw, Mami, I can't wait."

"I can't either, sweetie."

They talked for a few more minutes before Jules ended the call to find her castmates and see what they were doing for lunch. But once she was in the hallway, she couldn't resist posing for a selfie by her name on the door.

"Oof. I hope you're not letting that go to your head."

She turned to find Sophie standing a little way down the hall, watching her with an amused smile. "Oh, please. Like you wouldn't take a selfie if it was your name on the door."

"I absolutely would," Sophie agreed. "Want me to take one for you?" She held her hand out for Jules's phone.

"Thank you." She handed her phone to Sophie, then posed for several photos in front of her dressing room door.

"Here you go." Sophie handed back the phone. "They ordered sandwiches for us upstairs."

"Really?" The production team for this show really seemed to be taking good care of them. That wasn't always the case, and it made her extra appreciative when she encountered a good working environment like this one.

"Yep. You coming?"

Jules nodded as she fell into step beside Sophie, trying out the stairwell Sarah had pointed out to her earlier. "So where's your dressing room? Are we all on this hallway?"

"I think so, yeah," Sophie said. "I'm down the hall, sharing a room with Tabitha."

"Oh cool. She seems nice."

They came out at the top of the stairs, in the hallway to stage left as Sarah had said. Together, they walked to the break room, which was already bustling with cast and staff members, busily filling plates as they talked about the morning's rehearsal. Jules and Sophie made their way to the food set up in back. They fixed plates and found empty seats across from each other at one of the tables.

Jules sat beside Tabitha, who was midway through a story about a bad date she'd been on over the weekend, and from there, they went around the table with everyone trying to outdo each other with terrible first date tales. "What about you, Jules?" Amir asked.

She thought for a moment. "The worst would have to be the time a guy invited me to see a show with him, but he thought it would be an amazing surprise when I got there to find out he was *in* the show. I mean, I would have been thrilled to watch him perform, but it was a bit much on our first date for me to sit alone in the audience, looking like I'd been stood up. Afterward, he took me out for a drink and asked me questions about his performance, to make sure I had fully appreciated his art."

Across the table, Sophie snickered.

Jules narrowed her eyes at her. "And you? What's your bad date story?"

"This girl showed up to our first date completely wasted and then fell asleep with her head on my shoulder during the movie we went to see, and she snored super loudly through the whole thing."

"Yikes," Tabitha said, giggling under her breath.

After lunch, they assembled on the stage to rehearse a group dance number. Jules was glad for the chance to work off some of the nervous energy that had been building inside her all morning. She hadn't counted on being in front, though, leading the routine as Simon taught them the steps.

Still, she was a competent dancer, so she threw herself into the choreography with the same enthusiasm she channeled whenever she was on stage. Things went fairly smoothly for the next hour or so, until Micki joined Jules up front.

Simon stood in front of them, demonstrating the next move. "And five, six, seven eight..." he called as he moved.

Jules and the rest of the cast followed, dancing their way across the stage. Micki took an extra step, hip-checking Jules so hard, she almost lost her balance. Micki gave her an exasperated look, as if the mistake had been Jules's. She ignored Micki, moving to the side to give herself more room, but as hard as she tried, they couldn't seem to find their rhythm together.

"Not like that, Jules," Micki exclaimed when they bumped into each other for the fourth time. She proceeded to repeat the movement in an exaggerated fashion to demonstrate it for Jules.

"I've got it," Jules told her, clinging to what remained of her patience.

"Let's try it again, ladies," Simon said, and started them from the top.

But as the afternoon wore on, she and Micki struggled to get in sync with each other. Eventually, Jules got so flustered she couldn't tell which one of them was messing up. Maybe she was the problem after all. Kari sat quietly in the audience, watching with a slight frown, and Jules's cheeks grew uncomfortably hot. What if Kari decided she'd made a mistake in choosing Jules for the lead?

"Let's take ten," Kari called, and Jules winced.

She went down the hall to grab a bottle of water from the break room before making her way back to the now-empty stage. She clasped her hands in front of herself, gazing out at the rows of seats in front of her. This was something she'd always loved to do, steal a moment on stage by herself to stare into the empty theater, to imagine what it would feel like, standing here in front of a packed crowd, the spotlight in her face, singing her heart out.

This time, it wasn't a dream. It was really happening.

Unbidden, she remembered sneaking her dad onto a stage not unlike this one. It must have been seven or eight years ago, right after she'd landed her first bit part in an off-Broadway show. He'd stood beside her, tall and strong as he told her how proud he was that she'd never given up on her dreams.

And he knew what he was talking about. The son of Cuban immigrants, he'd worked tirelessly to achieve his own dreams here in America. He'd graduated top of his class and gone on to found an investment firm that had become one of the biggest and most profitable start-up companies in Miami. He'd given Jules his work ethic and the belief that she could be anything she wanted to be, if she wanted it badly enough and never gave up.

"Hey," Sophie said from behind her. "You okay?"

"Yeah." Jules turned toward her. "Just frustrated."

"Can't say I blame you," Sophie commented.

Jules sighed. She wasn't one to bad-mouth her costars,

but Sophie clearly understood without her needing to say a word.

"Why don't you show me the sequence before everyone else comes back out?" Sophie suggested.

"Right now?" Jules swept her gaze around the empty theater.

"Yep. Just dance like no one's watching."

"No one but you," Jules said, tossing a smile over her shoulder at Sophie as she walked to the front of the stage. Behind her, she heard Sophie begin to tap her toe against the stage, keeping the beat for her.

Jules moved easily across the stage. No fumbles. No missed steps.

"See? That was great," Sophie said. "You've got it. Don't let her distract you, that's all."

"Thank you," Jules told her. "Want to try it with me?"

"Sure," Sophie agreed.

They ran through the whole sequence together, their bodies effortlessly in unison. If only Jules could recreate this with Micki. Over the next few minutes, the rest of the cast trickled back onto the stage. Kari and Andrew returned to their seats in the audience, and Simon resumed his spot in front, guiding them. He started them at the top, and this time, Jules focused on herself, ignoring Micki as much as possible, as Sophie had suggested.

They kept at it for the rest of the afternoon, working through the number until everyone had it down. By the time they finished, Jules's confidence had rebounded. Still, she had to contain the urge to roll her eyes as Micki flounced off stage ahead of her.

Jules went downstairs to get her coat and purse. When she left her dressing room, Sophie was at the other end of the hall.

"Walking home?" Jules called to her.

Sophie nodded, pausing to allow Jules to catch up. "I have to hustle, though. Gotta go home and change before my date tonight."

"Oh yeah? Someone new?" she asked, because the last she knew, Sophie was single.

"Yep. First date. Wish me luck."

"Good luck," Jules said. "I hope things go infinitely better than any of the first dates we shared during lunch today."

Sophie laughed. "Yes. By those standards, I should have nothing to worry about."

"That's the spirit." Jules wondered if she should be looking for a little of that spirit for herself. It had been months since she'd gone on a date, and longer than that since she'd had a serious boyfriend. She had a tendency to focus on her career to the detriment of everything else in her life, but lately, she'd been feeling lonely. No matter how many people she surrounded herself with during her daily life, when she went home, it was just her and her cats.

"See you tomorrow," Sophie told her as they reached Carroll Street.

"Yep. Hope your date goes well."

With a wave, Sophie was off.

Jules walked the rest of the way home, relieved to enter her apartment. It was cold tonight, a reminder that they were already halfway through November. The show opened for previews just after the new year. After bending to greet Pippin, she poured herself a glass of red wine and headed to the bathroom for a hot bath.

Hopefully, she and Micki would find their footing together. What if they were as out of sync when they had to kiss onstage as they had been for today's choreography?

ophie was wasting her time. Worse, she was wasting time she didn't have. Between rehearsals for *It's in Her Kiss* and finishing up her last few shifts at the diner, she had her hands more than full. And here she sat next to a bubbly blonde named Kim, who'd spent the last fifteen minutes telling Sophie about her cat.

Jules had cats. That was the random thought circling Sophie's brain. If she was going to listen to a beautiful woman talk about her cat, she'd rather hear about Pippin and Phantom. Theater names. It made Sophie smile. And obviously, her plan to date until she'd gotten over her silly crush on Jules wasn't working.

"Doesn't she have the most beautiful eyes?" Kim asked, holding up her phone to show Sophie a photo of a gray-striped cat with amber eyes.

"Yes," she answered honestly. The cat's eyes were striking. Unfortunately, she couldn't care less about Kim or her cat.

"Do you have any pets?" Kim asked.

"No," Sophie told her.

"Do you at least *like* cats?" Kim pressed, as if this was a deal breaker for her, and Sophie almost lied and said no, just to let them both off the hook, but lying had never really been her style.

"I do, and I'd love to have one someday." She finished her beer and set enough money on the bar to cover both of their drinks. "I'm sorry to duck out so soon, but I have to be at work early tomorrow."

"Oh, I totally understand." Kim stood, offering her a shy smile. "I need to get home to Twinkle anyway. Can I call you?"

"I think maybe not," Sophie told her apologetically. "My schedule's really crazy right now, and I'm just realizing it was foolish of me to think I'd have time to date."

"Right. Gotcha." Kim's eyes fell, as she no doubt heard the rejection in Sophie's words. "Well, thanks for the drink. I had a great time tonight. Good luck with your new play."

"Thank you." Sophie dawdled with her coat as Kim headed for the door, so they wouldn't end up awkwardly walking to the subway together. Sophie gave her a five-minute head start, then buttoned her coat, wound her scarf around her neck, and set out.

She rode the 2 train to Brooklyn and walked the last few blocks to her apartment. Luckily, Nathan and Anthony were already in their bedroom watching TV when she got home. She called a quick hello from the living room as she rummaged through the armoire containing her belongings.

"How was your hot date?" Anthony asked.

"She talked about her cat the whole time."

"Well, at least you know she likes pussy," Nathan joked, causing Anthony to cackle with laughter.

"Ha-ha," Sophie said, fighting a smile as she carried her pajamas into the bathroom to get ready for bed.

"Hey, one of the dancers at work is going through Tinder hell right now too," Nathan said when she came out of the bathroom. "I think you two might hit it off. I could get her number for you if you want?"

"Thanks, but I think I'm going to put dating on the back burner right now so I can focus on the show."

They said goodnight, and she started removing cushions from the couch, her nightly ritual. As she unfolded the sofa bed, she realized how tired she was of living this way. Her roommates were great, but they probably didn't love having her on their couch every night any more than she enjoyed sleeping here. Like it or not, though, they all needed each other's help to afford this place.

For now, at least.

Sophie climbed into bed to read on her phone until she fell asleep. First, she checked tomorrow's rehearsal schedule, annoyed with herself for the little flutter she felt when she saw that both she and Jules would be there all day. Dammit, how was she going to get over this crush?

The next morning, she got up and remade the couch, packing away her things in the armoire in the corner. She took a quick shower and had the coffee pot running when the guys came out of their bedroom.

"Morning," she called as she started tossing things into her bag for the day. Water, snacks, a protein bar that would have to serve as lunch.

"Morning, dearest," Anthony called as he sauntered into the room, script in hand, already humming under his breath as he prepared for today's audition. Ah, living with actors. It was a special kind of crazy, and she really did love it. They maneuvered around each other like a carefully choreographed dance as they all got ready for their day.

Sophie filled her travel mug with coffee and headed out,

earbuds in, eager for the "peace and quiet" of her walk to the theater. Sometimes, it was the quietest part of her day. This morning, the sky was heavy with impending rain, cold and damp. She shivered, wishing she'd brought a scarf to keep her neck warm.

After a brisk thirty-minute walk, she let herself in through the back door of the theater, heading downstairs to her dressing room to drop off her stuff. Her gaze automatically fell on Jules's dressing room as she passed, but either she wasn't here yet, or she'd closed her door, which wasn't her usual style.

Sophie set down her bag and slipped out of her coat, taking a moment to fix her hair in front of the mirror. Tabitha came in, and they chatted for a few minutes as they got ready together, stretching and warming up their muscles for another day of dance rehearsals.

When Sophie headed back down the hall, Jules's door was open. She was inside her dressing room, wearing yoga pants and a figure-hugging blue top, bent in a forward fold as she stretched, giving Sophie a spectacular view of her ample cleavage. "Morning," she called, dropping her gaze to Jules's shoes, which seemed the only safe place to look.

"Good morning." Jules straightened, cheeks flushed, hair piled in a messy knot on top of her head. She grabbed her water bottle and stepped into the hall with Sophie and Tabitha.

"Don't tell me you're one of those naturally peppy people who doesn't drink coffee," Sophie said, giving the water bottle a skeptical look.

"God, no. I drink mine at home before I leave," Jules said. "And Cuban coffee is basically a sweetened shot of espresso, so yeah, I'm caffeinated."

"That sounds amazing, actually," Sophie said, feeling suddenly less excited about her boring vanilla roast.

"I'll make it for you sometime," Jules said with one of her effortless smiles, leading the way up the stairs.

Simon and Andrew were waiting for them on stage. For their first number, the cast joined up in a line, with Sophie holding hands with Tabitha and Jules as they danced. Unlike yesterday, Jules never missed a step, not even with Micki adding her extra flair to every move.

At the end of the day, Jules and Sophie walked home together, which seemed to have become a habit, one they continued for the rest of the week.

"I invited a few people over to my place on Sunday to run lines," Jules said as they left the theater together on Friday afternoon. "Want to come?"

"Who did you invite?" Sophie asked, torn between the desire to jump on this chance to spend more time with her castmates and the knowledge that, with her persistently inconvenient attraction to Jules, hanging out in her apartment this weekend was probably not the best idea.

"Amir and Micki," Jules said. "And you. What do you say?"

Sophie hesitated, but as the understudy for both Jules and Micki, the chance to run lines with them this weekend could be invaluable. "Yeah, sure."

"Great." Jules beamed. "Around four? We can run lines for a few hours and order food or something."

"Sounds great."

They headed their separate ways. Sophie's weekend had already been busy, as she was working her last shift at the diner tomorrow and then she had a voice lesson on Sunday morning. But busy was good. Really, she tried to avoid her apartment as much as possible. Without her own space to relax in, she often found herself heading to various coffee shops or the library to sit with her earbuds in and have some "alone" time.

By Sunday afternoon, Sophie found that she was looking forward to going to Jules's. She confirmed with her via text that they were still on, and then she fussed with her hair and makeup for longer than she probably should have before grabbing her copy of the script and heading out. As often as they walked home together, Sophie hadn't realized how close she and Jules actually lived to each other until she began her walk to Jules's apartment.

Ten short minutes later, she pushed the buzzer on a three-story brownstone. Jules buzzed her in, and Sophie climbed two flights of stairs. She knocked on the door Jules had indicated, and it swung open to reveal her standing there in skinny jeans and an oversized red sweater, her honey-brown hair loose around her face. And *damn*, it really wasn't fair for her to look so good.

"Hi," Jules said, gesturing for Sophie to come in. "You beat the others here."

"Oh. Am I early?"

"Nope. They're just late."

Sophie stepped into the living room. The wall to her left was exposed brick. To her right, a brightly colored curtain hung across the room, presumably hiding Jules's bed from visitors. She'd strung white lights around the ceiling, which made the whole room seem to glow. "This is really nice."

"Thank you." Jules motioned her toward the couch, where she'd set out a tray of snacks and a bottle of wine. "I do love this place. I've been here about five years."

"It's great. I would give my left arm to be able to afford something like this," Sophie said, grimacing at her admission, but Jules just rolled her eyes.

"My parents helped me out with rent at first, but I'm able to pay for it myself these days."

"How?" Sophie blurted.

"I've done some modeling, voiceover work, a walk-on role on *Law & Order: SVU*. And I've had a consistent run of theater work over the last few years."

"Impressive." Sophie sat on the couch and reached for a chip. "You're living the life I dream of."

They were interrupted by the buzzer, announcing Amir's arrival, and Micki got there a few minutes later. They sat around chatting for a while, enjoying snacks and wine, before they got down to business. Jules, Amir, and Micki read their own roles, while Sophie filled in for the remaining parts. After breaking for pizza, they were back at it, working until past nine. Sophie got the chance to read for both Bianca and Melissa, the first time she'd gotten to practice her understudy roles with her castmates.

She hadn't done this since high school, mostly because she hadn't had many speaking roles since, but also, the rapport among the cast of *It's in Her Kiss* was a lot more collaborative than some of the shows she'd worked on. That was partly due to the cast itself and partly because it was a brand-new production, so everyone was learning their lines together for the first time.

Micki wasn't Sophie's favorite person, but she wasn't awful either. Behind her dramatic tendencies, she was a hard worker and seemingly well-intentioned. As Micki, Sophie, and Amir got ready to head home from Jules's apartment, they made tentative plans to do this again next Sunday. Sophie was already looking forward to it.

The following morning at rehearsal, they started blocking scenes, which was a painstaking process that involved figuring out where everyone would stand, how best to orient themselves to the audience, and where all the props should go to make it happen. Some of the set work was already done, but they were winging it for most of the details, using metal folding chairs in place of the furniture they'd eventually have.

Monday and Tuesday were fairly tedious for Sophie and the rest of the ensemble, while Jules, Amir, and Micki did most of the work onstage. After the leads had their marks, the ensemble would find their places around them. By lunchtime on Wednesday, they hadn't even made it to the end of the first act. Sophie ate a power bar in her dressing room before wandering back to the stage.

Jules came to stand beside her, gesturing toward the empty balcony across from them. "I sat somewhere up there for a performance of *Romeo and Juliet* when I was eighteen. If you had told me then that I'd be back here again twelve years later, performing on stage, I might have leaped out of the balcony in my excitement."

"And the star to boot," Sophie said, nudging her shoulder against Jules's.

"The lead, anyway. I wouldn't call myself a star just yet."

"I'd say you're on your way." Sophie paused, glancing at the script in her hands. "Ready for the next scene?"

"Yes." Jules kept her gaze on the empty seats in front of them. The next scene was the one with Bianca and Melissa's first kiss. Jules's first onstage kiss. That had to be at least somewhat nerve-racking.

Sophie didn't envy her having to kiss Micki either. Not that she was hard to look at or anything, but her showy attitude and tendency to offer unsolicited advice made her a potentially awkward person to practice a stage kiss with.

As if on cue, Micki strode onto the stage. "Hey, ladies."

"Hi," Jules responded, and Sophie couldn't quite read

her expression when she looked at Micki, but she was definitely feeling some kind of way about this upcoming kiss.

"I'll leave you guys to get ready for your scene," Sophie said. "Good luck," she added, glancing at Jules, who gave her a tight smile in return.

Jules and Micki were the only two actors in the scene, but most of the cast and crew gathered off stage to watch, as had been the case all week. Everyone was eager to see the show come together for the first time, whether they were in the scene or not. And so Sophie found herself standing between Tabitha and Elena, watching as Jules and Micki ran through the scene, scripts in hand.

Maybe watching Jules kiss Micki would help Sophie get over her crush. A girl could hope, anyway.

Jules was standing on what would be their "stage on a stage," as large parts of the production were set in a television studio. Bianca was an actress at the top of her game who was struggling to come to terms with her sexuality. Kari directed Jules and Micki as they stood facing each other.

"I need to hear you say the words," Micki read. "I need to know that what I think is happening is real."

"It's real," Jules said, the script held loosely in her hands. She hadn't even glanced at it yet. "It wasn't supposed to be you, Melissa, and yet, you're the only one I can think about."

"And for me, it's only ever been you," Micki said. "Please kiss me, Bianca."

Sophie's fists clenched. Okay, she wasn't going to enjoy watching this. There was just no way around it. Kari paused the actors while she adjusted their positions. Jules put down her script so she could reach out and take Micki's hands, clasping them in hers.

"Raise your hands a little higher?" Kari suggested, walking from one side of the stage to the other. She had to have paced miles across that short expanse this week, tire-lessly checking their positioning from every angle.

Jules and Micki did as she'd asked, lifting their clasped hands between them.

Just kiss already. Sophie was dying from the anticipation —and not in a good way.

"Jules, turn toward the audience just a bit more," Kari said.

Jules adjusted her position, gaze still locked on Micki. There was nothing left for them to do but kiss. The script called for Jules to lean in, pressing her lips briefly against Micki's. But she didn't. She stood there for several long seconds, frozen in place. And then she stepped back, releasing Micki's hands. "I'm sorry. I just...I need a minute."

Jules rushed off the stage, leaving the rest of the cast staring after her in stunned silence.

6

J ules sat at the makeup table in her dressing room, staring resolutely at herself in the mirror as emotions churned like a turbulent sea inside her. This was a mess—a mess of her own making—and since there was no way out of it, she was just going to have to suck it up and get it over with, no matter how uncomfortable it made her. She was a professional, dammit.

There was a light knock at her dressing room door.

"I'll be right there," she called, frowning at her reflection.

"It's me," Sophie said from the other side of the door.

Jules flinched. Talking to Sophie could either make this less awkward, or...much, much worse. "Come in."

The door opened, and Sophie stepped through it, shutting it softly behind herself. "Everything okay?"

Jules shrugged, fingers tapping restlessly against the table in front of her. "Just need to get out of my head, I think."

Sophie leaned a hip against the wall. Her posture was

casual, but her eyes were sharp and questioning. "Anything I can help with?"

Jules pressed her fingers over her eyes. How did she tell Sophie—or anyone for that matter—that kissing a woman for the first time felt like an important milestone for her? As she stood there on stage, she just couldn't imagine sharing that milestone with Micki of all people. Never mind that she didn't want her first kiss with a woman to be in front of a room full of spectators. *Ugh.* "No. Thanks, though."

"Are you weirded out about kissing a woman?" Sophie pressed.

Worse. This conversation was definitely making things worse. Jules stood, turning to face her. Hysteria bubbled in her throat. She really just needed a minute alone to calm herself down before she went back on stage. "Sophie..."

"Look, it's not that different from kissing a dude," Sophie said. "Just close your eyes and picture your favorite actor instead of Micki."

Jules slapped her hands against her thighs as tears pricked at her eyes. "I'm not upset because I don't want to kiss a woman. I'm upset because I *do*."

Sophie froze. "What?"

Jules felt flames licking across her face. Why couldn't she just turn off her brain, shut her mouth, and do the scene like she was supposed to? This was so ridiculous. And mortifying. She could only remember feeling this embarrassed once before, and it had been a dream, one of those cliché nightmares where she'd gone on stage for her first starring role, only to realize she was standing in front of a packed crowd without any clothes on. She turned toward the wall so she wouldn't have to face Sophie...or her own reflection.

"Jules..."

"Look, I lied to you that night when I said I'd never thought about kissing a woman, okay? I have. I've thought about it."

Sophie was quiet for a long beat. "You've thought about it as in, you were curious? Or as in, you were attracted to a woman?"

"The second." Jules closed her eyes. Her skin crawled uncomfortably, and her stomach was in knots. She'd never said these words out loud before, and even though she knew Sophie was a safe person to tell, that it didn't have to go any further than this dressing room, she couldn't help feeling like everything was different now.

"Okay," Sophie said evenly. "Do you want to talk about it?"

"No. Yes. I don't know."

"Here, come sit with me." Sophie tugged at her fingers, and Jules followed her to the couch. They sat side by side. Sophie's expression was gentler now, nothing but kindness and empathy in her eyes.

Jules sucked in a deep breath and blew it out. "I thought I was ready to do the scene, but then, it just felt so...wrong for my first kiss with a woman to be staged, with a crowd watching. And knowing Micki, she'd tell me I was doing it wrong or something. I just...I panicked."

Sophie nodded. "Okay, I get that. So, am I the first person you've talked to about this?"

"Yes."

She took Jules's hand, giving it a reassuring squeeze. "Well, first of all, thank you for trusting me, and second, congratulations. It's a big step to acknowledge your feelings out loud. I'd love to talk more with you about this, but I don't think we should keep them waiting upstairs too long. Maybe we could get a drink together after we leave tonight?

I mean, only if you want to talk. I could be a good sounding board for you, I think."

"Yeah, okay. Thanks." Jules's cheeks were burning again at Sophie's words. Yep. It all felt a *lot* more real now, and she had no idea how to feel about any of it. Maybe talking to Sophie later would be a good idea.

"So, what do you want to do about the scene upstairs with Micki?"

God, it was going to be a thousand times more awkward now. Micki was an out-and-proud lesbian, and something told Jules she'd just love to share her expertise on the subject. Jules pressed a hand over her eyes. "I can*not* tell her anything I just told you. I've just got to suck it up and get it done."

Sophie sighed. "Your first kiss should be special, not something you're dreading."

"Ideally," Jules agreed. "But I don't really have a choice."

Sophie pressed her lips together in frustration, drawing Jules's attention to her mouth. If only Sophie had been cast as Melissa. For some reason, kissing her felt way less intimidating.

"Do you think…" Jules blurted, cheeks flaming all over again. "Could I practice with you in here where no one's watching? And so the first woman I kiss doesn't have to be Micki?"

Sophie's eyes rounded. "Oh, um, yeah. We could do that."

"Is that weird?" Jules looked down at her hands. "I'm sorry. I shouldn't have asked."

"No, it's not weird," Sophie said quickly. "You shouldn't have to do this in front of an audience, or with Micki."

Jules grinned in spite of herself. "Okay, then." As first kisses went, she could do a lot worse than Sophie. She was pretty, and funny, and Jules enjoyed her friendship. "Ready?"

Sophie nodded, her gaze dropping to Jules's lips.

Without giving herself a chance to second-guess things, Jules leaned in, eyes sliding shut as her lips met Sophie's. *Soft.* That was the first thought that reached her brain. Sophie's lips were unexpectedly soft. They lingered like that for a long moment, lips pressed together, exactly what she would do upstairs with Micki, but Jules couldn't help thinking this was somehow better, and not just because no one was watching.

Sophie tilted her head to the side, changing the angle of the kiss, and wow, that was good. Jules leaned in a little more, thrilled by the faintly fruity taste of Sophie's lip gloss and the way her lips moved against Jules's. There was a tingle in her belly, an awareness that spread warmth over her skin and ignited a yearning ache deep inside her. *Whoa.* She lifted her head, dazed. She could hear herself breathing, blood pumping hard and fast through her veins. Was this her reaction to kissing a woman, or was it a reaction to kissing Sophie?

Sophie grinned at her, lips glistening from their kiss. A flush had spread over the pale skin of her chest, which was heaving for breath, the same as Jules's. "That was nice."

Jules nodded, reaching up to fuss with her hair, suddenly not sure what to do with her hands. "Very nice."

"I *really* don't want to rush you, but we'd better get back up there before Andrew comes looking for you," Sophie said, and was Jules imagining things, or did she seem a bit flustered too?

She nodded. "You're right. I'm ready."

They stood, and Sophie opened the door. Jules didn't know where to look, what to say, how to act as she followed

Sophie. She felt like her whole world had been knocked off its axis, like she was spinning sideways, careening out of orbit. Really and truly, she needed a few minutes alone to collect herself, to calm her emotions and figure out how she felt about that kiss, about confessing her sexuality to Sophie, about all of it.

"You sure you're okay?" Sophie asked, giving her an inquiring look.

"Yes." Because this wasn't the time for her to sort herself out. She had a job to do and a whole stage full of people waiting for her to get back out there and do it. She touched Sophie's shoulder as they stepped into the hallway together. "Thanks."

"Any time." Sophie led the way to the stairs.

Jules walked a step behind her, taking the opportunity to compose herself before they reached the stage. The other actors seemed to have gone on their break. Only Kari, Andrew, and Simon remained on stage, deep in conversation.

"Everything okay?" Kari asked as she caught sight of Jules and Sophie.

"Yes," Jules said with a nod. "Sorry about that."

"No problem," Kari said, giving Jules an assessing look. "Unless there *is* a problem I should know about?"

"Nope. First-onstage-kiss jitters, but Sophie talked me through it." Among other things...

"Great. Well, please let me know if you're feeling uncomfortable with anything, but otherwise, let's finish blocking this scene."

"I'm ready," Jules told her with a nod.

Micki sauntered onto the stage, giving Jules an odd look. "I don't bite, you know."

"I know," Jules said. "Sorry about that."

"Okay, then," Kari said. "From the top."

Jules and Micki ran smoothly through their lines, hitting their marks. Their hands clasped. Their eyes met. And then, Jules leaned in, pressing her lips firmly against Micki's. Unlike her kiss with Sophie, this time she felt absolutely nothing.

"A BIT more to the front, ladies," Kari called.

Onstage, Jules and Micki angled themselves toward the audience, lips still pressed together. Sophie looked down at her shoes. She'd already been dreading watching Jules kiss Micki. And now that Sophie herself had kissed Jules? Yeah, this was torture.

She ducked behind Amir and made her way down the hall to the break room. After snagging a bag of chips from the table in back, she sank into a chair and began to eat, crunching through her feelings. Oh, she was so screwed. And still reeling from Jules's confession. Her vulnerability in that moment, the weight of her choosing Sophie as the first person she came out to, the wonder in her eyes as she brought their lips together...

Well, suffice to say, Sophie's crush had grown exponentially. But at the same time, she was no closer to acting on her feelings. Because, while Jules definitely seemed to enjoy the kiss as much as she did, she probably wasn't looking for a relationship while she was still sorting herself out, and Sophie didn't date people who weren't out.

She'd learned that lesson the hard way when she fell head over heels in love with a woman who'd kept Sophie in the shadows of her life, not willing to introduce her to her friends or family, despite constant promises that things would change. Eventually, Brianna had gotten cold feet entirely and dumped Sophie rather than come to terms with her sexuality. Sophie refused to put herself in that situation again.

She crunched through the rest of her chips, washed them down with some water, and made her way back to the stage, hoping Jules and Micki were finished kissing. And apparently, she was in luck. Two theater employees were in the process of wheeling the piano onstage for Jules's solo. Sophie went down the steps into the audience and sat beside Tabitha and Elena to watch.

"What happened earlier when Jules ran off?" Tabitha whispered.

Sophie shrugged. "She was just nervous about her first onstage kiss."

"And you talked her through it?" Tab's eyebrows rose questioningly.

"Yep." And that was all she was going to say on the matter.

Onstage, Jules began to sing, her rich voice filling the theater. She glanced toward the audience, looking straight at Sophie. A smile touched her lips before she shifted her gaze to the musical director, Francesca.

By the time they'd worked through Jules's solo, it was almost five, and Kari sent them home for the night. Sophie headed downstairs with Tabitha, who was in a hurry to get ready for a date. Sophie gathered her things and walked down the hall, finding Jules's door open. "Still on for that drink?"

Jules looked down at her hands as she nodded, a hint of her earlier insecurity reappearing. "Yeah."

"Cool. I thought Dragonfly might be a good option. It's kind of on our way home, and—"

"It's a gay bar?" Jules gave her an amused look. "Yeah, that's fine." She slipped into a navy-blue wool coat that belted at the waist and grabbed her purse.

They didn't talk much as they walked to the bar. Sophie figured their conversation would be easier once they'd had a drink or two to loosen up. She had so many questions, but she knew her role here was to listen and provide support. She had to keep her personal feelings out of it.

Dragonfly was comfortably empty when they arrived, a handful of people at the bar and two tables occupied in the back. A steady hum of conversation mixed with the bar's jazz music, just enough to keep them from feeling self-conscious about being overheard, but it wasn't too loud to hear each other talk.

Josie and a male bartender were behind the bar, mixing drinks. She waved them over with a smile. "Hey! How are my two favorite Broadway actresses?"

"Do you actually know any other Broadway actresses?" Jules asked as she slid onto a stool.

"Well, no, but you'd still be my favorite, because you named my theater kittens," Josie said playfully. "Hey, speaking of theater, what happened with that audition you guys had been on the last time you were in here?"

"Jules landed the lead," Sophie told her.

"No shit?" Josie looked delighted. "Your first starring role?"

Jules nodded. "Sophie's in it too."

"Well, this is fantastic news." Josie slapped her palms against the counter. "When does it open? You know Eve and I will be there to cheer you on."

"Previews start the first week of January," Jules said.

Josie took out her phone and looked up *It's in Her Kiss* while they talked. "Okay, I've got it bookmarked. Now, what can I get you to drink? Actually, do you guys want to be taste testers for something new I'm working on? There's prosecco in it." She dangled that last bit with an enticing lift of her eyebrows.

"You had me at prosecco," Jules told her.

"Sure, I'm game," Sophie agreed.

"If you like it, maybe I'll name it after you," Josie told them as she started mixing their drinks. "Broadway Bubbles or something like that."

"Love it," Jules exclaimed. She and Sophie watched as Josie prepared their drinks, adding an orange mixture and a splash of gin before topping it off with prosecco.

"On the house," she said as she slid them across the bar. "For being my taste testers and in celebration of your new show."

"Aw, thanks," Jules told her.

"Just make sure you let me know what you think," Josie told them. "Honest opinions, please."

"You got it." Sophie lifted her drink and sipped. It was sweet and fizzy with a hint of citrus. Josie moved down the bar to check on her other customers, and Sophie caught Jules's eye, gesturing to an empty table in back. "Want to move over there so we can talk?"

Jules nodded, lifting her drink and following Sophie to the table. "So."

Sophie settled herself on the bar height stool and looked at Jules. "So."

Jules dropped her gaze to her glass, trademark confidence missing from her expression. It was a big deal, coming to terms with your sexuality, and Sophie had seen the cross pendant that Jules wore around her neck. She imagined that only complicated matters for her.

"How are you feeling about this afternoon?" she asked carefully.

"Good," Jules answered quickly. "I mean...confused, I guess, but not in a bad way."

"Is this a new realization for you?"

Jules took a thoughtful sip of her drink. "In some ways, yes."

"I don't mean to pry, but it might help to talk it out with someone who's been there," Sophie said. "Whatever you're comfortable with."

"I guess...I've been attracted to women before, but for a long time, I ignored it. I like men too, and that just seemed easier." She winced. "I know that sounds terrible."

"It doesn't," Sophie told her.

Jules lifted her drink and took a hearty gulp. "I thought this role might help me figure myself out, like the universe was telling me it was time to kiss a woman."

"Maybe it was," Sophie said with a laugh.

"I just didn't expect it to be so...scary." There was something vulnerable in her voice.

Sophie had been out for so long, sometimes she forgot what it was like to be where Jules was. "Well, of course it's scary, and I would think it's probably more confusing figuring out where you fit when you're attracted to more than one gender. I knew when I was really young that I liked girls. I had a boyfriend my senior year of high school, just to see what the fuss was about, but it only made me absolutely certain that I was gay."

Jules's brows pinched as she took a big swallow of her drink. "See, it wasn't like that for me. In high school, it had never even crossed my mind that I wasn't straight."

"Everyone's story is different, Jules. It doesn't make yours any less valid. I have plenty of friends who didn't come out until much later in life."

"This is all so surreal." Jules shook her head. "Everyone in my life assumes I'm straight, including me sometimes. I mean, how do you know for sure?"

"You just have to trust your gut, and it's okay if it takes you a while to figure it out, or even if you change your mind."

Jules pressed her fingers against her forehead. "I don't want to change my mind. That's not my style."

"Then maybe just accept that right now, you're curious. You could try dating a woman and see how it goes, if that feels right for you."

"Maybe." Jules polished off her drink and set the glass on the table with a solid thunk. Something in her seemed to have loosened as the alcohol kicked in. She looked up, catching Sophie's gaze. "It felt right when I kissed you earlier."

"Oh?" Sophie asked casually, trying to ignore the little ping radiating through her stomach at Jules's words.

"I mean...not that I...shit." Jules scrubbed a hand over her face. "I'm not trying to come on to you or anything, but I don't think I would have enjoyed our kiss as much as I did if I was entirely straight." A very attractive blush spread over her cheeks.

"Then maybe that's your answer." Sophie lifted her own glass and gulped the last of her drink, feeling the warmth of liquor spread through her belly, mixed with the attraction already simmering there.

Jules sighed, resting her elbows on the table. Her gaze dropped to Sophie's lips, and surely it wasn't entirely Sophie's overactive imagination that the table between them seemed to vibrate with sexual tension. "I didn't enjoy my kiss with Micki nearly as much," Jules whispered.

Sophie couldn't seem to get enough oxygen into her lungs. She wished for another drink to distract herself with, anything to keep from staring at Jules, from noticing the swell of her breasts beneath her purple top or the way her plum-colored lips shone beneath the overhead lights. Sophie's hands tightened around her empty glass.

"What did you think?" Josie asked, appearing at their table and snapping them out of the sexually charged trance they seemed to have fallen into.

Jules startled, glancing at Josie with a slightly guilty look on her face. "It was great, if you couldn't tell by how quickly I drank it."

"Yay," Josie said. "Sophie?"

"It was good," Sophie said.

"But?" Josie pressed.

"I love the bubbles and the citrus, but I feel like if you gave it a little something extra, it might really sparkle."

"Hmm," Josie said, pressing a finger against her lips. "I might know just the thing. Another round?"

"Sure," Sophie said as Jules nodded eagerly.

"Coming right up." Josie took their empty glasses and headed back to the bar, pink-tipped hair bouncing over her shoulders.

Jules tucked a lock of hair behind her ears. "My sexuality feels a lot more real to me now, after today."

"In a good way?" Sophie asked.

Jules nodded, a smile tugging at the corners of her lips. "I think so."

"Good."

"Were your parents supportive?" Jules asked.

"Yeah. They've been great. My whole family has been super supportive."

"I'm glad," Jules said.

"How do you think yours would react?"

"That's the million-dollar question, isn't it?" Jules's smile wilted slightly. "I want to say my mom would be cool about it. She's always been my biggest supporter and my best friend, and she's a lot more progressive than, say...my grandma. But we're Cuban, and my whole family is super Catholic, and the reality is, they might *not* be cool about it."

"I'm sorry," Sophie told her. She'd been so envious of Jules when they first met, thinking she had this perfect, charmed life, but really, who did?

Josie arrived with their new drinks, and she and Jules sipped in silence for a few minutes.

"I don't know what she added, but this one is the winner," Sophie said thoughtfully. There was something vaguely spicy about the drink now, a hint of extra flavor that really made it pop.

"Yep," Jules agreed.

"I hope your family pleasantly surprises you," Sophie said.

Jules blanched, shaking her head. "I'm nowhere near ready to think about telling them yet."

And that was the dash of reality Sophie needed to keep her hormones in check. "Hungry?" she asked instead.

"Starving, actually," Jules said. "This alcohol is going straight to my head."

"Want to finish these and go find something to eat?"

"Josie has menus at the bar," Jules told her. "We could order takeout and eat it here."

"Really? Yes, let's do that."

So, they perused the menus at the bar and placed an

order from a Thai restaurant down the street. They gave Josie their thumbs-up on the new drink and returned to their table. Two hours—and a third round of drinks—later, they stepped outside into the chilly November night. Sophie was feeling pretty tipsy, and based on the relaxed grin on Jules's face, so was she.

They chatted comfortably as they walked, talking mostly about rehearsals, until they reached the corner where they would part ways. Jules hesitated for a moment, tongue darting out to wet her lips, and all Sophie could think about was kissing her again, a real kiss not in any way inspired by their roles in the show.

She cleared her throat. "So, I'll see you tomorrow, then."

Jules nodded, touching Sophie's coat-clad arm before she turned to cross the street. "Bye, Sophie. And thanks again for everything today."

leasure. Jules was swamped in it. Sophie's soft lips met hers as their bodies moved together, skin sliding over skin. Delicate fingers trailed down her stomach and dipped between her legs, lighting her on fire. Jules whimpered, lost in Sophie's brown eyes and the hot press of their bodies, rocking, arching, climbing. Harder. Faster. She was so close, *so* close...

Her eyes popped open, and she blinked into the darkness, confused and disoriented. Her fingers were clenched in the sheets. Her heart was pounding, and arousal pulsed in her core. She rolled over, checking the time on her phone as she gathered her wits. It was three fifteen in the morning, and she was apparently having sex dreams about Sophie now.

"What in the world," she murmured as her thighs pressed together uncomfortably. If only she'd woken just a minute later... She rolled toward the wall, closing her eyes, but memories of the dream lingered behind her eyelids, and dammit, she was throbbing.

She pushed a hand into her underwear, gasping as her

fingers slid through her wetness. Her hips arched instinctively, seeking more friction. She circled her clit, imagining it was Sophie's hand, Sophie's fingers, Sophie whispering dirty words in her ear. Jules whimpered, stroking herself faster. She rolled to her stomach, thrusting her hips against her hand, Sophie's name on her lips as she tumbled over the edge. Her body stiffened as the orgasm swept through her, and then she collapsed, exhausted, against the bed.

She lay there, eyes closed, as her breathing slowed and her pulse returned to normal. And then, sated, she drifted back to sleep.

The next time she woke, the room had started to brighten with dawn and the alarm on her phone was chiming. Groaning, she reached over and silenced it. As she flopped back in bed, one arm thrown over her eyes, her mind drifted to the dream. Had that really happened? Well, she'd either dreamed the first part or all of it, and wow, that was...unusual.

She honestly couldn't remember the last time she'd had a sex dream about anyone. Apparently, kissing Sophie yesterday had fully awakened her bisexuality, because as she got up and stepped into a hot shower to get ready for another day of rehearsals, she found herself wondering what sex with a woman would be like. And more specifically, what sex with *Sophie* would be like, what her hands would feel like on Jules's skin, what kind of lover she was, how she sounded when she came.

Jules swiped a hand over her face, washing away the soap and attempting to cleanse her brain at the same time. She could *not* fantasize about Sophie like this. If she kept it up, she was going to make things awkward between them at the theater. And they had to work together for months to come.

To change the subject in her suddenly sex-starved brain, she mentally ran lines as she finished getting ready. The only problem was, Bianca was as obsessed with kissing a girl as Jules was. Perfect, really. She'd become her character.

"Ridiculous," she muttered under her breath as she bundled into her coat and headed for the door. It was just a dream. She and Sophie were just friends.

Weren't they?

Because maybe there'd been a bit of a...vibe between them last night at Dragonfly. There'd been a few moments that could have been flirty. Or not. Jules usually had pretty good intuition for when a guy was interested in her. But women were harder to read, or maybe she just didn't know how to read them yet.

Maybe everything she was feeling was just a reaction to kissing a woman for the first time. It might not have anything to do with Sophie at all. The kiss had made her curious about sex with a woman, so she'd dreamed about it. That was all. Mystery solved.

Blowing out a relieved breath, she walked briskly down the sidewalk, eager to get to the theater and out of the cold morning air. At this point, she'd lived more than half of her life in New York, but Miami was still in her blood, because she could never seem to get warm here in the wintertime.

She went in through the theater's back door and headed downstairs to her dressing room, unraveling her scarf as she walked. She put away her coat and left her bag on the sofa, closing the door behind her as she left.

"Hey."

She turned at the sound of Sophie's voice to see her walking down the hall toward Jules, morning coffee in hand. And *whoa*, Jules's whole body went haywire at the sight of her. Her heart thudded inside her chest, and a jolt of electricity sparked in the pit of her stomach. "Good morning."

"How are you today?" Sophie asked, giving her an inquiring look that was probably in reference to everything they'd talked about yesterday, but Jules's mind was still in fantasyland, and she felt a hot blush spread across her cheeks.

She averted her gaze, leading the way to the stairs. "I'm fine. You?"

"No complaints."

They were the first two to arrive on stage. Jules darted a glance at her, and there it was again. Heat. Awareness. Oh, this was going to be a problem. When she'd been attracted to a woman in the past, it had often been more akin to a crush. She'd never felt anything this intense. It was like their kiss had unleashed something inside Jules, and now there was no reining it in.

Amir joined them on stage. "Morning, ladies."

"Morning," Jules said, smiling at him over her shoulder.

"Hey, are we still running lines at your place again on Sunday?" he asked.

"Yes! I meant to bring it up yesterday, but I got distracted. Yes, definitely."

"Cool," he said. "Looking forward to it."

"Are you coming?" she asked Sophie.

"Yeah, of course," Sophie said. "It was a lot of fun last weekend."

Jules had no idea whether she was imagining the awkwardness between them this morning. Maybe she was the only one feeling awkward. Maybe for Sophie, this was just any other morning. She probably hadn't had a sex dream about Jules last night...

Her cheeks were flaming again.

"Are you okay?" Sophie asked, giving her a funny look.

"Yes."

Luckily, Kari saved her by stepping onto the stage. Within minutes, she had them on their marks and beginning their first scene of the day. As they approached the end of their second week of rehearsals, Jules could start to see the show coming together, and she was ridiculously excited about it. One thing about being the lead: rehearsals were exhausting. The rest of the cast came and went, but Jules was almost always on stage. It was a good kind of exhausting, though, and she was loving every minute of it.

She didn't get a chance to talk to Sophie again that day. Kari sent the ensemble home early since the last scene of the day only required Jules, Amir, and Micki. Consequently, Jules set out from the theater alone that evening. She was still feeling out of sorts about their kiss. She needed to talk it through with someone. That was how she solved most of her problems, and surely this one was no different.

The problem was, her usual sounding board was her mom, and she wasn't ready to talk to her about this. Similarly, her brothers were out of the question. And while she had literally dozens of friends that she could call to meet her for a drink after work today, she wasn't close enough with any of them to trust them with this either.

As she walked, an uncharacteristic melancholy settled over her. What was she going to do?

The answer came to her as she glanced to her left and caught a glimpse of people seated inside a bar. She'd go to Dragonfly. Bartenders were supposed to give good advice, and Josie knew a thing or two about being attracted to a woman.

Relieved, Jules turned around and started backtracking toward the bar. With every step, she became more sure of her decision. Josie was exactly the person she should talk to about this. Ten minutes later, she walked through Dragonfly's front door. Josie's friend Adam was behind the bar with a brunette Jules didn't recognize. Unfazed, she slid onto an empty stool and caught his eye. "Where's Josie?"

"She's off tonight," he told her. "Hey, you're the actress, right?"

She nodded, deflating slightly at his news. "Jules."

"Right." He slid a drink menu toward her, tapping it with a smile. "I hear you had something to do with this."

She looked down at the glossy lavender card in front of her. Broadway Bubbles had been added to the list of signature drinks. "Oh, wow. That's really cool."

"She had them printed up this morning. Should I make you one?" he asked.

"Please." She snapped a picture of the menu and shared it to her Instagram, tagging Dragonfly in her post. The drink was fun, but she was no closer to finding someone to talk through her feelings with. While she was thinking about Josie, though, she should remind her to figure out a time to come see the cats. She picked up her phone and composed a text message.

I'm at Dragonfly, and you're not. She inserted a sad face emoji. *If you still want to stop by and see Pippin and Phantom, lmk and let's figure out a time that works.*

"Here you go," Adam said, placing a fizzy orange drink in front of her. "Broadway Bubbles for you."

"Thank you," she told him, lifting the glass for a sip. "I hope it's popular."

"If tonight's any indication, it will be." He gestured down the bar to a couple of women with matching glasses.

Jules's phone chimed with an incoming text, and she picked it up as Adam moved off to serve other customers.

Aw, I'm sad I missed you! Will you be around for a while? I could stop in and say hi when I get home. And I definitely want to see the kitties. Josie inserted a string of cat emojis and heart eyes.

Jules smiled. *I'm going to finish my drink and head home. I'll catch you next time!*

Actually, we'll be leaving this gallery event pretty soon. Mind if we stop by tonight? Or are you tired? Josie asked.

Jules nodded to no one in particular. *I'd love that! I was hoping to see you tonight.*

Perfect! See you around 8?

Yes. See you then.

Jules's night was looking up after all. As she sipped her drink, her thoughts drifted to Sophie. What was she doing tonight? Was she thinking about their kiss even half as much as Jules was?

She pressed a palm against her forehead. Oh boy. She really needed to get a grip. She'd been obsessing about Sophie and their kiss all day. Not to mention the sex dream...

She finished her drink, caught Adam's eye as she placed cash on the bar, and headed for the door. Luckily, the alcohol helped to numb the cold as she braved the blustery walk home. She jogged up the stairs to her apartment and let herself inside, exhaling gratefully as the warm air enveloped her.

Pippin came running toward the door, meowing in greeting.

"Hey, Pepito." She stooped to pet him. "Josie and Eve are coming over to see you in a bit. I wonder if you'll remember them."

Pippin purred, rubbing against her legs.

Jules hung up her coat and tossed her bag on the bed

before pulling the curtain to hide it. She spent the next ten minutes or so straightening up since she had company coming over. Then she settled on the couch with a bottle of water and her tablet to read until they got here. About an hour later, the buzzer rang.

Jules hopped up to buzz them in, and a minute later, she pulled the door open to invite Eve and Josie into her apartment. Eve had on a slinky black dress, her brown hair pulled back in a neat twist. Josie wore black pants, a silver top, and more makeup than Jules was used to seeing on her. "Wow, you guys look super fancy tonight."

"We were at an art exhibition at the Met," Josie told her. "Eve's turning me into an amateur art connoisseur."

"I'm not sure that's a thing," Eve said, giving her girlfriend a faux exasperated look.

"It's *my* thing," Josie countered. "Oh, and we come bearing wine." She held up a bottle with a shiny blue label.

Jules felt her brow scrunch. She'd only invited them over to see the cats. It hardly called for a hostess gift. "Uh, thanks? I didn't..."

Josie laughed at her confusion. "We won it in a raffle, and since I own a bar, the last thing I need is more wine, but I thought we could drink it while we play with the kitties, if you like." Josie's smile widened. "Oh, hey, sweetie!" She dropped to her knees as Pippin trotted up to her.

"It's really good wine," Eve said as she took the bottle from Josie and handed it to Jules.

"Well, in that case, how can I say no?" Jules brought the bottle into the kitchen to get her corkscrew. Once she had it open, she poured three glasses. She carried two into the living room, where Josie now sat in the middle of the floor with Pippin in her lap, talking nonsense at him while she rubbed him under his chin. Eve sat on the couch, watching her in idle amusement.

Jules handed a glass to each of them and went back for her own. She sat in the oversized chair across from the couch, tucking her feet under herself. "Phantom's probably under my bed. He hides when people come to the door."

"Well, he'd better get out here and say hello," Josie said jokingly as she sipped wine while petting Pippin.

"I would say I can't believe how big they've gotten," Eve commented. "But I can, because mine are just as big."

"They've come a long way since you pulled them out of that trash can." Jules sipped her own wine, its rich flavor exploding on her tongue. She didn't drink much red wine, but... "Wow, this is seriously good wine."

"Told you," Eve said with a nod.

"They were serving it by the glass at the event," Josie said. "This is not our first glass of the night." She let out a slightly tipsy laugh. "So, how are things going with the play?"

"Good," Jules answered. "Great, really."

"Oh, here he is," Josie exclaimed as Phantom darted into the room, flopping belly up a few feet away from her. She leaned over to give him a quick pet.

"Aw, he definitely remembers you," Jules told her. "He doesn't do that for any of my other visitors."

"Of course you remember me, don't you, sweetie?" Josie cooed over the black cat, and he batted at her playfully with his paws as she rubbed him.

Eve turned to pet Pippin, who had hopped up beside her, affection in her eyes.

"You and Sophie sure looked cozy last night at Dragon-fly," Josie said, giving Jules a sly look. "Anything happening there, or are you just friends?"

Well, here was the opening Jules had been looking for. Instead of taking it, though, she took a rather large gulp of her wine and choked on it.

"I think that's a yes," Eve said knowingly.

"It's an...I have no idea what I'm doing," Jules said, still spluttering from the wine.

"Well, tell us what's going on, and maybe we can help," Josie said from her position on the floor, rubbing Phantom as she sipped her wine.

"We kissed yesterday," Jules said. "I mean, I had to kiss another actress onstage, for the show. But Sophie helped me with sort of a...practice kiss in my dressing room beforehand."

"Ooh, do tell," Josie said, looking delighted.

"A practice kiss like, you just wanted an excuse to kiss for real, or were you actually rehearsing something for the show?" Eve asked, as usual getting right to the point.

Jules's face felt uncomfortably warm, so she took another sip of her wine. "It was more of an 'I've never kissed a woman before' kind of kiss."

"Well, good for you," Josie said. "Welcome to the club. So, you liked it, I presume?"

"I pretty much can't stop thinking about kissing her again," Jules admitted.

"Have you been attracted to a woman before?" Eve asked.

"Yes, but I had never acted on it."

"And now?" Josie asked. Pippin hopped down from the couch and dashed over to win her attention back from his brother.

"I'm so confused." Jules pressed a hand over her eyes. "I mean, how do I know if what I'm feeling is attraction for

Sophie or just a reaction to kissing a woman for the first time?"

"Oh, that one's easy," Josie told her as Pippin placed his front paws on her chest to rub his head against her chin. "The first time I kissed a girl—granted, this was in high school—I definitely did *not* want to kiss her again. So, I kissed a different girl the next time. Took me a few tries to find someone I wanted a second kiss with."

"What about this other actress?" Eve asked. "The one you have to kiss on stage. What was that like, for comparison?"

Jules took another sip of her wine. "I didn't feel anything when I kissed her."

"Well, that's your answer," Josie said, nodding briskly.

Jules glanced from Josie to Eve. "So you're saying…"

"Whatever you're feeling is because of *Sophie*, not her gender," Eve confirmed. "That doesn't mean you have to act on it, though. You work together. It could be incredibly awkward if you tried a relationship with her and it didn't work out."

"Don't listen to her," Josie said, waving a hand dismissively in Eve's direction. "She's such a romantic buzzkill. She tried this shit with me too, you know. 'We can't do this, Josie. It's in the contract.'"

"Well, it was," Eve told her sternly, even as the corners of her mouth quirked. "I could have lost my job."

"But you didn't, and look at us now." She winked at her girlfriend before turning her gaze on Jules. "If you've been attracted to women before, but Sophie is the one who inspired you to go for your first kiss, maybe you need to take that momentum and run with it."

8

On Sunday, Sophie went to Jules's apartment to run lines with her, Micki, and Amir. They had another fun afternoon, and Sophie was so grateful for the chance to practice her understudy roles with her castmates. When they parted ways that night, they made tentative plans to get together again the following Sunday.

They didn't really need a third session. By now, they all knew their lines, but they seemed to enjoy the comradery, and since Thanksgiving was later that week, they'd be away from rehearsals for a few days and could probably use a chance to brush up before they returned to the theater on Monday.

Neither Sophie or Jules had mentioned their kiss—or their conversation at Dragonfly. For the most part, things between them had returned to normal as they headed into their third week of rehearsals. Sophie's crush definitely hadn't gone away. On the contrary, she was more attracted to Jules than ever, and she was fairly sure Jules felt something for her too.

But for now, Sophie was content with their friendship.

Jules needed time to come to terms with her sexuality. She might not ever be ready to take the next step, and that was okay. They both needed to focus on the show anyway.

This was a short week of rehearsals. They finished at lunchtime on Wednesday, and most of the cast—including Sophie—left town that afternoon to visit family for Thanksgiving. She took a quick flight to Syracuse, grateful that her new paycheck meant she didn't have to fret about the cost.

Four days—and a lot of food—later, she was back in Brooklyn and ready to get back to work on *It's in Her Kiss*. She texted Jules to make sure they were still on to run lines that afternoon before spending the next few hours running errands. She did laundry and bought groceries, and then it was time to go to Jules's. Sophie had been looking forward to it all weekend, excited for another chance to practice with her castmates.

And to see Jules, of course, although Sophie was doing her best to keep her hormones in check. Still, she spent a few extra minutes in the bathroom styling her hair and touching up her makeup before she headed out, because it never hurt to look nice. She stopped at a deli on the way for a sandwich platter for them to share while they worked. Ten minutes later, she rang the buzzer at Jules's building. The door unlocked almost immediately, and she walked up to knock on Jules's door.

She pulled it open with a wide smile. Her hair was down, and Sophie had the irrational urge to run her fingers through it. Would it be as soft as it looked? Jules waved her in. "Amir is apparently fighting a cold and wants to rest his voice. Micki's flight back to the city was delayed, but she's hoping to be here in a little while."

"Oh, bummer." Sophie walked into the apartment, setting the sandwiches on the table.

"Thanks for bringing that," Jules said. "Want something to drink? Water? Soda? Wine?"

"Just water for now, thanks."

"Sure. Did you have a good Thanksgiving?" Jules asked as she walked to the kitchen.

"I did. It was great to see my family for a few days. Did you fly home too?"

Jules shook her head. "My aunt and uncle came up, so I spent Thanksgiving here with them. It was really nice." She filled two glasses from a pitcher in the fridge and handed one to Sophie. Their fingers brushed, and Sophie's heart gave a happy dance in her chest.

She turned to leave the kitchen, letting out a little shriek when she found herself face-to-face with Jules's black cat, who was peeking out at her from one of the cabinets.

"Phantom," Jules said in an exasperated tone from behind her.

"He lives up to his name, doesn't he?"

"He sure does. He's always slinking around." Jules lifted the cat out of the cabinet and set him on the floor. He was out of the kitchen in a flash of black fur, darting behind the curtain that surrounded Jules's bed.

She and Sophie walked to the living room, where Sophie sat in the chair and Jules took the couch. Her apartment was as warm and bright as Jules herself. The windows overlooking the street let in plenty of natural light, and the walls were painted a muted gold. The rest of the room was done in various earth tones. The beige couch was offset by bright orange and burgundy throw pillows, and plenty of colorful paintings adorned the walls.

Sophie let her gaze wander the room. Maybe she was just trying not to stare at Jules. The other cat, the gray one, hopped up in the chair beside Sophie, and she reached over to pet him. In the corner, a tabletop Christmas tree twinkled with white lights and branches laden with shiny, colorful ornaments.

"Going home for the holidays?" Sophie asked.

Jules nodded. "Can't wait, honestly. I've had enough of this weather, and I need some time with my family."

Sophie smiled. Even now, despite the comfortable warmth of her apartment, Jules had on a thick sweater paired with leggings. "What's Miami like at Christmas?"

"Warm," Jules said with a laugh. "But you probably guessed that much. I guess the traditions are what I love the most, baking *pastelitos* with my *abuelita*, the chance to get my whole family together under one roof. We laugh *so* much, and there's so much food."

"Sounds amazing," Sophie said.

Jules blinked, her eyes suddenly glossy. "It is."

"Must be hard, being so far from home."

"The hardest," Jules agreed. "But I go visit them as often as I can, sometimes for weeks at the time if I'm between jobs, and they come here a lot too. It'll be tough, during *It's in Her Kiss*, but I mean, for an amazing reason. I'll just have to FaceTime them a whole lot."

Sophie nodded.

"And you?" Jules asked. "I don't think you told me where you're from."

"Oh, my family's in Syracuse, only a few hours away."

"Is it just you and your parents?"

"And my older brother, Tanner," Sophie told her.

"Christmas will be our last break for a while," Jules commented, reaching out to rub the gray cat as he jumped into her lap. It was true. Once the show opened, they'd be working solidly into April, with only a day off here and there. Sophie was looking forward to it, though, and she thought Jules was too.

While they talked, they ate some of the sandwiches Sophie had brought, and then, since they were still waiting for Micki, they opened a bottle of wine and started rehearsing.

"This is a great chance for you to practice as Melissa," Jules said.

Sophie nodded happily. "Yes."

Half a bottle later, they were on their feet, reading the scene where Bianca confesses her feelings for Melissa. The scene ended with the now-infamous kiss, and while there was no reason for Jules and Sophie to act that part out—Jules and Micki hadn't kissed during their previous Sunday sessions at Jules's apartment—Sophie found herself hoping they would. There were a million reasons why dating Jules would be a terrible idea, but sharing a harmless kiss with her seemed like a really good one. Or maybe that was just the wine talking.

Jules reached out and clasped Sophie's hands the way Kari had directed her and Micki on stage. She moved subtly closer, her gaze locked on Sophie's as she seemed to consider how far to take this. Sophie held her breath, afraid even to blink and somehow ruin the moment. Anticipation hummed through her body as Jules leaned in.

Their mouths met quietly, just a gentle brush of lips against lips. Jules's fingers clenched around Sophie's, eyes fluttering shut as she lingered there, seemingly at a crossroads between acting or making this real. Sophie made the decision for her, breaking the kiss. She pressed her lips gently against the corner of Jules's mouth in parting. Jules's breath hitched, and then she turned her head, bringing their mouths back into alignment.

Sophie's heart pounded as a slow warmth spread through her system, a combination of wine and lust. This was a mistake, but it was a mistake she *really* wanted to make. "Jules..."

"I want to kiss you," she whispered. "For real."

"Then do it." Sophie nipped at Jules's bottom lip, eliciting a whimper. "Please."

Jules's lips parted, inviting Sophie into the heat of her mouth. She tasted like wine and something else, something sweet, something uniquely Jules. Their hands were clutched awkwardly between their bodies, so Sophie released them. She brought her hands to Jules's waist, gently drawing her closer.

Jules gasped as their breasts pressed together. Her hands lingered on Sophie's hips before sliding up, tracing the contours of her body, making goose bumps rise on Sophie's skin in the wake of her touch. There was wonder in Jules's eyes as her hands reached Sophie's breasts. "You feel so good."

Sophie pressed forward, sinking her fingers into the honeyed depths of Jules's hair, and *oh*, it was impossibly softer than she'd imagined, like silk between her fingers. "Feel free to keep exploring."

"Okay," Jules whispered as she brought her lips back to Sophie's. She edged closer, hips bumping Sophie's, hands skimming up and down her sides.

Sophie's breathing was out of control, chest heaving as her body came alive beneath Jules's touch. A restless anticipation grew inside her, but she held herself back, letting Jules move at her own pace. Sophie slid a hand down Jules's back, toying with the hem of her sweater.

"Yes," Jules mumbled as Sophie's fingers slipped beneath her sweater, encountering endless soft, smooth skin.

She cupped Jules's breasts over her bra, teasing her nipples until they hardened beneath the lace. Jules pressed closer still, needy sounds escaping her throat as her kisses grew steadily hungrier and more confident.

Sophie's whole body hummed with awareness, a heady feeling she wanted to capture and cherish forever. Briefly, she wondered what would happen if Micki walked in on them like this, but Jules would need to buzz her in, so really, there was no reason for them not to spend the rest of the evening making out if they wanted to. They kissed and explored, mouths growing increasingly sloppy as the heat between them built.

Jules let out a sound of frustration as her hips pressed into Sophie's, fingers grabbing at the beltloops of her jeans, trying to bring their bodies into alignment.

"Like this." Sophie pushed her leg between Jules's thighs, hands on her ass, guiding her.

Jules gasped, moving herself against Sophie's thigh. Her eyes fluttered shut, mouth falling open in silent pleasure, and Sophie was so turned on, she could hardly stand it. This position wasn't doing much for her, but the look on Jules's face sure was.

"Sophie..." Jules's voice was a whine, her fingers groping at Sophie's sweater.

"Couch," Sophie responded, nudging her in that direction.

Jules disentangled herself and stepped back, taking Sophie's hand, but she led her to the bed instead of the couch, sitting on the edge of it and gazing up at Sophie with a lust-drunk expression.

Sophie put her hands on Jules's shoulders and pushed her flat on the bed before climbing on top of her. She lowered her head, bringing their mouths together.

Jules gasped, fingers tugging at the waistband of Sophie's jeans.

"I think maybe we should use the fact that Micki might show up at any moment as an excuse to keep our clothes on today," Sophie said quietly.

Jules's brow wrinkled, lips pursing as she considered Sophie's words. "Only because of Micki?"

"Well, that, and I just...I don't want to rush into anything you're not ready for."

Jules rolled her eyes. "I'm hardly inexperienced. Just because you're the first woman I've been with..."

"Jules, can you honestly say you've thought this through?"

She huffed in frustration. "Well, no."

"I rest my case." Sophie lowered herself so that her body pressed against Jules's from head to foot.

Jules groaned, and then they were kissing again, moving together on the bed as they familiarized themselves with each other's bodies. Sophie popped Jules's bra clasp, taking her bare breasts into her hands. They kept on like that, kissing and touching, until Jules was writhing beneath her, panting for breath.

Sophie could relate. She was fast approaching the point of no return, and since that wasn't an option today, she rolled to the side, putting a little space between them. "We'd better slow this down before we lose control."

Jules grumbled, lips swollen and glistening from their kisses. "I don't like you right now."

"Oh really? Because I thought we were getting along pretty well." She leaned in for a quick kiss.

"Too well, I guess," Jules told her with a goofy smile.

"It's a problem," Sophie agreed. They lay on their sides facing each other.

Jules reached out and tucked a curl behind Sophie's ear. "So what are we going to do about it?"

Sophie blew out a breath, shivering with pleasure as Jules toyed with her hair. "I would never rush you or pressure you in any way, but for me to get involved with you, I need to know that you do plan to come out, at least to your closest friends and family."

Jules nodded, swallowing hard.

"I had a bad experience with a girlfriend a few years ago who kept me a secret from everyone in her life, and I won't put myself in that situation again."

"That's fair," Jules said. "And, while the thought of coming out to my mom is kind of terrifying, I also couldn't imagine doing this and *not* telling her. She doesn't need to know about my sex life, but she does deserve to know who I'm dating."

"Okay." Sophie nodded, the purple-patterned quilt tickling her cheek, thrilled with the possibility that this might really happen. "So, take whatever time you need to be sure, and then, you know, invite me over again."

"Or you could invite *me* over," Jules said coyly.

"Negative. I sleep on a pullout couch."

"Ah." Jules's hands slid down to grip Sophie's. "This is nice, you know. It's better than I thought it would be, even if we're just fooling around for now."

"I'm glad," Sophie told her. It had been a long time since she'd been anyone's *first* of any kind, and there was a sense of responsibility to it that she wasn't sure she liked. She was barely managing her own life, let alone guiding someone else's.

"Tell me more about your family," Jules said.

"We're close, but maybe not as close as you are with yours," Sophie told her. "They're pretty great. My dad owns a lawncare service, and my mom's a teacher. My brother, Tanner, is a fitness instructor. He got married last year."

"Do you like your new sister-in-law?"

"Yeah, she's pretty cool. No complaints."

"And you said they're supportive?" Jules asked.

"They are, but..."

Jules squeezed her fingers.

"They're...practical, I guess. They were amazing when I came out, and they were fully supportive when I first moved to the city to pursue my Broadway dreams. But now they're pressuring me to give it up and come home, or at least get a more stable job with a steady paycheck."

"Why?" Jules asked. "What's changed?"

"I guess now that I'm pushing thirty, they want to see me more settled. They feel like I've given Broadway a good try, and now it's time to move on. The truth is, I've struggled a lot financially over the last few years. It's why I'm sleeping on a couch." She scrunched her nose. "I haven't found much acting work. I've been mostly waiting tables while I go from audition to audition, but I can't even hold down a decent waitressing job while I'm focused on my Broadway career, you know?"

"I do know," Jules said with a sympathetic expression. "How do they feel about *It's in Her Kiss*?"

"Oh, they're thrilled. Like, beyond thrilled. Don't get me wrong. They're super happy for me, but what happens once my contract is up and I'm back to waiting tables?"

"Well, what do *you* want?" Jules asked, nudging her toes against Sophie's. "Is there another career you've considered?"

She shook her head. "Theater is the only life I've ever wanted, and I'm not ready to give up on it yet. I think my parents were hoping I'd spend a few years performing and then move to the suburbs, get married, and give them grandkids, but that's their dream, not mine."

"You don't want to get married?"

"I don't have strong feelings on it one way or the other," Sophie said. "If I meet the right person? Sure. But Broadway has been my focus, and it still is."

"Fair enough." Jules edged closer to her on the bed, reaching out to trace Sophie's lips with her fingers. "I always assumed I'd get married, and I always imagined it would be to a man. But I've been more focused on my career than my love life too, and now...well, I don't know about the man part either."

"Your options have increased," Sophie teased.

"Yes."

"I don't think Micki's coming."

Jules shook her head, and a lock of hair fell across her face. "I don't either."

Sophie scooted forward, and their lips met. This kiss was softer and gentler than its predecessor, an ending—at least for today—rather than the start of something more.

Jules pulled back to give her a lazy grin. "Maybe next Sunday, I won't even invite her...or Amir."

9

When she was a little girl, Jules loved to build "sand islands" at the beach. Not castles. What was the point of building a castle that wouldn't last? She would scoop sand into a mound and cover it with shells and seaweed and anything else she could find to decorate with. Then she'd sit back and watch as the tide came in, waves sliding around her island to surround it, until finally, they grew so big and strong, they swallowed it whole.

She felt like one of those sand islands at rehearsal that week. She could see the approaching tide, waves lapping at her toes. On the surface, nothing between her and Sophie had changed. But there was a current running beneath all their interactions now, secret smiles and touches that hinted at their burgeoning relationship. Every day, it grew a little bit stronger, swelling with the tide.

Sophie had been clear about her wants and needs, and now Jules had to decide what *she* wanted. Was she ready to come out to her family and make things with Sophie official? Or should she put that aside for now and focus on the show? Opening night loomed ever closer, and she couldn't afford to let her focus slip, not for her love life, not for anything.

Either way, she needed to make up her mind, and soon. Because right now she felt mired in quicksand, and it was slowly sucking her down.

As she walked to the theater on Wednesday morning, her phone started to ring from inside her purse. She tugged off her gloves to retrieve it, revealing her mom's name on the screen. "Hi, Mami," she answered.

"How is my favorite Broadway star?" Paula asked.

"Currently freezing my butt off while I walk to work."

"Rehearsals still going well?"

"Yeah. Exhausting but good," Jules told her.

"And how's Sophie?"

Jules's cheeks heated. She'd talked a lot about Sophie ever since they met during auditions, but her mom thought Sophie was a friend, and nothing about Jules's feelings for her this week were very friendly. "She's great. We've been spending a lot of time together."

"It's so nice that you two have become friends."

"Yeah," Jules agreed.

"Any new men in your life?" Paula asked.

"No." Jules felt an uncomfortable pinch in her stomach. She hated lying to her mom, even by omission.

"No handsome costars? What about the one you told me about—Amir? Didn't you have him over to your apartment to run lines together?"

"Yeah, as part of a group. And I like him a lot, but I am absolutely not interested in him that way."

"Okay, okay," her mom said with a laugh.

"What about you?" Jules asked, turning the tables on her. "Have you done anything with that Match.com profile we set up when you were here last month?" It was something of a sore subject. Her mom insisted she wasn't ready to date, but Jules's dad had been gone for five years now. Her mom was only fifty-three. She deserved to have a second chance at love.

"Well…" Paula hedged. "I did exchange a few emails with a man last month, but I don't know. It just didn't feel right."

"Mami," she warned. "You know I'm going to push you on this when I'm home for Christmas. You should at least go on a date. Have some fun."

"We'll see."

"Okay," Jules agreed. "My fingers are freezing, so I'm going to let you go, but I'll talk to you soon."

"Yes. Stay warm."

"I'll try." She ended the call, sighing as she tucked the phone into her purse and sank her frozen fingers into her pockets. There was an unsettled feeling deep inside her that only seemed to grow with each step she took.

The tide was coming in, swirling around the island on which she stood, and she couldn't hold it back much longer. But…maybe she didn't want to. She didn't want to deny her attraction to Sophie, and she didn't want to lie to her mom. She had to trust that even if her mom was uncomfortable with Jules's sexuality, they'd get through it together. It was going to be a terrifying conversation, but Jules had to have faith.

She could do this. She was going to have to do it, for her own sake. She blew out a breath, watching as it crystalized in the cool morning air, giving weight to her decision. Ahead, she spotted Sophie approaching the back door of the theater, brown curls protruding from beneath her hat.

"Sophie!" she called.

Sophie turned with a smile, waving in Jules's direction. She held the door open for Jules as she approached. "Good morning."

"Morning." Jules sighed in relief as the warmth of the theater enveloped them. "Want to grab a drink after rehearsals tonight?"

Sophie's eyes were questioning. "Sure."

It was all Jules could do not to lean in and kiss her right there in the hallway. All day, she found herself impatiently checking the clock. She was practically vibrating from the pent-up energy of a decision made but not yet set into motion.

When it was finally time to leave, they walked to Dragonfly on their way home. Josie served them Broadway Bubbles, giving Jules a discreet wink as she left them alone at their table.

"I've been doing a lot of thinking since you left on Sunday," Jules told Sophie.

"And?"

"And I'm ready," she said, exhaling in relief to have finally said it out loud. "I think it's a conversation to have with my family in person, so I'll tell them when I go home for Christmas, but unless you want to wait until after then, I was thinking maybe we could go out for a real date on Friday and...see what happens."

"Yeah," Sophie said, lips curving as she reached for her glass. "I'd like that."

SOPHIE RUMMAGED through the pitiful selection of clothes she kept in the armoire that served as her closet. What should she wear tonight on her date with Jules? They were going to dinner at a restaurant Jules had suggested, a seafood place here in Brooklyn that was supposed to be really nice. Sophie had never eaten there before. Fancy dinners hadn't been in her budget or on her radar the last few years, but with her paycheck from *It's in Her Kiss*, she could afford to broaden her horizons. And she was really, *really* looking forward to their date.

Finally, she decided on dressy black pants and a purple top that she'd been told flattered her complexion. She messed with her hair in front of the bathroom mirror, adding some cream to better define her curls. As she touched up her makeup, she realized she was spending a lot more time on her appearance tonight than she had for her date with Kim a few weeks ago, which was ludicrous because she and Jules saw each other almost every day. They'd seen each other barely two hours ago. There was no need to impress.

And yet, she wanted to. She wanted to impress Jules.

What would Jules wear? A dress, probably. Sophie zipped her coat, picked up her purse, and headed for the door. The restaurant wasn't far, so she opted to walk rather than wait on the subway just to go one stop. She didn't mind the cold air, and hopefully the exercise would help to settle her before her date. She refused to think about where tonight might lead them, because it might just be dinner. Jules might not be ready for more, and honestly, that might be for the best. Starting a relationship with a costar was risky.

It was also exciting. Thrilling. Sophie had always had a risky streak when it came to relationships, which was probably why she was still single, because they always seemed to blow up in her face.

And Jules wasn't out yet. That knowledge lingered in

Sophie's periphery, threatening to dampen her excitement about tonight. She was content to date Jules for a few weeks until she'd had the chance to go home and tell her family in person. But what if she didn't actually go through with it? Brianna had promised Sophie over and over that she'd come out to her family, only to back out at the last minute every single time.

Sophie was going to do her best not to think about it tonight. This was their first date, a fresh start, a time to look forward, not dwell on the past.

She arrived at the restaurant slightly out of breath. In her excitement, she'd speed walked the whole way. So it was probably a good thing that she'd gotten here ahead of Jules, because it would give her a minute to catch her breath. She took off her coat, glancing around the restaurant as she folded it over her arm. It had a nice vibe, with décor in various shades of blue and turquoise, an ode to the sea, perhaps. A Christmas tree to her right was strung with white lights and glossy aquatic ornaments.

The front door opened, and she turned toward it in anticipation, but a couple stepped inside, arm in arm as they headed toward the hostess desk. Sophie reached into her pocket for her phone to make sure she hadn't missed a text, surprised at the nervous tingle in her stomach. How could she be this eager for a date with a woman she'd already spent all day rehearsing with? It was bizarre and not at all like her.

The only notification on her phone was a text from Kit asking if she wanted to meet for lunch tomorrow. Sophie replied that she wasn't sure if she'd be around but would check in tomorrow, because…maybe she'd be with Jules.

Speaking of Jules, the front door opened again, and there she was, wearing a navy wrap coat that revealed her bare shins—she *had* worn a dress. Her cheeks were rosy from the cold, brown eyes shining as she caught sight of Sophie.

That tingle in Sophie's stomach zapped her like an electrical shock as Jules smiled at her. They certainly weren't lacking for sparks. "Hi," she said, sounding as breathless as she had been when she first walked into the restaurant.

"Hey," Jules said. "You look amazing."

"Thanks. So do you." Sophie closed the space between them, brushing her lips against Jules's cheek. "Can't wait to see what you've got on underneath that coat."

"Well, you're going to have to wait a minute until I've thawed out."

"We'd better get you warmed up, then," Sophie joked.

Jules led the way to the hostess desk. "Reservation for two under Julia Vega."

"Absolutely, Ms. Vega. We'll be ready for you in just a moment."

Jules nodded, stepping to the side.

Sophie leaned in. "Sometimes I forget your name is Julia."

"My brothers started calling me Jules when we were kids, and I guess it stuck."

"Well, I think Julia is a beautiful name, but Jules seems to suit you," Sophie told her. "Imagine the billboard at the theater, though. 'Starring Julia Vega.' It has a nice ring to it."

Jules ducked her head, biting her lower lip to hide her smile. "It does. I don't think my name'll be on the billboard this time, though."

It was true. Only stars with name recognition got that kind of placement. But still... "Someday, if not this time."

"Same for you, Sophie Rindell."

They were grinning at each other like smitten fools when the hostess interrupted to show them to their table. She seated them at a table for two in the center of the restaurant. Not exactly the romantic location Sophie would have preferred, but she doubted anything could dampen their mood tonight.

Jules untied the belt on her coat and shrugged out of it, revealing a figure-hugging rose-pink dress embellished with a white floral design. It hit just below the knee, highlighting all her curves, and Sophie couldn't wait to get her hands on it, even if it was just a quick kiss at the door before they said good night.

"Worth the wait," Sophie said, sliding her gaze over the dress.

Jules gave her an amused look as she sat across from Sophie. They picked up their menus and studied them quietly, stealing glances at each other as they decided what they wanted to eat. When their waitress arrived, they ordered cocktails to start.

"Costume fittings today kind of hit home how soon the show opens, didn't it?" Jules said, fingers tapping absently against her menu.

"Yes, totally. The mockups look amazing too. I can't wait to see you in that blue dress you wear at the end. It should be stunning."

"I like it too." Jules got a dreamy look on her face. "All those rhinestones. I love sparkles."

"And bubbles," Sophie teased as their drinks arrived. She'd gotten an apple martini, and Jules had something pink and fizzy.

"It's true," she agreed as she lifted her glass, holding it toward Sophie. "To new beginnings."

"I'll drink to that." They clinked glasses.

"Mm." Jules closed her eyes for a moment, savoring her drink, and *God*, she was gorgeous tonight.

Sophie could hardly take her eyes off her. She leaned forward. "It's really not fair, you wearing that dress tonight and expecting me to sit here and have a civilized dinner with you."

Jules's cheeks flushed almost as pink as her dress. "I'm glad you like it."

"I *love* it." Sophie dropped her gaze to Jules's breasts, highlighted beneath the snug fabric. Her cross pendant dangled above her cleavage, glinting beneath the restaurant's lighting.

"Jules?" a man's voice said, interrupting the moment.

Jules glanced to her left, and her eyes widened. "Stephen, wow. What a surprise."

Sophie followed her gaze. A tall, dark-haired man stood there, smiling at Jules, who had popped out of her seat to hug him. Stephen's hand lingered possessively on Jules's lower back as he spoke to her.

Sophie's fingers clenched around her martini glass.

Jules turned toward her, an apology in her eyes. "Sophie, this is Stephen Robichaux, an old...friend."

The hesitation gave her away. "Nice to meet you," Sophie said politely.

He extended a hand, his expression relaxed and friendly. Either Jules was far enough in his past that he no longer carried a torch, or he had failed to realize Jules was on a date. If Sophie were a betting woman, she'd put her money on the latter.

"A pleasure," he told her as they shook hands. "Jules and I go way back. We even dated for a while."

Shocker.

Jules's cheeks had gotten impossibly darker. "Briefly,"

she said as she disentangled herself from Stephen's grasp and slid onto her chair.

"What are you up to these days?" he asked, clearly not in a hurry to leave.

Sophie reached for her drink, toe tapping impatiently beneath the table.

"I'm rehearsing for a new show," Jules told him.

"Oh, how wonderful. Tell me about it."

This led to an obnoxiously long conversation about *It's in Her Kiss*, during which Jules never mentioned anything about it being a coming out story or that she herself was in the process of coming out. And Sophie was trying not to read anything into it, because Jules was probably caught off guard being confronted by an old flame during her first date with Sophie. It was perfectly understandable, despite the sting Sophie felt over the slight.

Stephen was talkative and overbearing, regaling them both with tales of his work at the television studio where he and Jules had apparently met when she did voiceover work for a commercial.

"Well, I don't want to keep you," Jules said pointedly, hands clasped tightly in her lap.

"Oh, I'm in no hurry," he said, although whether he was truly clueless to her meaning or just willfully ignorant, Sophie didn't know him well enough to say. "In fact, maybe we should get together sometime and catch up."

"I'm very busy right now," Jules said. "It was great to see you, though."

Still, he lingered, pressing her about scheduling an interview with someone at his studio to talk about the show. Luckily, the waitress arrived with their entrees, and not even Stephen was rude enough to interrupt them while they ate their dinner. As he finally headed for the door, Sophie let out a sigh of relief.

"I'm really sorry about that," Jules said quietly. She set her napkin on the table and stood. "I'll be right back."

Sophie watched her go, as uncomfortable about Jules's reaction as she was with Stephen's interruption. She sat there for a minute, staring moodily at her tuna steak before she left her seat and followed Jules to the bathroom. She found her standing at the mirror, swiping at watery eyes.

"Shit," Sophie mumbled as she stepped up behind her. "Jules..."

"I'm sorry." She shook her head, not meeting either of their eyes in the mirror. "I know I screwed that up."

"It's fine. Are you okay?"

Jules blew out a breath, casting her gaze toward the ceiling. "If I'm not, it has nothing to do with Stephen. Truly, he's ancient history."

"What happened between you two?"

"We dated a few months. He was screwing around on me the whole time." Jules waved a hand in front of her face. "It was years ago, and it sucked, but I'm over it. I'm just upset that he crashed our date and that I...I let him think you were a friend."

Sophie felt her own hurt evaporate in the face of Jules's shame. "It's fine. Really. Come on, let's eat before our food gets cold."

But as she led the way back to their table, Jules's mood was noticeably dimmer than it had been before Stephen's interruption, and if Sophie were being honest with herself, so was hers.

～

"Would you like to see the dessert menu?" their waitress asked.

Jules caught Sophie's eye with a wink. "No, thank you."

After she'd walked away, Sophie gave Jules a peeved look. "What if I wanted dessert?"

"I already got us dessert," she said. "Assuming you want to come over, that is. Otherwise, I'll get the waitress back over here."

Sophie's eyebrows lifted. "No, I like your original plan."

"Good," Jules said, injecting as much confidence into her tone as she could. Generally, she was bold and in control when it came to her sex life, and there was no reason for tonight to be any different. Especially after her run-in with Stephen, she needed to reclaim the rest of the evening. She wanted the second half of their date to be perfect.

When the waitress returned with their check, she insisted on paying. She'd invited Sophie out, after all, and while she wasn't accustomed to paying for a date, she found a kind of power in that too. She could get used to dating a woman. There was the thrill of something new and uncharted, but beneath it was a sense of ease she hadn't expected, although that might be due to Sophie herself, regardless of her gender.

They wrapped up in their coats and headed out, opting to walk to Jules's apartment since it wasn't too far. She slid her gloved hand into Sophie's as they strolled down the street, pausing to exclaim over a particularly charming little Christmas tree in the courtyard of an apartment building as they passed. The city really was beautiful at Christmastime, despite the cold.

"It's odd spending all my time in Brooklyn like this," she commented.

"Why? You've lived here awhile, haven't you?" Sophie asked.

"Yeah, but I'm not sure I've ever lived, worked, and dated someone here at the same time before. I'm used to making the trek into Manhattan much more often than this."

"Yes, that's true," Sophie agreed. "Can't say I've missed it."

"I haven't either, although I do want to go in and do some Christmas shopping, maybe some sightseeing."

Sophie gave her a skeptical look. "Sightseeing at Christmastime? Are you crazy?"

"I'm a sucker for all the decorations," she said with a shrug. "It's so different from what I grew up around in Miami, and apparently, I just can't get sick of it. Want to come with me?"

Sophie shook her head in amusement. "Let's see how the rest of our date goes first." Then she grinned. "But yeah, you could probably convince me to come, as long as hot chocolate is involved."

"Deal," Jules told her, and then, because she couldn't quite help herself, she leaned in for a quick kiss, annoyed with herself for the way her pulse raced...and not from arousal. What if someone saw them? She definitely had some work to do, but tonight was just for her and Sophie.

Jules tugged at Sophie's hand, leading her in the direction of her apartment. They walked in a hushed rush, footsteps quickening as her building came into view. She used her key to let them in, and Sophie gave her another kiss before they climbed the steps to her apartment. Jules unlocked the door, and finally, they were inside.

"Can I take your coat?" she asked as she untied the belt on her own. She slipped out of it and reached for Sophie's, moving to hang them both in the closet.

"Been waiting to do this," Sophie said when she returned, sliding her hands down Jules's sides. Her fingers traced the floral pattern on the dress, making goose bumps rise on Jules's skin, and they had nothing to do with the temperature.

"Is that so?" She sank her hands into Sophie's curls, drawing her in for a kiss. "Still want dessert?" she murmured against Sophie's lips.

"I don't know if you mean that literally or not, but either way, the answer is yes," Sophie told her as she gripped Jules's ass, pressing their hips together.

"Either. Both. Whatever you want." A thrill ran through her as she absorbed the feel of their bodies together, the warm swell of Sophie's breasts against hers, hot breath and roaming hands. It was unfamiliar and intoxicating.

"Show me your cards, Vega," Sophie said, releasing her.

Jules walked to the refrigerator and took out the bottle of champagne and white bakery box she'd bought earlier, setting them both on the counter. "Just to warn you, I don't cook, at least, not very well, so you should probably appreciate that I bought this instead of trying to be a romantic fool and make it myself."

"A woman who knows her own limitations," Sophie said as she joined her in the kitchen. "I have mad respect for that."

"And I have mad respect for Maribel's Patisserie." She opened the box to reveal a variety of pastries.

"Damn, girl, you are speaking my language." Sophie picked up a pink macaron and held it to Jules's lips. She took a bite, and Sophie popped the rest in her mouth.

Jules opened the bottle of champagne, pouring two flutes as Sophie poked around in the box of pastries.

"So how is it that the woman who told me stories about

baking with her grandma at Christmas doesn't know how to cook?" Sophie asked as she accepted the flute of champagne Jules held toward her.

Jules gazed into the sparkling depths of her own champagne. "Well, I guess it's mostly because I moved here for school when I was so young. I helped my mom in the kitchen, but I was pretty busy with classes and performances, and also...I'm just not good at it, no matter how hard she tried to teach me."

"Well—spoiler alert—I'm not much of a cook either," Sophie said. "So, no judgment here."

They sipped champagne as they polished off a few more pastries. Anticipation and anxiety mixed in Jules's stomach. Sophie seemed more reserved than usual tonight, letting Jules take the lead. And she was ready. *So* ready, despite her insecurities about this "first." She wrapped an arm around Sophie's waist, pulling her close. "I've been thinking about this all day...all week, really."

"Same." Sophie tapped her flute against Jules's. "To tonight."

10

They sat side by side on the end of Jules's bed, champagne flutes in hand. Sophie felt a tingle in her belly that had nothing to do with the fizzy liquid she'd consumed and everything to do with the woman sitting beside her. In unison, they drained their flutes and set them on the floor.

"Finally, I get to fully explore this dress," Sophie said, sliding a hand over the fabric covering Jules's thigh. It was impossibly soft, just stretchy enough that it bunched between her fingers, begging her to give it a little tug.

She leaned in, capturing Jules's mouth, kissing her the way she'd been wanting to all night, deep and searching. Their tongues met, mouths moving messily as they scooted closer, hands roaming and groping. She pushed Jules flat on her back, crawling on top of her. Sophie's thigh nestled between Jules's, and *yes*, this was what she'd been thinking about since the last time she was in Jules's bed.

She pressed feather-light kisses across Jules's chest as her hands slid over her dress, cupping her breasts before sliding lower. She gripped Jules's waist as she grazed her teeth over the tender skin between her breasts, and then her hands were moving again, sliding over Jules's thighs, relishing the freedom to touch her. Jules raised her knees, pressing herself more firmly into Sophie's touch, eyes glinting in the dim light.

Tonight, there was none of the hesitance in her expression that Sophie had seen the first time they'd made out in her bed. Tonight, Jules looked like a woman who wanted to be ravished, and *fuck*, Sophie wanted to ravish her. Already a restless ache was building between her thighs.

It had been so long since she'd enjoyed an evening like this. Tonight, she wanted to take her time and explore every inch of Jules's body. She wanted to make Jules's first experience with a woman suitably memorable. Sophie wanted to make her scream, and then she wanted to lose herself completely in the pleasure of Jules's touch.

Tonight, she wanted it all.

Jules reached for her, fingers unhooking the buttons on Sophie's blouse one by one to bare the black satin bra she wore beneath. She ran her hands appreciatively over it, smiling as Sophie's nipples hardened beneath her touch.

"Are you sure?" Sophie murmured as her fingers traced the hem of Jules's dress.

She nodded, the answer gleaming in the molten depths of her eyes. "Yes."

"Good," Sophie said. "Me too."

Jules gave her a searching look. "I don't know how the safe sex conversation goes with a woman, but just so you know, I've been tested, and I'm negative."

"There's much less risk," Sophie told her. "But it's always a good conversation to have. I had a checkup this summer, and I haven't been with anyone since."

"No need to make sure someone's got condoms," Jules quipped.

"Nope."

Jules pushed the blouse from Sophie's shoulders, helping her to disentangle her arms from it and toss it off the bed. Then it was Sophie's turn as she inched Jules's dress up her thighs. Sophie's fingers slid beneath the fabric, brushing against the front of Jules's underwear.

"Sophie," she gasped, hips arching into her touch.

"Let's get you out of this dress," Sophie whispered.

Jules wriggled, and Sophie tugged, sliding the fabric over her head. She gripped it in her hands for a moment as she took in the sight of Jules before her in nothing but a pale pink bra and panties. The color contrasted beautifully with her olive-toned skin.

"You're stunning," she murmured, raking her gaze over Jules, thrilled at the way her chest heaved beneath Sophie's stare and the blush blooming on her cheeks...almost as pink as her lingerie. Everything about Jules was delicate and feminine, from the lace trim on her underwear to the matching pink polish on her toes.

"Funny, I was thinking the same thing about you," Jules said, rising up on her knees to give Sophie another kiss. She popped the button on Sophie's pants and pushed down the zipper, easing them over her hips.

Sophie kicked her pants to the floor and pulled Jules close, bringing their bodies together, bare skin against bare skin, underwear against underwear.

Jules gasped. "This is... I really like it."

"Different?" Sophie asked.

Jules nodded, pressing her hips more firmly against Sophie's. They took their time touching and kissing, bodies moving together as the heat between them grew. Jules rolled them, pinning Sophie to the bed, bottom lip pinched between her teeth and a look of wonder on her face. She rolled her hips, making them both gasp. "Tell me if I'm doing things wrong."

"You aren't," Sophie told her, reaching up to cup Jules's breasts over her bra. She'd intended to take the lead tonight, to guide Jules through her first experience, but if Jules wanted to explore on her own first, Sophie wasn't exactly complaining.

Jules slid down to straddle Sophie's thigh as she touched her over her underwear. Sophie's hips arched off the bed, a hiss escaping her throat.

Jules's gaze darted up to meet Sophie's. "You like that?"

Sophie nodded. "A lot."

Jules grinned as she returned her focus to Sophie's body, fingers exploring, and Sophie's hips pressed into her touch. She wanted to hurry Jules along, and at the same time, she wanted this to last forever. She wanted to savor every moment, because when was the last time someone had looked at her the way Jules was right now, like she was mesmerized by every detail of their encounter?

Jules's fingers slid inside Sophie's underwear. "Oh, wow, you're so wet for me."

"Yes," Sophie said, her voice gone hoarse, hips jerking involuntarily beneath Jules's touch. "Wait."

Jules froze, her eyes darting to Sophie's.

"You first," Sophie said, pushing herself up on her elbows.

Jules shook her head. "I want to do this for you. Please?"

Her expression was impossibly earnest, and how could Sophie say no? Maybe Jules felt like she had something to prove, or maybe she just preferred to give before she took. Whatever it was, her comfort tonight was Sophie's priority, so she wasn't going to argue with her, especially not when her fingers were pressed intimately against Sophie, driving her mad with need. She nodded breathlessly.

Jules touched her hesitantly at first, fingers ghosting over her skin, exploring as she got her bearings. She bit her bottom lip, a wrinkle appearing between her brows as she concentrated, and if Sophie had found her sexy before, well...this was next level. Jules's fingers slid through her folds, and Sophie couldn't help the whimper that escaped her throat.

Jules smiled, and then she was stripping away Sophie's underwear, pushing them down her legs before moving up to pop the clasp on her bra. She paused there, taking in Sophie's naked body with such an appreciative look, Sophie felt herself blushing from head to toe.

Jules took her time exploring Sophie's breasts, and she was dying in the very best way. Their eyes met as Jules's hand crept down her stomach, dipping between Sophie's thighs.

Sophie gasped, arching into her touch.

Jules seemed to gain confidence with each stroke, increasing pressure as she found a rhythm. She teased Sophie's entrance, dipping lightly inside her, and Sophie was so turned on, she could hardly see straight. Her hips moved, matching Jules's rhythm. It was all perfect and perfectly infuriating because Jules hadn't yet touched the part of her that was begging most insistently for her attention.

Almost as soon as she'd had the thought, Jules's fingers brushed against her clit. Sophie jerked beneath her. "Yes," she gasped.

"Oh." Jules's eyes went wide, and her fingers returned to circle Sophie's clit.

"Don't stop," she panted, hips grinding against Jules's hand.

Jules nodded, adjusting her position, still with that look of intense concentration on her face. Her lips parted, hair hanging messily around her face as she worked. Her fingers circled and stroked, faster and harder, as Sophie mumbled her encouragement, hips moving frantically against Jules's hand.

Sophie gripped Jules's waist, needing something to ground her as the pressure inside her mounted. "I'm going to come," she gasped, and she had just caught sight of the thrilled smile on Jules's face before she squeezed her eyes shut, moaning as release ripped through her in a scorching wave, leaving her boneless and panting against Jules's bedspread.

Sophie opened her eyes to see Jules hovering over her, cheeks flushed, pride gleaming in her eyes, and holy *hell*, she was sexy.

"Not bad for my first time?" she asked, lips quirking.

Sophie was on her in a heartbeat, pinning her to the bed and bringing her lips to Jules's for a blistering kiss. "I'd say you're a fast learner."

JULES WAS on fire beneath the warm weight of Sophie's body, achingly alive from her scalp to her toes. She'd been wholly focused on providing pleasure, on exploring Sophie's beautiful body, on being assertive to keep from feeling like a fish out of water, and now...now, with Sophie's hands roaming her overheated skin, she was about to lose her mind.

"Yes?" Sophie asked, tugging at the band of Jules's underwear.

She nodded. "Yes."

Sophie popped the clasp of her bra, and Jules wiggled out of it, dropping it to the floor as Sophie brought her mouth to Jules's exposed nipples. She licked and nipped, bringing first one and then the other to tight, aching peaks as Jules squeezed her eyes shut, swamped in sensation.

Sophie's fingers gripped her underwear, and Jules lifted her hips, helping her strip them away. When she opened her eyes, Sophie was staring at her in a reverent kind of way. Heat rolled over Jules's skin, her chest heaving, heart racing.

"Ready?" Sophie asked.

"So ready," she whispered, hips shifting restlessly.

Sophie grinned, her hand sliding up Jules's leg. She paused just before she reached her destination, fingers teasing the delicate skin on Jules's inner thigh, and it was the most exquisitely frustrating thing she'd ever felt. Her entire body tensed in anticipation, arousal throbbing in her core.

And then Sophie's fingers pressed against her right where she ached for her. She swirled them, making Jules whimper in pleasure, before beginning to move, stroking her with an expertise that had her writhing within minutes. "Yes, *yes*. God, Sophie."

Sophie circled her clit before sliding two fingers inside her, positioning her hand to let Jules grind against her palm, and *yes*, that was perfect. Sophie pumped her fingers in and out, retreating periodically to pay extra attention to her clit. Jules was too far gone to do anything but hold on for the ride, hips rocking to Sophie's rhythm. She could hear herself moaning and panting, and well, she'd never been very good at keeping herself quiet.

"That's it," Sophie murmured, capturing her mouth for a kiss. "Let go."

"Yes," Jules gasped. "Please don't stop."

"Wouldn't dream of it." On the contrary, Sophie stroked harder and faster.

Oh, she was *so* close...

Jules dug her fingers into Sophie's skin, pulling her closer, breasts and hips bumping together, and just like that, she broke. Her back arched as she came, release pulsing through her. "Yes," she moaned. "Yes, oh..." She collapsed against the bed, limp and dazzled.

Sophie rolled to lie beside her, one of her legs resting between Jules's thighs, their skin hot and damp where it touched. She reached out to brush a strand of hair out of Jules's face. "Okay?"

"So much better than okay," Jules told her. Deep down, she'd been a little afraid that sex with a woman might be somehow...less. She loved the feel of a big, strong man's body against hers, the hard press of a cock between her legs.

But she needn't have worried. If anything, being with a woman brought something extra to the experience. The weight of Sophie's breasts, the brush of her hair on Jules's shoulders, the way their bodies fit together... It was all thrilling and intensely erotic. She'd felt a heightened awareness of her senses, every movement of their bodies increasing her pleasure.

"I'm not quite finished with you yet," Sophie said, looking smug.

"No?"

She shook her head, giving Jules a firm kiss before she dipped her head, pressing hot, openmouthed kisses over Jules's neck and across her chest. She lavished her breasts with attention until Jules was panting all over again, squirming beneath her. Sophie kissed her way down her stomach, swirling her tongue around Jules's navel before venturing lower.

Her breath caught in her throat as she realized where Sophie was headed, and a warm ache built between her thighs. Sophie gripped Jules's legs as her mouth descended on her clit, her tongue flicking gently from side to side.

"Fuck," Jules whimpered.

"That's the idea," Sophie said, her breath teasing Jules's sensitized skin, and oh yeah, she was going to enjoy this.

Sophie set to work, exploring Jules's most intimate parts with a combination of long, leisurely licks and the gentle suction of her mouth. After kissing every inch of her, she returned the delicious heat of her mouth to Jules's clit, entering her with her fingers at the same time.

Jules arched off the bed, an embarrassingly loud cry escaping her lips. From there, she lost the ability to think beyond the hot pleasure of Sophie's mouth and the orgasm building inside her. Her thighs shook, muscles straining as she grew closer to her release. She buried her hands deep in the mahogany depths of Sophie's hair, holding on to her as she came apart.

"Sophie," she cried, hips bucking as she came in a blinding rush. Aftershocks sizzled inside her, as if her blood had been infused with the champagne she'd drunk earlier.

Sophie slid up to lie beside her, and for several long minutes, they just lay there, facing each other. Jules's body hummed with the bone-deep satisfaction that came from two powerful orgasms and a deeply intimate experience with her partner. Beside her, Sophie looked just as satisfied, a relaxed smile toying with the corners of her mouth.

"More champagne?" Jules asked, because she was thirsty and also because their evening seemed worthy of further celebration.

"Sure."

She sat up, rummaging in her dresser for a couple of comfy T-shirts for them to wear. She handed a plain navy blue one to Sophie before pulling on an oversized gray tee with the ocean wave crest of her dad's investment firm printed over the left breast. It was softened from years of washing, her favorite "lounging around the apartment" shirt.

They wandered into the kitchen to find Pippin sniffing at the box of pastries they'd abandoned in their rush to the bed. Jules shooed him off the counter while Sophie retrieved their champagne flutes. Jules filled them.

"Dessert part two?" Sophie snagged a snickerdoodle from the box.

"I think we've earned it."

"Definitely."

They brought the whole box—and the bottle of champagne—with them into the living room and sat together on the couch to indulge a post-sex sugar rush.

Jules rested a hand on Sophie's thigh. "Stay the night?"

Sophie grinned. "I was hoping you'd ask."

11

"Suck it up, Vega," Sophie teased, wrapping an arm around Jules's waist. "This was your idea, remember?"

Jules shivered dramatically, pressing her face into the shoulder of Sophie's coat. "But it's so cold tonight."

"It'll be worth it." She gave Jules a squeeze, not at all bothered by the cold and positively thrilled by the chance to wander Manhattan with Jules at her side, even if it meant braving the crowds in Rockefeller Center at Christmastime.

After spending the better part of twenty-four hours in bed, exploring all the different ways to make each other come, they'd finally left Jules's apartment. They posed for silly selfies in front of the oversized ornaments across from Radio City Music Hall before making their way toward the world-famous Christmas tree.

They were jostled by the crowd, bumping into each other frequently, which Sophie was pretty sure neither of them minded. She sure as hell wasn't complaining. Jules's gloved fingers gripped her own, her cheeks flushed from the cold, golden hair fanning out from beneath her red knit cap, stirred by the winter breeze.

"Not to sound like a cliché, but you look so gorgeous right now, I can hardly stand it," Sophie told her.

Jules nudged her playfully. "Flatterer."

"I only speak the truth." Sophie pressed her free hand against her heart.

Jules kissed her cheek, her lips cool against Sophie's skin. "You're sweet. And you also look lovely all bundled up in winter gear."

They made their way into the plaza, weaving through the crowd as they drew closer to the tree. They waited for a spot to open up against the railing above the ice-skating rink, the perfect spot for a selfie.

"Just don't try to get me down there," Sophie joked, gesturing to the ice.

"God, no," Jules said. "I'm pretty sure any kind of winter sport would be frowned upon this close to making my off-Broadway debut." She paused, and a funny look passed across her face. "Wow, I think that just hit me a little bit."

"Starting to feel real?" Sophie gave her hand a squeeze.

"Maybe," Jules said, "but I doubt it'll really sink in until the curtains go up on opening night."

"Wish I could be in the audience to watch you," Sophie said.

"But I'm more glad you'll be on stage with me." Jules squeezed her hand back.

A family stepped away from the railing, and she and Jules moved in before someone else could snag the spot. They leaned in close, framing the tree over the ice-skating rink behind them as they snapped selfies with both of their phones.

"Mind if I share these on my social media?" she asked Jules.

"No, I was going to share one too. Just, you know, don't caption me as your girlfriend or anything." She ducked her head. "At least, not yet."

"Don't worry. It's a bit soon to make that kind of announcement anyway. Maybe I'll be sick of you by Monday." She elbowed Jules in the ribs as they stepped away from the railing, making room for the next group.

"Hey," Jules said in mock affront.

"You never know," Sophie said with a shrug. "You might be hiding a super annoying habit I don't know about yet."

"I might," Jules agreed, giving her an amused glance.

They leaned against the side of the nearest building as they uploaded pictures. Sophie didn't have much of an online following. She'd followed Jules on Instagram shortly after they met and knew Jules had a much more active presence, with most of her photos garnering several hundred likes. She combined vibrant, engaging photos with witty captions, documenting behind-the-scenes moments of her life as a theater actress with snapshots around the city and funny pictures of her cats. Her personality shined in her posts, and no wonder so many people followed her. Sophie couldn't imagine meeting her and not wanting to spend more time with her. She'd been captured by Jules's presence from the moment they'd met.

They spent the next hour wandering midtown Manhattan, taking in all the Christmas sights and doing some shopping at the craft booths in Bryant Park, before Jules exclaimed dramatically that she needed to get inside before she caught hypothermia.

"I know just the place," Sophie told her. "And it's not too far from here."

"Lead the way," Jules said.

Sophie led her down the street, around the corner, and a few more blocks down a quiet, mostly residential street. Jules followed willingly, her expression bemused. Clearly, she had no idea where they were going. "I heard about it from a friend of mine. It should be romantic...and also warm you up."

"Sounds perfect."

At the end of the block, the bar came into view. Its windows had been spray-painted around the edges to appear frosted. The interior glowed with hundreds—maybe thousands—of twinkling, multicolored Christmas lights. Glistening ornaments and glittering garland were strung across the ceiling, and as the front door opened, the chorus of "Jingle Bells" spilled into the otherwise hushed street.

"Oh," Jules exclaimed, her face glowing almost as brightly as the bar. "Wow."

"I don't think Josie will mind if we visit another bar just this once," Sophie joked as she held the door for her.

"Definitely not." Jules looked around in awe as they stepped inside. The whole place smelled vaguely like peppermint and spice, and the bartenders wore green-tassled elf hats.

Sophie and Jules headed for a small table in back. The art on the walls had been wrapped to look like gifts, a combination of Christmas, Hanukkah, and Kwanzaa paper on display. A variety of holidays were represented in the decorations around them as well.

"I love it already," Jules proclaimed, reaching down to untie the belt on her coat. Drink menus rested on their table, and naturally, the drinks were all holiday inspired. They hung their coats on a nearby hook before settling in to peruse the drink options, although Sophie was halfway distracted by the woman on the other side of the table, smiling delightedly as she slid a finger over the menu, her red sweater shimmering beneath the strands of lights criss-crossing the ceiling overhead.

"I know what I want," Jules announced.

"Wait. Let me try to guess." Sophie scanned the list of drinks in front of her. "The Peppermint Party."

Jules pursed her lips. "You're good."

"Well, you're kind of predictably a sucker for bubbly drinks," she said, pointing to champagne under the list of ingredients. "Also, mint."

"True," Jules agreed. "Hey, I like what I like. Okay, let me try to guess yours." She spent a long minute studying the menu. "The Gingerbread Snap."

"Hm," Sophie said, keeping her expression neutral. "What makes you think so?"

Jules gave her a searching look. "You ate a gingerbread cookie last night, and you seem to like spicy things."

That was actually pretty astute of her. "It was between that and the Mistletoe Martini."

"But you decided on the martini?" Jules asked, looking disappointed.

"I did, but it was close. I might try the gingerbread one next."

"I would have one of everything on the menu if you wouldn't have to scrape me off the floor at the end of the night," Jules joked.

A waiter approached their table, and they placed their orders, holding hands across the table after he'd left. They'd been together a full twenty-four hours now, and Sophie would be perfectly happy to keep this date going indefinitely, which was kind of scary, considering how quickly things between them seemed to be progressing.

"We still need food at some point," Jules said, glancing around the bar. It was long and narrow, smaller than its opulent decorations initially suggested, and as such, it didn't serve food, only cocktails. "But how do you feel about takeout?"

Takeout meant they'd be heading back to Jules's apartment, and maybe that should feel like too much for this weekend, but it didn't. "I'd say it sounds like I need to stop by my apartment and get some clean clothes."

"Deal," Jules said. "Do you have plans tomorrow?"

"Just need to run some errands before we're back in rehearsals on Monday."

"Same," Jules said. "And I have a piano lesson in the afternoon."

"Brushing up before your big debut?"

Jules nodded. "I've been practicing as much as I can."

"Want to play for me later?" Sophie asked. "I'd love to hear."

Jules gave her fingers a squeeze. "I'd like that a lot."

The waiter arrived with their drinks, and they both paused to take pictures of them for social media because they were just too pretty not to. Jules's drink was minty green and frothy at the top, while Sophie's was a deep red thanks to the cranberries infused into it as well as mulled wine. The green garnish gave it extra Christmassy flair.

"Mistletoe?" Sophie said, remembering the name of her drink. She lifted it above their heads.

"Pretty sure that's mint," Jules told her.

"Well, pretend for me, then," Sophie teased, leaning in to press her lips firmly against Jules's.

Jules gave her a quick kiss before sitting back, gaze darting around the bar.

Sophie looked at her drink, determined not to be bothered by Jules's hesitance to kiss her in public. They'd only been dating since yesterday, after all. Sophie lifted her glass and took a sip. Her Mistletoe Martini was rich and spicy, with a tanginess from the cranberries that was absolutely delicious. "Don't tell Josie, but this is amazing."

"Mine is too," Jules agreed. "Want a taste?"

They swapped glasses, sipping and laughing, holding hands through three rounds of drinks. By the time they left the bar, between the two of them, they'd tried almost every drink on the menu and were delightfully tipsy.

"I'm so hot from all the alcohol, it actually feels good out here," Jules said, tipping her face toward the night sky.

"You say that now..."

"True." Jules hooked her arm through Sophie's. "I'm sure I'll be shivering in no time."

"By the time we reach the subway, I predict," Sophie teased.

"Probably right. Should we stop at your place on the way back to mine?"

"Uh, yeah. Sure." She hadn't exactly planned to bring Jules to her apartment. Generally, she steered her dates away, embarrassed about her couch-sleeping arrangement. But Jules already knew about that, so really, there was nothing for Sophie to hide.

"Unless you'd rather meet me at my place?" Jules said, obviously having sensed Sophie's hesitation.

"No, it's fine. If we get off at 10th, we'll walk right by my apartment on the way to yours."

"Perfect," Jules said.

"Once you've seen my couch, you'll be glad for your bed," Sophie told her, hoping to keep the tone light.

"Oh please. I have so many friends who've slept on

couches. It's almost a necessity in this city at some point, isn't it?" Jules said. "Especially for struggling actors."

"Not for you, though," Sophie said, old insecurities rearing their ugly head at the reminder of her and Jules's different financial status.

"I'm very lucky that my parents were able to help me when I needed it," Jules said quietly.

"Some people might take that for granted," Sophie said, shaking it off, because neither of them deserved to be poisoned by her chronic bitterness tonight. "But again, not you."

"Never," Jules said. "It's just what we do for each other, right? I'd help anyone in my family in a heartbeat if they needed me, even if meant letting them sleep on my couch." She gave Sophie a playful nudge.

"They're all coming for opening night?" she asked.

"God, yes," Jules said. "My mom and grandma are staying for almost a week when we open for previews, and they've got tickets to every show. Then, of course, they'll be back for opening night."

"Aw, that's so sweet."

"And yours?" Jules asked, glancing at her as they walked.

"Mine will be here for the first night of previews and opening night, yes."

"I guess we might be playing 'meet the family' in a few weeks, then, huh?" Jules said, a hesitance in her expression that hadn't been there before. This was a big deal for her, coming out to her family and then potentially introducing them to the first woman she'd ever dated.

"I imagine the whole cast will be meeting each other's families," Sophie said, hoping to ease her mind. "It won't have anything to do with our relationship."

"Yes, true."

They boarded the subway together and rode to Brooklyn, exiting at 10th. Sophie led the way to her apartment and let them in, but although she'd been kind of looking forward to introducing Jules to Nathan and Anthony, her roommates weren't home. Instead, Jules sat on Sophie's couch while she packed a quick bag, and then they were on their way back to Jules's apartment. They'd barely made it inside before they were on each other.

Jules pushed her against the wall, kissing her deeply as they fumbled with their winter clothes. Kisses turned to laughter as they unzipped coats, tugged off gloves, and tossed hats, finally reaching their regular layers of clothing. Jules's fingers strayed beneath Sophie's sweater, touching her with a confidence she had lacked yesterday, the awe of discovery replaced now with the assurance of what was to come.

They scrambled out of their clothes as Jules stepped Sophie backward to the bed. Her fingers dipped between Sophie's legs, stroking her just the way she liked. Sophie reached for her, cupping her breasts in her hands, and Jules threw her head back with a soft gasp. They tumbled onto the bed, arms and legs entwined.

"Together this time?" Jules asked, rocking her hips against Sophie's.

"Yes." She loved how assertive Jules was in bed. It was unbelievably hot.

Together, they touched and explored, fingers stroking and mouths roaming. They moved as if they'd been choreographed, heat and friction building everywhere. Jules slid down to straddle Sophie's thigh, stroking her as she began to rock her hips. She settled into a rhythm, matching it with her fingers as they swirled and plunged. Sophie groaned in pleasure, gripping Jules's hips.

Jules leaned forward, shifting the angle between them, eyes fluttering shut with a gasp. "Is this okay?" she whispered.

"Really fucking great," Sophie said breathlessly.

"For me too," Jules said, hips moving frantically, a steady stream of whimpers and cries escaping her lips. Her tits bounced to the rhythm she'd set, a caramel waterfall of hair tumbling over her shoulders. Her fingers worked tirelessly, rapidly driving Sophie past the point of no return, but even without that stimulation, Sophie had a feeling the sight of Jules above her might be enough to do the trick.

Jules let out a cry as she came, fingers curling inside Sophie's body, which sent her right over the edge. The orgasm rushed through Sophie hard and fast, leaving her limp beneath the warm weight of Jules's body. They lay together, hair tangled and twisted between them, bodies sticky and sweaty with the aftermath of sex. It was all messy and wonderful, so wonderful, Sophie's heart was full to bursting with the power of it.

"That was…" She couldn't quite find the words.

"Yeah," Jules said, sounding similarly awed. She raked a hand through her hair, sweeping it over her shoulders as she rolled to the side, snuggling in beside Sophie. They lay like that for a few minutes, catching their breath. "Shower?" Jules suggested eventually.

"Definitely," Sophie agreed.

They got up, and Jules lent her an elastic for her hair while they rinsed off in the shower. Afterward, they ordered a small feast from a nearby Greek restaurant, both having realized they were famished. They ate, rehydrating with tall glasses of water after their Christmassy drinks and extracurricular activities.

"How were you going to play the piano for me?" Sophie

asked, glancing around the studio apartment. "You don't have one."

Jules gave her an amused look. "Ye of little faith. Do you really want me to play for you?"

"Yes," Sophie told her. She'd been thinking about it while they ate, and yes, she wanted to experience *all* of Jules's talents tonight, up close and personal.

Jules stood and walked to the closet, bringing out a keyboard, which she set up on the desk in the living room. "The best I can do in this place, but it's almost as good as the real thing."

"Perfect," Sophie told her. "Will you play your solo for me?"

Jules gave her a shy smile. "Yeah, but go easy on me, okay?"

"I won't have to," Sophie said.

"I also have to keep the volume turned all the way down, because...neighbors," Jules told her, making a silly face. She was nervous, and it was impossibly adorable.

"Fair enough," Sophie said.

"Here goes," Jules whispered as she splayed her fingers over the keys and cleared her throat. She shook her hair over her shoulders and straightened her back, tossing a shy glance at Sophie.

And Sophie found herself holding her breath, poised on the edge of the couch, hands clasped tightly in anticipation, even though she'd already heard Jules perform this song dozens of times during rehearsals.

Jules began to play, hands moving gracefully over the keys. Her voice filled the apartment, rich and clear. Tonight, there was a hush to the way she sang. No doubt, she was keeping her voice down for the neighbors, but somehow, it added an extra layer of emotion to the song.

This would be Jules's breakout moment. There was no doubt in Sophie's mind. *It's in Her Kiss* was going to launch Jules's career, and Sophie was so happy for her, she could hardly stand it. Jules deserved this. She'd worked so hard, and she had the talent to back it up. More than enough talent.

Jules finished the song, and Sophie clapped, grinning at her. "It was even more beautiful this way. Seriously. It's powerful when you belt it out from the stage, but this quiet version was really, really special."

"Thanks." Tears shone in Jules's eyes. "Want to sing it with me?"

Of course, Sophie knew all the words. She'd observed Jules's every move from the sidelines as she prepared for her role as understudy and then gone home to practice alone in her apartment. "Yeah," she said. "I'd like that."

"Me too."

And so they sang it together, harmonizing on the chorus and alternating lines during the verses. Sophie squeezed in next to her on the chair, resting a hand on Jules's waist as she played the keyboard. When they'd finished the song, Jules rested her head on Sophie's shoulder.

"I think that might be my new favorite version," Jules said softly.

"Nah, your version is the best. I'll be first in line to buy the cast recording."

"Wish they'd cast you as Melissa," Jules said. "Then I could kiss you on stage in front of all those people."

Sophie shrugged. She wished a lot of things, but this wasn't the time for them, because she and Jules were having the most perfect night, the most perfect weekend, and none of her bitterness was going to creep in and ruin it. "It will all work out the way it's supposed to, right?"

"Yes," Jules agreed. "And your moment is coming, Soph. I have absolutely no doubt about it."

"I sure hope so."

They climbed into bed that night tired and happy, and Sophie fell asleep almost immediately, with Jules at her side. When she woke, sunlight streamed into the apartment. As she rolled over in bed, she realized she was alone. Curious, she tugged at the curtain that surrounded the bed. There was Jules, standing in the kitchen wearing a white robe, thumbing through messages on her phone as she waited for the espresso machine to heat up. Her hair hung loose over her shoulders, her face bare of makeup, giving her a fresh-faced, youthful look that Sophie couldn't seem to get enough of.

"Morning," Jules called.

"Morning. I was going to complain about waking up alone, but I can't complain when I see that you're making me Cuban coffee."

Jules tossed her a coy look. "Who says it's for you?"

"Smartass."

Sophie went into the bathroom to freshen up, and when she returned to the living room, Jules was performing her magic as the espresso machine hissed and squealed. A few minutes later, she joined Sophie on the couch, carrying two impossibly small coffee cups. When Jules had presented her with one yesterday, Sophie had given her a skeptical look, never having seen anything quite like it, but now she knew to anticipate the amazing-ness of Cuban coffee.

"Thank you," she said as she accepted the cup Jules held out to her, lifting it to inhale the rich aroma. She sipped gingerly, careful not to burn her tongue. "This frothy stuff at the top is pure heaven."

"That's the *crema*," Jules told her. "And I agree. It's the best part."

They sipped their coffee together mostly in silence, occasionally commenting on the day ahead as they waited for the caffeine to kick in.

"Now I get why you fix your own coffee every morning," Sophie said as she set her empty cup on the table in front of her.

"I've spoiled you," Jules teased.

"In more ways than one," Sophie agreed. "But I really should get going."

Jules nodded. "It's been a great weekend."

"Amazing." Sophie leaned in for a quick kiss, tasting espresso on Jules's tongue. Then she stood, taking both empty cups to the sink before gathering her clothes. She dressed in a fresh long-sleeved tee and jeans and threw the rest of her things into the duffel bag she'd brought from her apartment last night. She bundled up in her coat and slung the bag over her shoulder as Jules joined her for one last kiss.

"See you tomorrow," Sophie told her.

Jules grinned. "Yes."

"Maybe we can go out again one night this week?" Sophie suggested.

"Definitely," Jules agreed.

"Okay. Bye, then."

"Bye." Jules waved as Sophie headed for the door.

Had she really just had a thirty-six-hour first date? That was crazy, and yet every moment had been amazing. Already, this felt like the start of something a lot more serious than any relationship she'd had since...Brianna.

Sophie walked home, stopping for a muffin from her favorite coffee shop on the way. The barista gave her a funny look when she declined a coffee, but she already had a nice caffeine buzz going, thanks to Jules. While she waited for her order, she scrolled through social media on her phone. Jules had tagged her on Instagram, so she clicked on the photos, smiling again to see how happy and carefree they'd looked last night in Manhattan. Jules had captioned the photos #girlsnight.

And Sophie's smile deflated. They'd agreed not to mention anything publicly about their date, but to call it a girls' night seemed to explicitly imply that they were just friends.

Don't overthink this.

Just because Jules was more cautious about their relationship than Sophie didn't mean things would end the way they had with Brianna. But still, as she collected her blueberry muffin and left the café, her mood was more subdued than it had been a few minutes before. She needed to tread carefully with Jules so she didn't set herself up for another heartbreak.

12

M usic swelled across the stage as Sophie took her position in the wings, surrounded by the other members of the ensemble. Jules stood center stage, running through a scene with Amir. It had been over a week since their thirty-six-hour date, and they'd spent a lot of it together, both on and off stage. They'd been on several more dates, and Sophie was more smitten with Jules than ever.

This was the last full week of rehearsals, and as such, they would also have fittings, a photo shoot for the program, and other tasks to prepare for opening night. This weekend, Sophie and Jules would leave Brooklyn to go home for Christmas. When they came back after the holidays, they'd see where they were and what came next for their relationship.

On cue, Sophie and the other members of the ensemble entered the stage, joining Jules and Amir for the next song. This was the part of the rehearsal process that Sophie loved best. Most of the hard work was behind them. They knew their lines. They knew the choreography. Fine-tuning their performance was fun and exciting, like putting the finishing touches on a painting, finding all the spots that could be improved with an extra dab of paint or another layer of color.

Being an understudy added some extra stress, though. Sophie would have a private rehearsal with Kari tomorrow, but she would never get the full experience that Jules had. Learning Bianca's and Melissa's lines in addition to her role in the ensemble was a challenge, but hopefully this would help her grow as a performer. It might even lead to a bigger role for her in the future.

At lunch, she and Jules sat next to each other in the break room, sneaking some time together during an other-wise hectic day.

"You looked great out there," Sophie told her.

"So did you," Jules said before popping a grape into her mouth.

It endlessly entertained Sophie that Jules brought such balanced lunches with her to the theater. Sandwiches, fruit, yogurt. Half the time, Sophie tossed a protein bar in her bag and called it a meal.

"Mind if I join you?" Tabitha asked, setting her bag on their table.

"Not at all," Jules told her.

"You guys excited for the shoot this afternoon?" Tabitha asked as she sat across from them and pulled an apple out of her bag.

"So excited." Jules's radiant smile said she meant it too.

"Same," Sophie said, but honestly, she was rather apathetic about photo shoots. She was more excited that this was one step closer to opening night. Although, on second thought, seeing Jules all done up for the shoot might make the whole thing worthwhile.

After lunch, they headed to the room in back where the hair and makeup team had assembled to get them ready for their photoshoot. Sophie, Tabitha, and the rest of the ensemble went to one end of the room, while Jules, Amir, and Micki headed the other way. Sophie sat patiently as the team spritzed and polished her hair, applied false lashes, and made her up.

Afterward, they were handed sample costumes to wear. Sophie's consisted of tight black jeans and a sequined purple top, and honestly, she couldn't be more thrilled. Tabitha received the same, except her top was turquoise. They retreated to their dressing room to get changed before assembling on stage, which had been fitted with lights and screens for the shoot.

Sophie and the rest of the ensemble went first. They posed for individual shots and a variety of group poses, including Sophie's favorite in which they all leaped into the air. She couldn't wait to see how they came out. Afterward, they sat in the audience to watch the leads do their photos.

Jules, Micki, and Amir took the stage, and Sophie had to bite her lip to keep from gasping. Jules wore the floor-length blue dress she would perform her piano solo in. It shimmered under the stage lights, highlighting the curve of her hips and the swell of her breasts. They'd put long, loose waves in her hair and pinned it back on one side, revealing the graceful column of her neck. The end result was nothing short of stunning.

Jules posed at the center of the stage, one hip effortlessly cocked, flashing the camera a million-dollar smile and reminding Sophie that she'd done modeling work in the past. Sophie made a mental note to Google her later.

"She's gorgeous," Tabitha commented.

"Mm-hmm," Sophie responded without taking her eyes off Jules.

"You like her."

"What?" Sophie darted a glance at her, to find Tabitha watching her in amusement. She and Jules were keeping things quiet for now, at least until after Jules came out to her family, but even so, there was no need to flaunt their relationship in front of their castmates.

"Just an observation," Tabitha said lightly. "You look at her the way I look at Amir."

"Oh boy," Sophie said with a laugh. "No harm in looking, right?"

"Right," Tabitha agreed.

Amir and Micki stepped up on either side of Jules, and they took a series of photos to illustrate the love triangle that would play out onstage, as Bianca found herself torn between the man her family wanted her to date and the woman *she* wanted.

"And now, the kiss," the photographer announced, gesturing for Jules and Micki to move closer to each other.

Sophie's stomach dropped. She'd already seen Jules kiss Micki dozens of times, but she still wasn't exactly thrilled about the idea of sitting here watching them pretend to make out for the photographer. She slouched in her seat.

Jules rested a hand on Micki's waist, leaning in to press their lips together as the photographer directed them on how to angle their bodies and where to put their hands. It was about as unromantic as a kiss could get, and it still made Sophie jealous as hell. For the sake of Tabitha's watchful eyes, she tried to keep her feelings to herself.

After a few shots with Jules and Micki, the photographer directed Amir to step in, taking one of Jules's hands as if trying to get her attention, while she leaned to the side to kiss Micki. It would make a hell of a shot for the promotional materials.

Finally, they called the rest of the cast onto the stage and took photos of them all together, a mixture of serious and silly poses. Afterward, Sophie and Tabitha headed back to their dressing room together. Sophie changed into her own clothes and gathered her things. She grabbed her bag, said goodbye to Tabitha, and headed down the hall to Jules's dressing room. The door was open as usual. Jules sat on the couch, typing on her phone.

"Hey," Sophie said as she stopped in the doorway.

Jules looked up. She was back in her jeans and sweater, but she still wore her camera-ready makeup, and her hair...

Sophie cleared her throat. "Heading out?"

Jules crooked a finger, gesturing for Sophie to come in. "Close the door."

Well, then. Sophie stepped in, closing the door behind her. Jules was off the couch in a flash, pressing Sophie against the wall as she kissed her. Sophie sank her fingers deep into the silky depths of Jules's hair, ruffling her perfectly constructed waves, anchoring herself in the feel of Jules's kiss, the whisper of her breath across Sophie's cheeks, and the firm grip of her fingers on Sophie's ass.

"What was that for?" she whispered when they'd come up for air.

"Because I missed you," Jules said. "And because I wanted to remind you that *you* are the only person I wanted to be kissing on stage today."

"It's just a stage kiss," Sophie murmured, her earlier jealousy leaking away. "We'll all have to do it sooner or later, right?"

"If we're lucky," Jules said. "Because it means we're getting the juicy roles, right?"

"Right."

"Okay, now I'm ready to head out," Jules said, wrapping up in her coat and grabbing her bag. "I've got dinner with my agent tonight, but let's get together later this week, even if it's just for a drink."

"I'd like that," Sophie said.

"Me too." Jules gave her hand a squeeze as they left her dressing room.

Tabitha, who was halfway down the hall on her way toward the back door, raised her eyebrows slightly as she took in their joined hands. "Night, ladies."

"Night," Jules said quietly, dropping Sophie's hand.

They followed her out, turning left toward their respective apartments while Tabitha turned right, headed for the subway. Jules chewed her lip, noticeably silent.

"Tabitha's cool," Sophie said. "She won't say anything."

Jules shrugged. "It's fine." But she didn't sound fine.

"She likes Amir," Sophie told her with a conspiratorial smile.

"I noticed that too."

"You did?" Sophie hadn't had a clue until Tabitha told her.

"The way she talks about him?" Jules said. "Not to mention the way she looks at him. Girl, please."

Sophie laughed. "Half the cast will be hooking up before we're finished here."

"I checked our contracts," Jules told her, serious again. "There are a few lines about proper conduct, but nothing specific. I think as long as we don't flaunt our relationship at the theater or let it affect our performance, we'll be fine."

"Good."

They chatted as they walked, and after a block or so, Jules took her hand again, holding on to it until they parted at Sophie's street.

"See you tomorrow at rehearsal," Sophie said, leaning in for a kiss.

"See you." Jules kissed her back, cheeks flushed as she walked away.

Phew. Sophie was so done for where Jules was concerned. She walked the rest of the way to her apartment with a smile on her face. It didn't even dim when she entered her apartment and found Nathan and Anthony sitting on the couch, watching TV. As much as she liked them, it sucked not having a space of her own, especially after a long day of rehearsal.

"Hey, guys," she said, dropping her bag on one of the kitchen chairs.

"Hey, Soph," Anthony said. "Haven't seen much of you lately. Got a new girl?"

"As a matter of fact." She grabbed a bottle of water from the fridge and settled in the chair across from them.

"Good for you," Nathan said, rubbing a hand over the stubbly beard he'd recently grown for a role. "It's about damn time."

"Tell me about it," she said, taking a gulp of water.

"I'm happy for you," Anthony said. "Bring her by and introduce us sometime."

"Geez, guys, you're not my parents," Sophie told them jokingly. "But yeah, I will."

"Can't wait to meet her," Anthony told her. "We have some news too, and unfortunately you may not like it."

Sophie made a face at him. "What? Spill."

"Well, you know our lease is up in a few months," Anthony said.

"The end of February," Nathan clarified, ever the one for details.

"Yeah," Sophie said. "Don't tell me. They're raising our rent?"

"Well, yes," Anthony said. "But nothing out of the ordinary. The thing is, some friends of ours are moving out of their loft around the same time, and it's an amazing space that we'd actually be able to afford on our own."

"Oh," Sophie said, taking another gulp of her water. *Oh.* "You're moving."

"Yeah," Nathan told her apologetically.

"Okay." She nodded, trying not to feel as if the rug had just been pulled out from underneath her. Their names were the only ones on the lease. They were basically doing her a favor letting her crash on the couch, although it had allowed all of them to get by in this impossibly expensive city.

Now, she had two and a half months to find a new place to live. It wasn't an insurmountable task. She knew a lot of people in the theater community, and it seemed like someone was always looking for a new roommate, but *ugh*, she wasn't looking forward to it. And despite her lack of privacy, Anthony and Nathan were actually perfect roommates. They were polite and considerate, did their share of the chores, kept their space clean, and even cooked her dinner on occasion.

"We'll put feelers out for anyone looking for a roommate," Nathan offered.

"I appreciate that."

"And if worse comes to worst, you can crash on our

couch in the new space until you find a place of your own," Anthony told her.

"You guys are the sweetest, but I'll be out of your hair by the time you move, I promise." And then, because she really needed a few minutes alone to sort out her emotions, she excused herself to take a shower.

13

J ules sat in the empty theater, watching Sophie's understudy rehearsal. Jules didn't have to be here for this. Everyone else had gone home, but she hadn't been able to resist watching. Andrew was reading for the other characters so Kari could make sure Sophie was ready to take the lead, should the need arise. And she obviously was. Even standing up there with no one but the stage manager, she had a powerful presence as she delivered Bianca's lines.

Jules lifted her phone and took a few discreet photos so that Sophie could share them on her social media. Since she wasn't in costume, there weren't any spoilers involved, and it was good publicity both for Sophie and the production. Jules had been sharing spoiler-free pictures and tidbits for weeks now.

Kari had Sophie run through Bianca's biggest scenes, ending with the piano solo. Sophie had a beautiful voice, deeper and throatier than Jules's. It brought a whole new vibe to the song.

"Wonderful," Kari said when she'd finished. "Now I'd like to have you rehearse as Melissa."

"I can read for Bianca, if you like," Jules called out, hoping her offer was helpful and Sophie wouldn't feel like she was somehow stepping on her toes. But it seemed silly for Andrew to read Bianca's lines while Jules was sitting here.

Kari, Andrew, and Sophie blinked down at her as if they'd completely forgotten she was there.

"Actually, that would be perfect," Kari said. "Thank you."

Sophie's expression was unreadable.

Jules pocketed her phone and jogged up the steps to the stage, grinning at Sophie as she took her mark beside her. To her relief, Sophie smiled back. Melissa only had four big scenes, and Kari asked them to read all four, including the one with the kiss.

Somehow, this hadn't even occurred to Jules when she offered to read with Sophie, but *hell yes*, she would get to kiss her onstage, even if it was only a rushed rehearsal with no one else in attendance but the two of them and a handful of production staff.

"What's the matter?" Sophie said, speaking as Melissa. "I thought your date with Trevor went well."

"It did, but..." Jules cast a longing look at Sophie, twisting her hands in front of herself, the way she'd done dozens if not hundreds of times now. Somehow, the entire scene felt different when she was standing across from Sophie instead of Micki.

"But what?" Sophie asked breathlessly, stepping forward, effortlessly hitting her mark without looking down at the strip of red tape on the stage.

"But, he's not...you."

"Oh." Sophie managed to appear cautious and shy while

simultaneously projecting her voice to carry through the theater, and Jules found herself hoping she'd get the chance to act this scene with her in front of a packed audience, even if only once. "Tell me what that means, Bianca."

"I think you know." Jules turned away, facing the rows of empty seats before her.

"I think I do too," Sophie said from behind her. "But I need to hear you say the words. I need to know that what I think is happening is real."

"It's real." Jules turned back to her, clasping Sophie's hands in hers. "It wasn't supposed to be you, Melissa, and yet, you're the only one I can think about."

Sophie was nodding the entire time she spoke, an almost giddy smile on her face. Jules had never seen that smile before. This wasn't Sophie smiling at her. It was Melissa.

"And for me, it's only ever been you. Please," Sophie said, lifting their clasped hands as she stared unflinchingly into Jules's eyes. "Please kiss me, Bianca."

They rotated slowly as they spoke, turning so that each of them was angled slightly toward the audience as they faced each other. Together, they raised their hands, holding on to each other as they moved closer, turning the moment into a dance, even if the music was lacking for this particular rehearsal.

Jules leaned in, brushing her lips against Sophie's. She closed her eyes, holding tight to Sophie's fingers, imagining the reaction of the crowd, applause, maybe even a few cheers. She opened her eyes, meeting Sophie's gaze. They parted, smiling at each other, hands still clasped. Jules remembered their first kiss, the flutter of excitement and awareness it had ignited in her, and she projected that now as Bianca reacted to her first kiss with a woman.

This was where the curtain would drop for the intermission.

"Great job, ladies," Kari said, one finger pressed thoughtfully against her lips. "A very different energy than I've seen from Jules and Micki in that scene."

Jules knew exactly where that energy had come from, but she just shrugged. Sophie was similarly mum on the subject. They ran through Bianca and Melissa's scenes from the second act, turning to Kari when they'd finished.

"Excellent work today, Sophie," Kari said. "I feel very confident about you taking the stage in the event that Jules or Micki have to miss a show."

"Thank you," Sophie said, looking uncharacteristically modest, almost shy.

"All right, then. Get out of here, you two," Kari said, making shooing motions with her hands. "I'll see you both bright and early tomorrow."

As they walked downstairs to their dressing rooms, Sophie was quiet, a pensive look on her face.

"You did amazing," Jules told her. "I was impressed, even more impressed with you than I already was."

"Thanks."

"Want to grab a drink?" Jules asked.

"Sure," Sophie said.

"Come get me on your way out."

Sophie nodded, walking down the hall toward her dressing room.

Jules ducked inside her own. She grabbed a drink of water and visited the bathroom before bundling up in her coat and scarf. She'd just tied the belt when Sophie appeared in the doorway, bag slung across her shoulders.

"Ready?" she asked.

Jules nodded, falling into step beside her as they headed

for the back door. "Kari seemed really pleased with your understudy rehearsal."

"I hope so."

"You were great. And that kiss made me hope Micki needs a night off at some point," Jules said, nudging Sophie with her shoulder.

Sophie scoffed at her.

"It just got me thinking about what it would be like to kiss you onstage in front of a packed house," Jules told her. "I think it would be magical."

Sophie gave her a look that Jules couldn't quite decipher, then shrugged. "It could happen, or I could be onstage kissing Micki, covering for *you*."

They walked outside, and Jules was relieved to discover it wasn't as cold this evening as it had been earlier in the week. She was still glad for her coat, but she probably wouldn't be shivering inside it as they walked to Dragonfly. She tried to imagine what it would be like to see Sophie onstage as Bianca. It wasn't a thought Jules had entertained in too much detail, since she was hoping not to miss any shows. And if it did happen, she wouldn't be there to see it. She'd either be out of town or at home sick.

As she pictured it now—Sophie seated at the piano in Bianca's blue dress—she was torn between a sort of awe at Sophie getting her moment in the spotlight and the ingrained disappointment that came with the thought of missing a performance.

They were quiet as they walked, quieter than usual. By the time they reached Dragonfly, Jules was starting to wonder if something was amiss. Maybe Sophie's rehearsal today had stirred up some weird emotions for her. She had taken it really hard when she was first passed over for the role of Bianca. Was she feeling that way again now? Jules's good mood had withered significantly by the time they entered the bar.

Instead of their usual table for two in the back, tonight Sophie led her to the bar, choosing two empty stools just inside the door. As Jules hung her coat on the hook beneath the bar, she saw that all the tables were occupied. Maybe this was just a coincidence. She shot Sophie a questioning look.

Sophie responded with a warm smile...for Josie, who was making her way toward them.

"Hey, ladies," Josie said. "How are you? I feel like I haven't seen you in ages."

"All good," Sophie told her. "Rehearsals have been keeping us busy."

"I bet they have," Josie said excitedly. "I meant to tell you. Eve and I will officially be there on the first night of previews. She bought our tickets last week."

"Oh wow," Jules said, feeling a ping in her stomach. A happy ping. A good ping. But also the ping of *oh shit, so many people I know are going to be there.* "That's so great. You guys are the best."

"Literally could not be more excited," Josie told her, pink curls bouncing for emphasis.

Jules really was lucky to have her and Eve as friends, however casually she knew them. In fact, she ought to make an effort to get to know them better. She was terrible about having a million casual friends but no *close* friends, and she really liked Josie. "We should go out sometime. Maybe a double date, you and Eve, and Sophie and me."

Josie's eyes bugged comically. Sophie's eyebrows rose. They were both staring at Jules, and her cheeks heated almost painfully as she realized what she'd just said.

"So, is it official, then?" Josie asked carefully, looking between them with a delighted smile. "You two?"

"It is now," Sophie told her jokingly. "Did you know we were...unofficial?"

Josie tugged at a pink curl, twirling it self-consciously. "Well, let's just say I had a hunch."

Bless her for not letting on to Sophie about the night Jules had asked her and Eve for dating advice. Not that there was anything wrong with what she'd done, but right here, right now, it would have been awkward to explain.

"This calls for a round of drinks," Josie declared. "What'll you have?"

"I couldn't possibly not get the drink you named for us," Jules told her.

"Broadway Bubbles for you," Josie said. "And Sophie?"

"I'll have the Whiskey Kiss," Sophie told her.

"Be right back with those," Josie said, waving over her shoulder as she walked off.

"A double date, hm?" Sophie said, giving Jules a searching look, reminding her of the awkwardness that had descended between them on their walk here. Had it been awkward, or was Jules projecting her own insecurities onto Sophie?

"I just blurted it out," Jules told her apologetically. "You don't mind, do you?"

"No," Sophie said, her expression softening. "It sounds fun."

"Good." Jules felt some of the rigidity go out of her spine. She reached over and gripped Sophie's hand under the bar. "I was afraid I had overstepped."

"You didn't."

Are we okay, she wanted to ask, but she didn't because

she was afraid she'd make things more awkward when she wasn't even sure anything had happened.

"I can hear your thoughts over there," Sophie said.

"I didn't know you were psychic."

"Well, they're pretty loud," Sophie said. "So why don't you tell me what's on your mind?"

Jules exhaled, looking at Sophie. "I just felt like things got weird after we left the theater tonight, and I don't know why, so I don't know how to fix it."

"To quote a cliché...it's not you, it's me," Sophie said, looking down at her hands. "I was just feeling some things after my rehearsal, that's all."

"Bad things?" Jules asked. "Because you were amazing."

"Not bad. Just complicated."

Josie arrived with their drinks, setting two glasses on the bar in front of them. "Be back to chat more, ladies." With a wave, she was off again to serve her other customers.

Sophie lifted her drink and took a hearty swallow, and Jules hoped the moment hadn't passed. She wanted to know what was on Sophie's mind. As if she could still hear the noise from Jules's thoughts, Sophie took another generous sip of her drink and looked sideways at Jules.

"I guess part of me was wishing I would get to do those scenes for real," she said. "This is the closest I've ever gotten, and standing up there today made me realize how far away I still am."

"I don't think you're that far away," Jules said quietly. "I really don't."

"Thanks," Sophie said. "Anyway, I'm fine. Although I was pretty surprised when you outed yourself to Josie just now."

"Oh." Jules flinched, reaching for her glass. "She already knew, not about us, but about me."

"When did you tell her?" Sophie asked, looking somewhat peeved.

"She and Eve came over one night to see my cats, since they were their foster moms when they were kittens. Anyway, I was in the middle of my sexual identity crisis, so I asked them for advice."

Sophie's expression softened. "I'm glad. It's good to have other queer friends."

"I guess it is." Jules sipped her drink, enjoying the fizz of the prosecco against her tongue. She really was a sucker for a bubbly drink. "It was fun kissing you onstage today."

"Yeah?" Sophie said, giving her a coy look.

"Didn't you enjoy it?" Jules asked, eyebrows raised.

Sophie shrugged, her eyes sparkling with amusement. "I can kiss you anytime I want."

"Oh really?" Jules leaned closer, pulse quickening. "Anytime at all?"

Sophie licked her lips. "That's what I said."

"Pretty presumptuous," Jules murmured, and then they were kissing, not the chaste press of lips they'd shared on stage or in that Christmas bar last week, but a real kiss, the kind of kiss that left the flavor of Sophie's whiskey drink on Jules's tongue and had her blood rushing through her veins.

They lifted their heads, grinning at each other. Jules felt bold and daring, kissing a woman in the middle of a crowded bar. But since it was a gay bar, no one even batted an eye, except maybe Josie who was staring in their direction with a distinctly delighted expression on her face.

Jules leaned in to press her lips against Sophie's again. "Want to come over tonight?"

"Yeah," Sophie said. "I'd like that."

~

JULES PUSHED through the theater's back door, flanked by Sophie and Tabitha. It was Friday afternoon, and they'd just wrapped their last day of rehearsals. Tomorrow, she'd fly to Miami while Sophie left for Syracuse, both of them heading home for the holidays. When they returned after Christmas, they would dive straight into dress rehearsals ahead of the first night of previews.

They walked to the pub next to the theater, the same pub they'd visited after the first day of rehearsals. Tonight, Kari had reserved the back room for them. They arrived in twos and threes, gathering to share one final night together, a celebration after weeks of hard work.

"I have a surprise for you all," Kari told them as she took her seat at the head of the table. Everyone turned to look at her, and Jules saw her own excitement reflected on her cast-mates' faces. "Playbills," Kari said as she reached for the large tote bag beside her chair.

Jules gasped, a thrill racing over her skin. Tears pricked her eyes in anticipation of seeing her face on the official artwork. Sophie's hand slid into her lap, finding Jules's and giving it a squeeze.

Kari pulled a stack of playbills out of the bag and began passing them around the table. The front cover was a vivid purple. Jules didn't look directly at it at first, accepting the stack as it reached her. She lifted a booklet off the top and passed the rest to Sophie. Only then did she look down, inhaling sharply.

She was at the center of the image in Bianca's blue dress, and she was kissing Micki. It was the shot they'd staged to illustrate the love triangle, with Jules leaning toward Micki, their lips barely touching as Amir held her other hand, attempting to get her attention. The words "It's in Her Kiss" hung above them in big, dramatic letters.

Tears overflowed her lids and spilled down her cheeks. It was a beautiful design, absolutely perfect. This image would be printed on posters all over New York City and grace the marquee on the Sapphire Theater.

"You okay, Jules?" Kari asked.

She swiped at her tears, nodding. "Dream come true."

"Happy to make it happen for you," Kari said. "You deserve this."

Jules glanced at Sophie, wishing she were on the cover of the playbill too, wishing Jules was kissing *her*, not Micki.

"It's gorgeous," Sophie said, her tone and expression sincere. "I'm so happy for you."

"I have even better news for you," Kari told them. "This went live on our social media a few hours ago, so you're free to share."

"Don't move," Sophie said, grabbing Jules's cell phone from the table in front of her, then handing it back with a sheepish look so Jules could unlock it for her. "Hold up the playbill."

Jules did as she said, holding the pamphlet in front of herself as she posed for a photo. Her cheeks were still wet with tears, and her fingers shook as they gripped the playbill.

"Perfect," Sophie whispered as she clicked several rapid photos before handing the phone to Jules.

She glanced at the screen, and *gah*, she looked a mess, but there was no mistaking the real, raw emotion on her face. Even if she ended up taking a more composed photo later, she was glad Sophie had captured this moment for her.

"Text it to your mom," Sophie urged, resting a hand discreetly on Jules's knee.

She nodded, not even bothering to type anything to

accompany the photo. It spoke for itself. She took a closeup of the playbill and sent that too. Almost immediately, her phone began to ring.

Beside her, Sophie grinned.

"Julia!" her mother exclaimed as she connected the call. "This is beautiful. It's amazing. Oh honey, I'm so proud I could burst." Her voice shook, and Jules was crying again, not even caring that the whole table was watching her with amused expressions. Probably, they'd all heard every word. People outside on the street could probably hear her mother's excitement.

"Thanks, Mami."

"I'm sending it to Rob and Alex right now," she said. "And all your cousins."

Jules rolled her eyes in mock exasperation. "I'll call you later, okay? I'm at dinner with the whole cast right now."

"Tell them hello from me," Paula said. "I can't wait to meet them in person after Christmas."

"I'm pretty sure they heard you," Jules said, unable to fight her smile as heads nodded all around the table.

"Congratulations, *mija*. I absolutely can't wait to see you up on that stage. It's going to be one of the proudest moments of my life."

Jules thanked her and ended the call, giving her castmates a sheepish look. "So, that's my mom. And yes, you'll all meet her when we open for previews."

And then she almost did a really stupid thing. She almost leaned over and kissed Sophie, right here in front of everyone. They'd spent most of their evenings this week together, soaking up every moment before they left Brooklyn for Christmas, and it felt so good, so comfortable. So much that Jules had almost forgotten they had to keep this under wraps in front of their castmates for professional reasons. Not to mention, she wasn't exactly sure what the rest of the cast had assumed about her sexuality.

The more time she spent with Sophie, the more secure and confident she felt about dating a woman, but at the same time, they'd kept their relationship in a protective bubble, separate from their day-to-day lives. No one knew, except Josie and Eve.

The enormity of what she had to do felt suddenly more real. Coming out was more than telling her family. That was only the beginning. She'd have to tell her friends, castmates, so many people in her life. Was she ready for this? She looked at Sophie, and the one thing she knew for sure was that she had feelings, *strong* feelings, for this woman. And that meant she would have to do the work to be able to acknowledge those feelings to the rest of the people in her life.

Their drinks arrived, and there were many toasts, a lot of celebrating, and even more photos shared on social media. The excitement around the table was palpable. They drank. They ate. They drank more. By the time they stumbled outside together, laughter spreading like wildfire through the group, they were all at least partly drunk and feeling *good*.

"Walk me home?" Sophie asked.

Jules nodded. "Unless you want to come over?"

"So tempting, but I have an early flight tomorrow, and unfortunately, I haven't even started packing yet."

"Okay, then." She fell into step beside Sophie, headed toward her apartment. "I'm going to miss you like crazy."

"Same," Sophie said, linking her arm through Jules's now that they had parted from the rest of the group.

"Get ready for me to call you a lot," Jules said, leaning over to give her a quick kiss.

"I'm ready," Sophie told her. "Are you ready to tell your family?"

Something cold and unwelcome washed through Jules's stomach. "God, Sophie, I'm terrified."

"It's okay," Sophie told her, giving her arm a squeeze. "Just go with what feels right."

"Even if that means not telling them yet?" Jules asked, darting a glance at her.

Sophie nodded. "Even if."

"I don't...I don't want to hurt you," she said, her eyes again filling with tears.

Sophie stopped walking, turning to face Jules on the sidewalk. "Jules, you have to do this for *you*. Not for me."

"But what about your girlfriend, the one who dumped you because she decided not to come out?"

Sophie's gaze dropped to the sidewalk. "I won't deny that's an issue for me. She hurt me, badly. And I don't want to put myself in that position again. But it's my issue, and you shouldn't let it pressure you into coming out before you're ready."

"I'm sorry." Jules squeezed her eyes shut, leaning forward until her forehead rested against Sophie's. "I hate that I'm struggling with this. I really do."

"You can't help how you feel," Sophie whispered. "And neither can I. You do what you have to do, and we'll deal with the rest after we get back from the holidays."

"Okay." They started walking again.

It was cold tonight, cold enough to chill the alcohol in her veins, sobering her up much more quickly than she'd anticipated, or maybe that was sadness that she was about to say goodbye to Sophie for the next week.

All too soon, they arrived at Sophie's building.

"I'm sure I'll talk to you tomorrow," Sophie said. "We'll text. Or call. Or whatever."

"Yes."

Sophie wrapped her arms tightly around Jules. "Good luck with everything, and Merry Christmas."

"Merry Christmas."

"Bye, Jules." Sophie brought their lips together for one last kiss.

"Bye." She buried her face on Sophie's shoulder, inhaling the scent of her hair, absorbing the feel of her arms around her waist. She soaked it all in, and then she pulled free, waving over her shoulder as she walked away.

14

───────

Sophie settled on the couch with a satisfied sigh, beer in hand as *It's a Wonderful Life* played on the TV. To her left, the tree glowed with multicolored lights and a lifetime of familiar ornaments, clay pressed stars she and Tanner had made as kids, paper cutouts adorned with sequins and glitter, and glass balls of all sizes and colors.

Home. She'd been back for twenty-four hours, in the house where she'd grown up, sleeping in her old bedroom. Right now, she was curled in her favorite spot on the couch while she waited for Tanner and his wife to arrive for family game night. Some things never changed. But others did. Her dad, who for decades had sat across from her with the Sunday paper spread across his knees, was now swiping through the news on his tablet, glasses perched on his nose.

"Need any help?" Sophie called to her mom, who was puttering around in the kitchen.

"Nope," her mom answered. "Casserole's already in the oven. I'm just tossing together a quick salad to go with it."

"If we're having salad, we also need dessert," Sophie reminded her. It was a Rindell family rule, one that her friends had been insanely jealous of when she was still in school.

"Then you'd better get in here and make something," her mom said.

"Coming." Sophie slid off the couch and walked to the kitchen, still carrying her beer. "What have I got to work with?"

"I think there's a box of brownie mix in the pantry somewhere," her mom said.

"On it." Sophie took a swig of beer and set down the bottle to rummage through the pantry. A minute later, she held up the brownie box triumphantly. "Bonus, they're dark chocolate."

"I might have bought those specifically with you in mind," her mom told her with a grin.

"Because you're the best." Sophie started gathering the ingredients she needed. There were no fancy chefs in her family. Her mom was an adequate cook and had made sure Sophie and Tanner always had a homecooked meal on the table at dinnertime, but she embraced easy favorites like pizza, casseroles, and spaghetti, and her brownies always came from a box.

"I have a proposition for you," her mom said as she chopped tomatoes.

"Oh yeah?" Sophie whisked together water, olive oil, and a raw egg in a large mixing bowl.

"Go see Stuart tomorrow at the theater."

"Stuart?" Sophie gave her a quizzical look. "Why?"

Stuart Grimmel owned the Alton Theater, where Sophie had spent practically every free moment of her childhood and teenage years. She'd acted in the theater's youth productions through elementary and middle school, and in high school, she'd graduated to the theater's main stage, taking any and every role she could get. Once she'd been old enough, she'd also worked there, soaking up as much of the backstage experience as she could. She'd painted sets and sewed costumes, worked the lights, and swept the stage after everyone else had gone home.

It had been her home away from home before she moved to Manhattan, and Stuart had been her mentor. She had nothing but fond memories of her years at the Alton Theater.

"Just go see him," her mom insisted. "He's expecting you."

"Mom," Sophie protested. "You've got to give me more to go on than that." Because this felt like a setup, and she didn't like it.

"Fine." Her mom lifted her hands in defeat. "Shirley's retiring, so he's looking for someone to lead the youth program, and you're the first person he thought of."

"Well, why didn't you just start with that?" Sophie scowled as she dumped the brownie mix into the bowl and began to stir.

"Because you'd tell me you don't want to work at the local theater. You don't want to be a manager. You want to be an actress. And I get that. I really do. I just think you should go see Stuart and hear him out. This could be an amazing opportunity for you."

"That's exactly what I'm going to tell you, Mom," Sophie said. "It's a great opportunity, but it's not for me."

"Go talk to him. That's all I ask."

"Okay," Sophie conceded. It would be good to visit the theater and to see Stuart. And honestly, it was flattering that he'd thought of her for the job. The Alton's Young Actors program had been such a foundational part of her career and still held a special place in her heart. She'd love to revisit that world, if it didn't mean giving up her current life.

"Thank you," her mom said. "Now tell me all about this girl you've been dating. Will I meet her on opening night?"

"I imagine you will," Sophie told her. "But whether I'm introducing her to you as my girlfriend depends on whether she comes out to her family this week."

"Yes, I guess it would," her mom said with a nod. "That certainly complicates things."

"It does."

"Do you have a picture?" her mom asked.

Sophie nodded, setting down the whisk she'd been using to mix the brownie batter to tug her cell phone out of her back pocket. She pulled up a selfie she and Jules had taken together last week at the theater.

"Oh, she's gorgeous," her mom exclaimed. "I can certainly see how she caught your eye."

"She is," Sophie agreed. "But she's also super fun to be around. She's smart and funny. I think we complement each other well, like she's bold where I'm jaded and vice versa."

"And that's so important to have in a partner, someone who challenges you to grow. Your father and I have that. It sounds serious, then? Or at least the potential to become serious?"

"I'd say potential at this point," Sophie said. "We've only been together a few weeks, and the whole relationship is on shaky ground until she comes out, so we'll see what happens."

"Well, I'll keep my fingers crossed for you two. Is she from New York?"

Sophie shook her head. "Miami."

"Ah, sounds wonderful right about now." She glanced out the kitchen window at the snow-covered yard.

"Sure does." Sophie had never lived anywhere but New York, though, so she couldn't really imagine celebrating Christmas without the cold weather. They didn't always have snow, but it was still a world away from the selfie Jules had sent earlier of herself outside in a sweatshirt and shorts, walking on the beach. At the thought, she pulled up the photo just to see Jules's face, her vibrant smile, and the way her hair blew around her face, tossed by the sea breeze.

Before her mom noticed and ribbed Sophie over her infatuation, she tucked the phone back into her pocket and poured the brownie batter into the pan. She slid it into the oven before sticking the spatula in her mouth to lick off the batter.

Her mom rolled her eyes at her good naturedly. "Some things never change."

Sophie shrugged, grinning around the spatula. She licked it clean and rinsed the bowl in the sink. Then she and her mom joined her dad in the living room. Tanner and Melanie arrived soon after, and they had dinner and played board games until her parents starting yawning around ten. Sophie, tipsy from beer and happy from a fun family night, excused herself to her room to curl up in bed and call Jules, hoping to catch her before it got too late.

"I was just thinking about you," Jules said as she connected the call.

Sophie lay in bed, twirling a strand of hair idly between her fingers. "Good thoughts, I hope?"

"Always. Hang on a minute." There was a pause and the sound of a door closing, and then the background music and conversation from Jules's end of the line disappeared. "Okay, now I should be able to hear you better."

"Sounds like a party at your house," Sophie said.

"Just my mom and grandma watching TV, actually."

"Okay, that's hilarious." Sophie snuggled against her pillow, wishing Jules was here in bed with her. "I'm so jealous that you were outside in shorts today."

"Well, you won't be shocked to know that I was freezing my butt off," Jules said, and Sophie could hear the smile in her voice. "It was only about sixty-five today."

"Only," Sophie teased.

"What did you do this weekend?" Jules asked.

"Not much of anything, and it was glorious. I spent a lot of time with the fam and finished my Christmas shopping. You?"

"About the same," Jules said. "And missing you, of course."

"Yeah. Same." She stared up at the rainbow-striped canopy above her bed. "I finally have my own bed to sleep in, and I can't even share it with you."

"A real shame," Jules agreed. "Is it the same room you grew up in?"

"The very same."

"Tell me about it."

"Let's just say, there are a lot of rainbows," Sophie told her. "And pictures from all the plays I acted in at the local theater." She felt a pang in her chest as she looked at the photos on her dresser. Those years had been magical for her. She'd been so excited to chase her dreams on Broadway, so sure she'd be a leading lady by now.

"Aw, take pictures after we hang up and send them to me," Jules said. "I want to see where little Sophie grew up."

"Only if you send me pictures of yours too," Sophie told her.

"I will, but mine's not as nostalgic. I basically moved out of this house when I was fourteen, even though I came back for summers and school vacations. All my teen flair happened in the apartment where I lived with my mom in Manhattan, and most of it got tossed when we moved, I'm afraid."

"So what does your childhood bedroom in Miami look like now?" Sophie asked.

"Well, my mom's been using it as a guest room, so it's got a lot of beige that teenage Jules would have hated."

"Is that where you are now?" Sophie asked.

"Yeah."

"In bed?"

"Yes." Jules's tone dropped, as if she was imagining Sophie in bed with her, the same way Sophie was right now.

"What are you wearing?" Sophie asked, picturing Jules in the pink bra and panties she'd been wearing the first time she undressed her.

"Sophie," Jules chided, laughter in her voice.

"Ever had phone sex before?"

"Actually, no." Jules sounded surprised by the admission.

"Want to?"

Jules giggled. "So romantic, my dear. But I would say...I could probably be convinced."

Sophie ran her free hand over her breasts. "When you sleep on a couch, you start to appreciate the little things, like being able to lie in bed and have phone sex with your girl-friend without having to worry about anyone walking in on you."

"That's very true," Jules said.

"And the thing is, I haven't had this kind of privacy in a *long* time. Do you know what it's like, trying to sneak my vibrator into the shower with me while my roommates are out? Let's just say, I haven't had many orgasms this year, and since I met you, I've been pretty much constantly horny."

"Oh." Jules's voice dropped deeper still, the way it sounded when she was aroused.

"I think about you, Jules. I want you. I need you. And I can't do anything about it."

"Tonight you can," Jules whispered.

"I'm already wet just thinking about it," Sophie told her, rubbing herself over her jeans, igniting the ache between her thighs.

"Tell me more," Jules murmured.

"I'm taking off my jeans, which is really not sexy, so imagine I'm lying here on my rainbow bedspread, naked and waiting for you."

"Mm," Jules said. "I bet you do look sexy taking off your jeans. Your tongue pokes out when you're concentrating on something, and it's hot."

Sophie blinked, realizing her tongue was indeed poking out from between her lips. She dropped her jeans on the floor. "Your turn. What are you doing right now?"

"I'm wearing a skirt, so I just slipped off my panties. I have to be quiet, though. My mom and grandma are just downstairs."

"Right." Sophie closed her eyes, imagining Jules in bed with her skirt hiked up around her waist, touching herself. Her core throbbed at the mental image.

"And you?" Jules asked. "Do you need to be quiet?"

"My parents' bedroom is downstairs, and they're probably already asleep, so I'm not too worried."

"I'll let you do most of the talking, then," Jules whispered.

"No fair," Sophie teased. She slipped out of her own panties, beginning to stroke herself. She couldn't hold back the gasp that escaped her lips. "Oh God, Jules."

"Yes," Jules moaned. "I'm imagining that it's your fingers touching me right now."

"I wish it were," Sophie told her fervently. "I love the feel of your body against mine. I love the way you're so uninhibited when we're together, so willing to experiment and see what feels good."

"Because it's all new with you."

"That might have made you cautious," Sophie countered.

"I'm not naturally a cautious person." Jules sounded breathless, and it only stoked the fire already burning inside Sophie.

"No, you're not, and I really fucking like that about you." Sophie rolled to her side, hips thrusting against her fingers.

"I wish you were here," Jules whispered. "Your fingers are like magic, and your mouth..."

"Imagine it," Sophie told her. "Pinch your clit and pretend it's me biting you there."

Jules whimpered in pleasure. "Yes."

"Listening to you is really turning me on."

On the other end of the line, Jules went silent. "Shit. Am I being loud? I'm so afraid my mom or grandma will hear me. These walls are so thin."

"I don't think they can hear you," Sophie said. "I'm right in your ear, and they're downstairs."

Jules let out a frustrated groan, and Sophie had the impression she'd stopped touching herself.

"Challenge yourself to be as quiet as possible," Sophie suggested.

"Okay." Jules exhaled into the phone, and the sound sent a shiver of pleasure through Sophie.

"Now tease yourself a bit," Sophie said, even as she increased the friction of her own fingers, need rising swiftly inside her. "Just ghost your fingers over yourself until you're so turned on, you can hardly stand it."

"You're bossy all of a sudden," Jules whispered, but she sounded relaxed again. "Now tell me what you're doing."

"I'm..." She paused, stilling her fingers before she carried herself over the edge. "I'm taking my own advice and slowing down for a minute while I wait for you."

"Oh." Jules gasped. "It's working. Sophie, I—"

"Good. You're doing good," Sophie told her as she drew teasing circles over her own clit, hips jerking. "Ready?"

"Yes." Jules's voice was a whine. "I'm so ready."

"Go," Sophie whispered. "Fuck yourself so hard and fast you can't breathe, and imagine that those are my fingers in you."

Jules muttered something unintelligible, and then there was a whole lot of gasping and breathing that was impossibly sexy. Sophie closed her eyes, listening to Jules on the other end of the line, letting it carry her right over the edge. She moaned as she came, burying her face in the bedspread to muffle the sound.

Afterward, they lay there, just basking in the satisfaction palpable over the line between them. They talked for a few more minutes before they said goodbye, and when Sophie fell asleep that night, it was with a smile on her face.

THE NEXT MORNING, Sophie borrowed her mom's car to drive to the Alton Theater. The day was clear and sunny, if cold. As she parked in the lot across the street from the theater, nostalgia washed over her. She hadn't made time to attend a production here in a few years, and now she regretted that. Shoving her hands into the pockets of her coat for warmth, she crossed the street and approached the white brick building. The marquee in front advertised a production of *Grease* beginning January 8th.

Sophie pulled the front door open and stepped inside. The lobby was empty on this Monday morning a few days before Christmas. She turned down the hall to her left, headed for Stuart's office, her footsteps echoing in the hallway. His door was open, so she paused there, smiling as she tapped her knuckles against the doorway to catch his attention.

Stuart sat behind his desk, squinting at a pile of papers in front of him. He looked up, his expression warming as he caught sight of Sophie. Stuart had to be in his late sixties now. There were more lines on his face than she remembered, and his white hair had receded to emphasis the shiny expanse of his forehead. "Sophie, it's so good to see you."

"I was about to say the same thing," she told him.

"Come in. Sit." He waved at the chair across from him. "How are you?"

They spent a few minutes exchanging pleasantries and catching up. He had two granddaughters in college now, one of whom was studying theater, much to his great pride. "It's wonderful that you're understudying the two female leads in *It's in Her Kiss*. An understudy isn't a glamorous role to people outside the business, but you and I both know how difficult it can be."

"It's true," she admitted.

"It shows your versatility as an actress and their faith in your talent," Stuart told her. "I'm proud of you. You've done well for yourself, just as I knew you would."

"Thank you." She twisted her hands in her lap. "I'm still not where I'd hoped to be, though."

Stuart waved a hand as if brushing away something

unwanted. "Well, that's the nature of the business, isn't it? There's always more to achieve, a bigger role, a shinier part."

"Yes."

"So I feel somewhat guilty for even bringing you back to the old Alton here, because I know Broadway has always been your dream, but sometimes dreams change as we get older, and you have exactly the skillset and experience that I'm looking for, not to mention a history here at the theater. I had to at least invite you in for a conversation."

"To be honest, when my mom told me about the job, my immediate response was a no."

"I figured as much," Stuart told her. "Let's take a walk. Let me show you what we've got going on these days. Hear me out, and then, if nothing else, this was a chance for us to catch up."

"Fair enough," Sophie agreed, standing to follow him out of his office.

"Thanks to the generous support of our patrons, last year we were able to upgrade our lighting system," he told her as they stood in the production booth, surveying the equipment. Sophie had only a rudimentary understanding of how it all worked, but she knew enough to know she was looking at a state-of-the-art system.

In fact, the more they walked and talked, the more she realized the Alton Theater was doing well. The paint was fresh. The seats were plush and pristine. It had a full roster of shows scheduled for the year, exciting and innovative shows, some of which featured names she recognized from Broadway.

Stuart told her about the job, about the responsibility she'd have in overseeing the Young Actors program and what productions were scheduled, about the Alton's commitment to strengthening its outreach in the local community and bringing in more diverse productions and casts. It was a dream job…if her dream wasn't to be the one on the stage. Stuart had said that sometimes dreams changed as people got older. Had hers? Or should it?

She'd worked on Broadway for over a decade now. Not everyone was meant to be a leading lady, and if she took this job, she'd have a steady salary that was more than she'd ever made as an actress. She'd work in this wonderful theater. She could find an apartment for a fraction of the cost of renting in the city. She could build a career here. A different career. A new life for herself.

But she would have to leave Broadway behind. She'd leave the thrill of the city, of auditions, of dancing and singing and acting on stage. She'd have to move away from Jules. She would have to give up on her dream, change it, evolve it into something new.

"So, have I swayed you even the slightest bit?" Stuart asked as they stood side by side on the stage, staring out at the rows of empty seats in front of them.

"Yes," she told him with a smile. "The slightest bit."

"That's fair," he said. "And obviously, there's time for you to think about it. Shirley isn't retiring until April, and I understand that you're contractually obligated to *It's in Her Kiss* until then anyway."

"I am."

"So give it some thought. Come back and see one of our productions. And in a month or so, let me know if this is something you're seriously considering, so I know whether to expand my search."

∿

"JULIA, PLEASE PASS THE WINE."

Jules reached for the bottle, passing it to her aunt. It was Christmas Eve, and she and the rest of her family had comfortably—or not—settled into the sort of food coma that came after hours of boisterous eating and celebrating, resting before Midnight Mass. On the other side of the table, her grandma was planning a shopping excursion with her mom in anticipation of their upcoming trip to New York.

"*Gracias,*" Tía Martha told Jules as she took the bottle and topped off her glass. "Will there be a way for us to watch your performance here in Miami?"

"Unfortunately, no," Jules told her. "Most theater isn't recorded. You aren't even supposed to take photos during the show."

"Oh, psst," her aunt said, making a dismissive motion with her hand. "I know Paula will sneak a few photos for us."

"She better not." Jules raised her eyebrows at her mom, who gave her a look of mock innocence.

"I would never break the rules," she said, not quite meeting Jules's eyes.

"Mami, you could get kicked out of the theater," Jules told her. "You know this."

Her mother waved her hands as if Jules had nothing to worry about, but she wasn't convinced. She'd talk to her about it again later.

"I hear you'll be kissing a woman onstage," Tía Martha said, eyes wide as if she'd just said something scandalous.

Jules lifted her wine and took a careful sip. "Yes."

"How...modern," her aunt said.

"I'm pretty sure women have been kissing women for as long as they've been kissing men," Jules told her, stomach tightening uncomfortably.

"Well, you know what I mean," her aunt said.

"Sure," Jules said. *It means you're uncomfortable with the idea.*

The conversation shifted to Jules's brother, Alex, and his wife Cindi, who had just announced she was pregnant with their third baby. They already had two adorable little girls, and the family was taking bets over whether number three might be a boy. Jules's youngest brother, Rob, had a new girl-friend that everyone was dying to meet. Inevitably, the next thing they wanted to know was did Jules have a boyfriend?

"Nope," she said, feeling absolutely sick about lying, even by omission. But she had to tell her mom first, and it wasn't a conversation to have on Christmas Eve in front of the whole family. There would be plenty of time for that after the holiday.

"I bet you'll have men lining up once your new show opens," her mom said, smiling proudly, and the vise over Jules's stomach tightened.

She set down her wineglass, desperately searching for a change of topic.

"I'm going to get more *coquito*," her grandma announced, rising from her seat.

The spiced eggnog was one of Jules's holiday favorites. "I'll get it, Abuelita," she told her grandma. "You stay here."

"*No seas ridícula*," her grandma said, stubborn as ever. "I said I'd get it."

Jules lifted her hands in defeat, fighting a smile. She loved her grandma so much and couldn't wait to spend a week with her and her mom when they came up for the show. How would her grandma react to Jules's news?

Her time with Sophie in Brooklyn felt a million miles away as Jules sat here in her childhood home in Miami, facing the reality of coming out to a woman who kept a framed photo of the pope on the table beside her bed. She reached for her wine and took a fortifying sip.

A crash echoed from the direction of the kitchen, the sound of glass breaking followed by another thump. All the heads at the table swiveled toward the doorway Beatriz had walked through moments before.

"You okay in there, Mami?" Jules's mom called, rolling her eyes playfully in anticipation of Beatriz's response to whatever she'd dropped...probably the bowl of *coquito*.

But there was no response.

"Mami?" Paula said again, already rising from her chair.

Jules watched her go, waiting for her grandma to yell at her for overreacting, but when Paula reached the doorway to the kitchen, she let out something between a gasp and a scream that stole all the air from Jules's lungs.

She lurched to her feet, knocking over her wineglass in her haste. It spilled bloodred across the white tablecloth. Everyone was on their feet, rushing toward the kitchen, and they were all in Jules's way. She pushed forward, legs oddly numb as she wedged herself in the doorway beside Rob.

Her grandmother lay on the floor beside the broken bowl of coquito, red blood mixing with the white liquid spreading across the tile. Jules heard the cry that escaped her lips as if she was outside herself, looking down at the chaotic scene in the kitchen. Already, Beatriz was surrounded by people, obscuring Jules's view.

Where is she bleeding? What happened? Oh God...

Through the din of concerned family members and her own thoughts, Jules heard her mother's sharp cry. "Someone dial 911."

15

J ules spent Christmas day in the hospital. After a while, the rhythmic beeping of the machinery seemed to blend with the holiday music playing softly from the portable speaker Alex had left beside Beatriz's bed. After several festive hours, opening gifts and celebrating with an endless parade of friends and family through her room, Jules's grandma had finally fallen asleep.

Two small stitches near her hairline were surrounded by a large purple bruise where she'd hit her head on the edge of the kitchen counter as she fell. She'd also twisted her left ankle, which was wrapped in a thick bandage. In a word, she was lucky. Due to a mild concussion and her age, the hospital had insisted that she stay for observation, but she was going to be okay. In fact, she had spent most of the day fussing about wanting to go home.

"I think this is our cue to leave," Paula said quietly from the other side of the hospital bed. The rest of the family had come and gone throughout the day, but Jules and her mom had been here since her grandma was admitted last night.

Between them, Beatriz began to snore.

"Yeah." Jules smiled as she stood from her chair. She leaned over to kiss her grandmother's cheek before gathering her purse and the gifts she'd received from family members while she was at her grandma's bedside today.

She and her mom didn't say much as they walked outside to the car, both of them exhausted by the last twenty-four hours. Neither of them had managed much sleep last night. They loaded their gifts into the backseat and exchanged a long hug beside the car.

"She can't fly to New York next week," Jules whispered, tears stinging her eyes.

"I know," her mom agreed.

"She'll fight us on it, even if the doctor forbids her to fly."

"You leave her to me," Paula said, patting Jules's arm before they got into the car.

It was a pretty drive home, Christmas lights twinkling from houses and businesses as they passed and the Miami skyline glittering behind them. The lights softened and blurred before Jules's eyes. Suddenly, she was so tired, she could hardly hold her eyes open.

Her mom parked in the driveway, and they walked into the house together, surprised and yet not surprised to find that the family had cleaned up after their chaotic departure to the hospital last night. The kitchen was pristine, no sign of Beatriz's fall or the food that had covered the countertops at the time.

In silent agreement, Jules and her mom went to the fridge and pulled out various containers of leftovers, fixing themselves a late dinner. They filled plates with roast pork, black beans and rice, and mashed yucca, then finished it off with a couple of the *pastelitos* Jules had made with her grandma yesterday morning.

Her phone buzzed with a text message.

Miss you! How's your grandma doing? It was from Sophie.

Jules had managed to sneak away from her grandmother's bedside this afternoon to give Sophie a quick call, but they'd only gotten to talk for a few minutes, and right now... yeah, Jules missed her a lot. A funny ache rose in her chest.

Miss you too! If all goes well, she'll be home tomorrow morning.

So glad! You must be exhausted, Sophie replied.

I am. My mom and I just got home. Eating dinner and then collapsing in bed.

"Who are you texting over there with that big smile on your face?" her mom asked in a teasing tone as she carried their empty plates to the sink.

"Just a friend," Jules answered quickly as her heart gave a kick in her chest. She could blurt it out right now, tell her mom and be done with it. But after the last twenty-four hours, she was just too tired. And so was her mom. This wasn't the right time.

"The same friend you've been sneaking off to call all week?" her mom asked playfully.

"Maybe," Jules hedged, ducking her head.

A new text from Sophie gleamed on her screen. *Sleep well! Merry Christmas!*

Same to you! xx

"Tell me everything," Paula said.

Jules stood and kissed her cheek. "Not tonight, Mami. It's time for us to sleep."

~

"Is your grandma still coming home this morning?"

Jules snuggled deeper under the comforter on her bed.

"Yeah. My mom is on her way to the hospital now. She should be discharged in about an hour."

"I'm so glad," Sophie said. "And how was your Christmas otherwise?"

"The usual chaos. Lots of people. Lots of food. We've never spent it in the hospital before, but we Vegas can be flexible when necessary."

Sophie laughed. "That's good."

"And how was your Christmas?" Jules asked.

"Fewer people and no hospital visits, but also great," Sophie said.

"I miss you," Jules told her, pressing a hand against her chest. Her time with Sophie felt so far away that sometimes she felt like she was losing her grasp on it. The longer she kept Sophie a secret from her family, the more surreal the whole thing felt.

"Same. This week has been a bit crazy for me too."

"How so?" Jules asked, because unless she was imagining things, Sophie sounded as distracted as Jules felt.

"Nothing compared to yours," Sophie said, and Jules could practically see her waving a hand in front of her face, wishing she hadn't said anything. "I'll tell you about it when I see you."

"Tell me now," Jules said quietly. "Please."

"It's just...I had an interesting job offer while I was here," Sophie said, and she definitely sounded guarded now.

"A job offer?" Jules traced the floral pattern on her sheets with a fingertip. "In Syracuse?"

"Yeah. I'd be managing the Young Actors program at the theater where I used to work in high school. It's a great opportunity, but I'm not going to take it." She seemed to rush at the end, and Jules's finger stilled against the sheet.

"Do you want to take it?" she asked hesitantly.

Sophie sighed deeply. "It's complicated. I'd have a steady job, earning a really good salary, and I love that theater. It might be a good change."

"Might?" Jules pressed, trying to ignore the sick feeling in the pit of her stomach.

"I wouldn't be performing. I'd have to give up my Broadway dreams," Sophie said. "And I'd have to move back here. It's...like I said, it's complicated."

"How soon do you have to decide?"

"I have a month or so to think about it," Sophie said. "I'm sorry, Jules. I wasn't going to tell you about this the day after Christmas and certainly not over the phone, especially after what you've been through with your grandma."

"No, I'm glad you told me," Jules said, burrowing deeper in the covers. She felt like she was drowning, like those perfect weeks she and Sophie had shared together before Christmas were drifting away from her.

"I don't want to leave the city," Sophie said, her voice gone quiet. "I don't want to leave *you*, not when we've just started something I can't seem to get enough of."

"I don't want you to leave either." Jules hugged her comforter, wishing it was Sophie. How could she think of giving up performing when Jules had never known her to want anything else? "But I also don't want to hold you back, if this is what you want."

Sophie sighed again. "I don't know what I want right now."

An uncomfortable silence descended between them. Jules sucked in a deep breath and blew it out. She'd already been out of sorts, already unsettled over the thought of coming out to her mom, especially after their chaotic holiday. She'd hoped this conversation with Sophie would settle her nerves, would remind her why she was doing this, would set the stage for Jules to introduce her mother to her girlfriend next week in New York.

And now...now she wasn't even sure she'd have a girlfriend on opening night.

"I'm sorry," Sophie said.

"Don't apologize. Things happen. People move." Jules knew it well. She'd given up her life in Miami and precious years with her dad to chase her dreams in New York. "I can't possibly be impartial here, because obviously I want you to stay, but I also don't want you to be too quick to give up on your dream. You've worked so long and so hard to get as far as you have on Broadway, and *It's in Her Kiss* may open doors for you."

"I want to believe that's true," Sophie said, a hint of vulnerability in her tone that Jules had never heard before. "But I've been auditioning for a decade, and I have so little to show for it."

"Your name might not be on the marquee, but you've accomplished a lot. I've seen you perform. I know how good you are and how much you love it. I believe in you, Soph."

"Thanks. I appreciate that," Sophie said. "I have a lot to think about."

16

S ophie climbed the stairs to Jules's apartment, excitement and nerves warring for dominance inside her. They hadn't seen each other in a week, and so much had happened during that time. The door opened before Sophie could raise her hand to knock, and Jules stood there in formfitting silver pants, a black top, and the kind of smile that knocked Sophie's knees right out from under her. Just as quickly, their arms were around each other, and Sophie was enveloped in the warmth of Jules's embrace.

"I missed you so much," Jules whispered against her neck.

"So did I." She turned her head, bringing their lips together as Jules tugged her into her apartment. Vaguely, Sophie heard the door click shut behind her as she kissed Jules, hands tangled in the honeyed depths of her hair. It was meant to have been a "hello" kiss, but neither of them seemed in any hurry to end it.

Jules's arms were tight around her, hands fisted in the back of Sophie's coat as her tongue slipped into Sophie's mouth. It felt good, so good, *too* good, after everything that had happened while they were apart.

Finally, Jules lifted her head, her expression dazed. "Wow."

"Yeah." Sophie reached out to tuck a lock of hair behind Jules's ear. "You know, I wouldn't complain if we stayed in tonight."

"No way," Jules told her. "The party will be so fun, and we can finish catching up after. You're staying here tonight, right?"

Sophie patted the bag slung over her shoulder. When Jules had called to invite her to a fancy New Year's Eve party overlooking Times Square that promised to be a "who's who" of the theater world, she couldn't say no, even if part of her would rather stay right here, strip Jules out of those sexy-as-hell silver pants, and have a private celebration of their own.

Sophie set down her bag, deciding to keep her coat on if they were indeed heading out. "So, are we attending together...or *together*?"

Jules's radiant expression dimmed. "I don't know. I think maybe because we're castmates, we should be discreet about it, don't you?"

"As castmates, yes. But if this wasn't a Broadway party?" Sophie couldn't help asking, because Jules hadn't said anything about coming out to her family, which made Sophie think that she hadn't.

Jules's gaze dropped, a pained expression crossing her face, and Sophie felt guilty for dampening the mood between them. "I didn't do it, if that's what you're asking. After my grandma fell, everything just went sideways."

Sophie blew out a breath. *This isn't like Brianna. Jules is truly trying.* But she'd been so counting on Jules coming out over the holidays, on being able to make things official between them as they headed into the new year. And now she couldn't seem to stop herself from taking a big step back from Jules, both physically and mentally.

"I'm sorry," Jules said quietly, her gaze falling to her shoes.

"I guess both of our Christmases went a bit sideways," Sophie said, closing the space she'd inadvertently created between them, determined not to let anything ruin their reunion. "What if we worry about all that tomorrow and just focus on celebrating tonight?"

"I like that plan," Jules said with a slightly brittle smile.

"How is your grandma? Is she recovering okay?"

Jules nodded, but the sadness on her face was unmistakable. "Her pride took the worst damage. She's not going to be able to fly up next week, though, and I don't know who's more disappointed about that, because I was really looking forward to her being here."

"I'm sorry," Sophie murmured. "Can she come later in the run?"

"I hope so. My mom's already offered to fly up again with her as soon as she's able."

"Good."

Jules reached for her coat and shrugged into it. She knotted the belt around her waist and swept her hair out from beneath the collar. Then she grabbed her purse and led the way to the door. "We can take the subway there, but I hired a car to drive us home. Public transportation will be a nightmare after midnight."

"No kidding," Sophie agreed, even as those ugly feelings rose again in her chest, because Jules could afford to hire a car for them on New Year's Eve. She never flaunted it, but

Sophie couldn't help feeling somewhat inadequate by comparison. "Thanks for doing that."

"Well," Jules said, leaning in for a kiss. "I do have ulterior motives to get you home safely and promptly, because we have some private celebrating to do later."

"Indeed we do."

Jules paused in the doorway, taking Sophie's hand in hers. "I really missed you, you know."

"I know." They had a lot to talk about, but tonight was for celebrating.

They went down the stairs together and out into the street. Sophie grinned as Jules shivered dramatically, shrinking into her coat. Together, they walked three blocks to the subway entrance. Jules stopped suddenly, drawing Sophie in for a deep, hungry kiss as people bumped into them from every direction.

"I'm sorry I didn't tell my family about you yet," she told Sophie. "But I just wanted to make sure you knew it has nothing to do with me being ashamed to kiss you in public, because I'm not."

"I can see that," Sophie said playfully as she led the way down the steps to the subway, thrilled by Jules's public display of affection. "And coming out is a big deal. I'm sorry if I rushed you."

"You didn't, and I'm going to do it," Jules said as they swiped their MetroCards.

They didn't talk much as they battled the New Year's Eve crowds on the subway, exchanging looks and smiles as they rode, shoulders bumping together from the movement of the train. Sophie was sweating by the time they exited— choosing to get off a few stops early and walk the rest of the way to avoid the Times Square traffic jam—but Jules still had her face burrowed in her scarf. She really was adorably cold-blooded.

She might have Miami in her blood, but she led Sophie through the crowded streets with all the confidence of a native New Yorker. They entered the Marriott Marquis through a side entrance and waited with the crowd at the elevator bank. Eventually, they stepped into a sleek, glass-sided pod bound for the rooftop restaurant.

Sophie and Jules were wedged inside with a dozen or so other guests. They faced the glass, alternately looking out at the hotel atrium passing by and exchanging covert kisses. Generally, Sophie preferred to stay home and watch the ball drop with a couple of friends—maybe go to a nearby bar if she was really feeling adventurous—but this was going to be fun, especially with Jules on her arm.

The elevator slid to a stop, and they stepped off, hand in hand. They checked their coats near the hostess desk before wandering into the restaurant, which was decked out in black and gold balloons and filled with people in fancy clothes. Right away, she recognized a prominent Broadway director and several actors. Soft music filled the room, and Times Square flashed brightly outside the floor-to-ceiling windows.

"Okay, I'm glad we came," Sophie said, giving Jules's hand a squeeze.

"We're going to have so much fun tonight." Jules led the way to the bar, where she ordered champagne. Sophie got a whiskey sour. And since no one seemed to be paying them any attention, they kept holding hands, leaned in close as they sipped their drinks.

"I'm glad we're in here and not out there," Sophie said, nodding her head toward the windows.

"I did it once," Jules told her. "Times Square."

"Of course you did." Sophie shook her head in mock exasperation.

"It was my freshman year of college, and a big group of us decided to go. We thought it would be *amazing*, and it was, but it was also super freaking cold, and I almost peed my pants because there aren't any bathrooms."

Sophie choked on her drink, covering her mouth with her hand as she snorted with laughter. "You know, a lot of people wear adult diapers to watch the ball drop," she said when she could speak again.

Jules scrunched her nose. "We were eighteen. We definitely never considered that option."

"It's never had any appeal for me," Sophie told her. "Too many people. Too many diapers. Just a big nope all around."

Now it was Jules's turn to laugh. "I'm glad I did it, but now I'm really glad to be in here, where it's warm, and we have drinks and music and bathrooms."

"A definite upgrade," Sophie agreed. "Want to go take a peek?"

With a nod, Jules led the way, weaving between people toward the windows that ringed the restaurant, which Sophie now realized was slowly rotating. *Whoa.* She sipped her drink as they edged closer to the glass. As another couple walked away, she and Jules stepped quickly into their place.

"Okay, this is amazing." Sophie gazed out at the city. Currently, they faced the Hudson River—the opposite direction of Times Square—but all they had to do was stand here and wait for their view to change.

"This has got to be the best view in the city," Jules said, the reflection of the city sparkling in her eyes.

"I know *I* have the best view," Sophie said, allowing her gaze to roam from Jules's face over the tight black top that highlighted the swell of her breasts to the silver pants that hugged her hips, all the way down to her black leather boots.

Jules scoffed, tossing an amused glance at Sophie as she sipped her champagne.

"I wasn't joking," Sophie told her. "You look stunning."

"Thank you," Jules said, cheeks darkening with a blush. "So do you."

Sophie wasn't going to argue with her, but she had on a black blouse and pants, nothing even remotely interesting. She'd already caught several men checking Jules out, and it made her want to move in possessively, to wrap an arm around Jules's waist and kiss her in front of this room full of people.

Jules's tongue darted out to wet her lips, drawing Sophie's attention to her mouth. They clasped their free hands, leaning subtly closer, helplessly drawn by the magnetic pull between them.

"Julia!" a man's voice called, and Jules straightened as her gaze darted toward the bar, a tight smile replacing the languid one she'd just given Sophie.

Sophie turned to see Timothy Rollins, a prominent Broadway actor, walking toward them.

JULES FELT Sophie's hand slide out of her grasp, and everything inside her that had been warm went cold in its absence, even though she was the one who had set the parameters for tonight. "Tim, how are you?" she asked as he reached them.

"I'm fabulous." He leaned in to kiss her cheek in greeting. "And yourself?"

"Great," she told him, imagining Sophie bristling beside her, although in this instance, she had nothing to be jealous of. Jules and Tim had never dated. She wasn't even sure he was straight. He was just an affectionate guy.

"Glad to hear it," he said before transferring his gaze to Sophie. He held out a hand. "Timothy Rollins."

"It's a pleasure to meet you," Sophie told him politely. "Sophie Rindell."

"The pleasure's all mine," he said. "Jules and I met years ago when we both worked on *Danger Zone*."

"He's being modest," Jules told her. "Tim starred in *Danger Zone*, and I had a walk-on role."

Sophie grinned. "A role I know all too well."

"Are you an actor as well?" Tim asked her.

She nodded, and for the next few minutes, they shared tales of the various productions they'd worked on. Sophie seemed completely at ease, smiling and laughing as she polished off her drink. Jules's champagne was long gone, and she was contemplating returning to the bar for a refill when Sophie turned to her.

"Another glass?" she asked, taking the empty flute from Jules's hand.

"If you don't mind," she told her gratefully. "Thank you."

"No problem." Sophie headed toward the bar, leaving Jules with Tim.

"Are you here with someone?" he asked, leaning a shoulder against the column behind him, his gaze lingering on hers with an intensity she couldn't quite place. It wasn't attraction, perhaps just curiosity.

Her stomach clenched, but maybe this was the perfect opportunity to flex her muscles, so to speak. "Yes," she answered carefully. "I'm with Sophie."

"Ah." His eyebrows rose, and a delighted smile crossed

his handsome face. "I thought so, but I didn't want to be presumptuous. Good for you. She seems great."

"Thank you." Jules's face was on fire, which was ridiculous, because Tim seemed completely unfazed. "We're not exactly..."

"My lips are sealed," he said. "I'm here with Jonathan." He tipped his head toward a tall, handsome man with mahogany skin who stood near the bar, one hand in the pocket of his slacks as he chatted with several other well-dressed men.

It was Jules's turn to smile. "Good for you too."

"Thank you," he said. "I was thrilled to hear about your role in *It's in Her Kiss*. Jon and I will definitely come and see it."

"Thank you," she told him. "My first leading role. I'm still pinching myself, honestly."

"I'd say it's been a long time coming," he said. "You have a lot of talent."

Jules pressed a hand against her cheek, which was still flaming. "I really appreciate that."

Sophie rejoined them with a drink in each hand, handing Jules a fresh flute of champagne. Tim chatted with them for another minute before heading off into the crowd. Jules sipped her champagne, watching Sophie.

"What?" Sophie said slyly.

"I guess I expected you to be jealous."

Sophie glanced at Tim, who was standing close to Jon. "Nothing for me to be jealous of. He clearly has his eyes on someone else tonight."

They shared a laugh, sipping their drinks as Times Square passed by beneath them. It was slightly disorienting, or maybe that was the alcohol talking. Jules rested a hand on the window to steady herself.

"Kari's here," Sophie said. "We should say hi."

Jules nodded, following Sophie's gaze to find their director in a stunning red dress, her black hair swept back in a neat twist, talking to a man she assumed was her husband. "Lead the way."

Sophie did, although she kept a respectable distance between them.

"Sophie," Kari exclaimed as she caught sight of them. "And Jules. It's great to see you both. Did you have a good holiday?"

They exchanged pleasantries and were introduced to Kari's husband, Bai. Jules thought she might have caught Kari giving her and Sophie a questioning look, but it could have been her imagination. For whatever reason—maybe it was the alcohol talking again—she wasn't too concerned about Kari having suspicions about them. As long as they didn't let it affect their performance, it shouldn't be a problem. And how could it affect their performance when she and Sophie didn't even interact during the show?

"Hi, ladies."

An arm slid over Jules's shoulders, and she turned to find Micki standing there, pink cocktail in hand.

"How are my favorite costars?" Micki asked, giving Jules a squeeze.

And where Sophie had been laidback at Tim's approach, her fingers were now clenched around the tumbler in her hand. Jules sidestepped Micki's embrace, sliding neatly out from under her arm as she offered her a polite smile. "Enjoying the party?"

"It's *fantastic*," Micki exclaimed, resting a hand on Sophie's shoulder as she swayed on her feet. "I can't get over the view. Best New Year's Eve party I've ever attended."

Sophie's eyes widened. Yeah, Micki was drunk. Very

drunk, if her slurred speech was any indication. They shared several minutes of awkward conversation—and even more awkward touching—before Micki stumbled off in the direction of the bar.

Kari's eyebrows lifted as she sipped her martini.

"She's going to have a hell of a hangover tomorrow," Sophie remarked dryly as she sipped her own drink.

"As long as she's over it before dress rehearsals start on Monday," Kari said.

Jules cringed internally at the impression Micki had just made on their director. Professionalism was key—always— but especially at an industry-heavy party like this one. Kari and Bai excused themselves to greet another director, and Sophie and Jules snuck off to a quiet corner of the restaurant to regroup.

"Can you believe Micki?" Sophie said.

"I know. That was not a good look."

"She may have regrets in the morning on top of her hangover," Sophie said.

"Something you and I will not," Jules told her, giving her hand a quick squeeze. "I'm having an amazing time."

And that didn't change throughout the night. Dinner was served buffet style, and they filled themselves with delicious food while Manhattan glittered outside the windows around them. It was beautiful and romantic and absolutely the perfect way to ring in the new year. After they ate, they sat for a while, sipping drinks while they exchanged the kind of effortless conversation that made Jules's soul hum with contentment.

Throughout her adult life, she'd been surrounded by so many people that she'd started to feel an odd sort of loneliness in the center of the crowd, a detachment from her friends. She'd become a master of casual conversations and carefully masked emotions, because none of the people in her life were the sort that she shared her fears and disappointments with. She'd begun to feel shallow.

And then she'd met Sophie.

As midnight drew near, they got fresh drinks at the bar and managed to squeeze into an empty space along the windows, using the crowd as an excuse to stand close enough that their hips touched. Jules snuck her free hand into Sophie's, giving it a squeeze.

"Do you make New Year's resolutions?" she asked.

Sophie's brow knitted. "Sometimes. I haven't thought about one for this year, though."

"I think I just want to make myself proud in *It's in Her Kiss*," Jules said, surprised when she heard the tremor in her voice. "I have no control over reviews or how the crowd will react to the show. I just want to feel like I gave it my best."

"I think that's perfect," Sophie said.

"And I want to own my sexuality. These last few weeks with you have shown me that this is a real, vital part of who I am, and I need the people in my life to know that."

"I'm glad," Sophie told her. "I think this is going to be an amazing, important year for you on many fronts."

"Big changes for both of us, maybe," Jules said. They'd been skating around Sophie's job offer all night, having agreed not to talk about serious topics tonight, but it felt disingenuous to completely ignore it too.

Sophie nodded pensively. "I have a big decision to make, that's for sure."

"Which means we need to be extra thankful for this night." Jules felt tears pressing behind her eyes. "I'm so glad to be here with you, Sophie."

"Same."

"Look." Jules tipped her head toward the window, Times

Square gleaming below. The crowd seemed to surge in waves, hands and signs in the air. "Five minutes to midnight. Looks like we'll be facing the Hudson when the ball drops."

"Actually, I think that will be perfect."

"How so?" Jules asked, because to her, it felt like a manifestation of the all the ways her life seemed to be backward these days.

"It'll be quieter," Sophie said. "Everyone will crowd to the other side of the restaurant to try to look down and see the ball drop."

"You're right," Jules said. "That *is* perfect."

They stepped closer, staring into each other's eyes as the TVs above the bar began the countdown to midnight. As Sophie had predicted, most of the party guests rushed to the windows overlooking Times Square, leaving them in relative obscurity.

"Five...four...three...two..." the crowd chanted, and Jules pulled Sophie into her arms, to hell with any potential onlookers.

"Happy New Year!"

All around them, people burst into applause and cheers as Jules lowered her lips to Sophie's, tasting whiskey on her lips as she rang in the new year with a kiss. She lifted her head, smiling into Sophie's dazed eyes.

"Happy New Year," she whispered.

"Happy New Year, Jules."

They tapped their glasses before polishing off what remained of their drinks, turning to face the room just in time to see a wide-eyed Micki watching them from the bar.

17

S ophie opened her eyes to find herself staring into the gauzy depths of the curtain that sheltered Jules's bed. She smiled as she registered the warm press of Jules's body against her back, remembering the party last night and the even more memorable celebration they'd shared here at Jules's apartment afterward.

Consequently, as she fumbled for her phone beside the bed, she saw that it was already almost noon. That was fine with her. It had been a late night, after all. Tomorrow, dress rehearsals started, so she hoped to spend today with Jules, soaking up this time with her before things got crazy.

Behind her, Jules stirred, sliding an arm around Sophie's waist. "Morning."

"Morning." Sophie rolled to face her, enamored by the naked and sleep-softened woman lying there.

"Love waking up beside you," Jules said, bringing their lips together for a gentle morning kiss.

"So do I."

"And other morning activities." Jules's hands slid over Sophie's equally naked body, and even though they'd already thoroughly had their way with each other last night, she felt a familiar fire awakening in her body beneath Jules's touch.

They moved together in the ruby-tinted oasis of Jules's bed, touching and kissing. Sophie melted into the sheets beneath Jules's talented fingers, coming in a hot rush of sensation. Rolling over, she returned the favor, carrying Jules swiftly over the edge.

Afterward, they showered and drank Cuban coffee together. Between the two of them, they even managed to make a batch of pancakes that tasted pretty damn good.

"This week will be busy," Jules said as she speared a bite of pancake with her fork, a wrinkle appearing between her brows. "And stressful."

"Yep to both," Sophie agreed. The days leading up to their first performance were always nerve-racking and exhausting. Sophie had the added stress of preparing for her two understudy roles on top of her position in the ensemble, and Jules had the added stress—and excitement—of her first leading role.

"I don't think it's fully sunk in yet," Jules said, but the twitch in her right eye suggested it might be starting to. On Friday, the show would open for previews. For three weeks, they would perform for audiences so that Kari could make changes and adjustments based on feedback from the crowd before the show officially opened.

In theory, previews were the time to work out all the kinks before critics saw and reviewed the show. In reality, reviews would likely trickle in from the beginning, so the pressure was on out of the gate.

"I have interviews this week," Jules said, a faraway look on her face. "Three of them."

"That's exciting," Sophie told her.

"I've never given an interview about myself before," she said, her voice seeming to shrink. "Not a drop quote about a show, but a whole interview about *me*."

"You'll do great."

"What if they ask about the kiss? What if they ask about my sexuality?"

Sophie watched the panic spread across Jules's face. "Well, first of all, no one should ask you that. It's rude and invasive, and you have every right to tell them it's none of their business. But you should also think about how you want to handle the question, because it might come up, at least in the context of how you feel about playing a queer character. You need to decide what you're comfortable with and how you want to respond."

Jules blew out a breath, nodding. "This week, I'm just going to play it coy and give them something about how I'm honored and glad for the chance to play this role, and let them wonder at my sexuality."

"I think that's perfect," Sophie told her. "Let them wonder. It'll be a good buzz for the show, and for you."

"Do you think Micki will make trouble for us at the theater?" Jules asked.

"She might try, but even if she went to Kari, I don't think anything would come of it."

Jules pushed her mostly uneaten pancake around her plate. "I just don't want any drama hanging over my head this week. I'm already pretty stressed out."

Sophie gave her a wry smile. "I hadn't noticed."

"We have to talk about your job offer too," Jules said hesitantly. "Whether you're leaving, and what that means for us."

"Yeah." Now it was Sophie's turn to fidget with her

pancakes. "There's another aspect to that I haven't told you about."

"Oh?" Jules gave her a questioning look.

"My roommates are moving when our lease is up at the end of February, so I'll have to find a new place to live. Either the universe is telling me to get out of town, or...I don't know. Maybe this is just another bump in my path."

"Damn." Jules took a bite of her pancake, frowning as she chewed.

"The opportunity in Syracuse is a good one," Sophie said. "Maybe I should listen to my parents for once and take it."

"But is it what *you* want?" Jules cocked an eyebrow at her.

"I'm not sure," she answered. "It's always been my dream to star on Broadway, to earn a living in the theater, doing what I love. Now I have to decide which part of that dream is most important to me. Because working at the Alton Theater would give me the second part. I'd have a reliable salary, a *good* salary, and I'd be managing the program that made me a performer. It's exciting, and I love that theater. I practically grew up there."

"But..." Jules pressed.

Sophie sighed. "But it means giving up my Broadway dream, giving up performing all together. Leaving the city. Leaving *you*."

"Those are big things." Jules said. "I haven't known you very long, but you're a performer, Soph. Would you really be happy directing kids?"

"I don't know," she admitted.

"I just don't want to see you give up on your dream too soon." Jules reached over and squeezed her knee beneath the table. "I keep thinking about the day I met you and how hungry you were for the role of Bianca. You come alive on stage. I know, because I'm the same way."

Sophie straightened in her seat. Everything Jules had said was true, but there was a flipside to the picture she'd painted, ugly cracks in the foundation of Sophie's dreams. There was the fear she wasn't good enough, that she'd never succeed on Broadway. How long should she stay and fight before she accepted that some things simply weren't meant to be?

"Just don't rush into anything, okay?" Jules said.

"Did we rush in?" Sophie couldn't help asking, because mixed in with everything else was the fear that Jules would leave her the way Brianna had.

"Maybe a little, but I don't have any regrets." She paused, glancing at Sophie. "Do you?"

"No," she said, but it didn't sound convincing, even to her own ears.

"I like you, Sophie," Jules said quietly. "I like you *so much*. And I'm going to do the work to make you a part of my life the way you deserve to be."

"I'm sorry," Sophie said, fighting a mounting sense of frustration with herself and everything about her current situation. "This is all so new for you, and I feel like I'm pressuring you with my baggage, but I can't help how I feel either."

"It's all going to work out," Jules said, eyes glossy. "I really think so, but we can slow things down if that's what you want."

"We're going to be so busy over the next few weeks anyway," Sophie told her, shaking her head as if it might help her to shake off her insecurities. "Let's just play it by ear, okay?"

Jules nodded. "Things are going to be crazy. Hopefully,

by the time we've found our footing with the show, you'll have decided whether you're moving, and I'll have had a chance to come out to my family. Then, if you're staying, we can take the next step."

"And what would that be?" Sophie asked.

"Anything. Everything. We could start with that double date with Josie and Eve."

JULES LEARNED another difference between dating a man and a woman that week, because as she woke on Thursday morning with nausea churning in her stomach, she didn't have to wonder if she was pregnant. Nope. This was just nerves. A lot of nerves. So many nerves she was beginning to wonder if she was cut out for a leading role after all.

Holding in a groan, she climbed out of bed. This was the final day of dress rehearsals. Her family was flying in this afternoon. Previews began tomorrow night. Shit was getting real. Her hands shook as she fixed herself a coffee. It burned all the way down, only worsening the ache in her stomach. She needed to eat something if she was going to make it through the day, no matter how unappealing food sounded. Remembering Sophie's on-the-go meal of choice, a protein bar, she decided to stop for one on the way to the theater.

She and Sophie hadn't seen each other outside of work since she left Jules's apartment on Sunday afternoon, and right now, Jules was missing her something fierce. She needed to hold her, to kiss her. She needed the peace she always seemed to find in Sophie's arms. With a sigh, she closed her eyes, remembering their New Year's kiss, that brief bubble of contentment they'd shared before the real world came crashing back in on them.

When she opened her eyes, Pippin was on the counter in front of her, amber eyes wide. He knew she wasn't herself this week. He just didn't know why. As they made eye contact, he leaned in, bumping his head against hers.

"Thanks, Pepito," she told him. "I'll be okay. I just need to get through tomorrow night." She gave him a quick rub before she bundled up and headed for the door. Downstairs, she pushed outside, only to be slapped in the face by Mother Nature. The air was heavy, the sky gray, and a frigid wind whipped down the street, tossing her hair in her eyes.

She tucked it under her hat, eyeing the sky with apprehension as she walked toward the market at the end of the block. Hopefully, it wasn't going to snow. She'd been so preoccupied with rehearsals, she hadn't checked the weather, but her mom hadn't mentioned anticipating bad weather for her flight. Jules didn't need anything extra to stress about today.

She entered the market and picked out a strawberry banana protein bar, not that the flavor mattered much. She was going to have to force it down regardless. After paying for it, she headed outside, walking quickly to keep warm as she took tiny bites of the protein bar, chewing until it was fruity mush in her mouth. Eventually, she managed to eat the whole thing, and by the time she arrived at the theater, she felt a little bit better.

Inside, she jogged down the stairs to her dressing room. She went in and closed the door behind her, needing a moment to prepare herself for the day ahead. The morning would be spent going over last-minute tweaks and hashing out all the details for their first performance.

After lunch, they would do one final run through in full costume and makeup. This was an invited dress rehearsal, and various friends and family of the cast and crew would be in the audience. If her mom made it here from the airport quickly enough, she'd be seeing Jules perform today. Regardless, she'd be giving her first performance as Bianca in front of an audience today. A few of her friends would be out there. Sophie's friends. There might even be a handful of industry people in attendance.

That protein bar was threatening to reappear. Jules pressed a hand against her stomach, steadying herself. Someone knocked on the door to her dressing room. Swallowing hard, she pulled it open to reveal Sophie standing there, a curious expression on her face. Everything inside Jules relaxed as she gestured Sophie inside, shutting the door behind her.

"You okay?" Sophie asked as Jules wrapped her arms around her, burying her face against Sophie's neck.

"No," she admitted. "I'm a nervous wreck."

"You're going to be great," Sophie told her, one hand rubbing up and down Jules's back. "I've been watching you all week, and you've got this, Jules. Your performance is flawless."

"Thank you," she whispered. "I wish I had your confidence in me."

"You will, after you've got a few performances under your belt."

She straightened, giving Sophie a shaky smile. "Thanks. Do you have anyone coming to watch this afternoon?"

Sophie nodded, excitement lighting in her eyes. "My roommates will be here. It's the only time they'll be able to come since they're both performing in the evenings right now too."

"I'm so glad they'll be here," Jules said. "Maybe you can introduce us."

"Definitely." Sophie leaned in for a quick kiss. "Ready?"

"Mm. Just one more of those..." She pulled her in for a deeper kiss, and the jittery feeling in her stomach magically disappeared. "If I could keep kissing you, I don't think I'd be nervous at all."

"Well, I'm available for discreet kissing whenever you need it," Sophie murmured against her lips.

"I may have to take you up on that." Reluctantly, she broke the kiss. After another hug, she opened the door, leading the way to the stairs.

"Did you hear about the snow?" Sophie asked.

Jules turned to her in alarm. "Snow? Really?"

"Tomorrow," Sophie said.

"Shit." Jules pressed a hand against her stomach. "A lot?"

"I don't think so. It shouldn't affect our first preview performance, but if a few people stay home, that might take a little of the pressure off, right?"

"True." Snow meant she could blame empty seats on the weather, not her performance. "I'm glad my family's flying in today, though."

"Mine are coming tomorrow. Hopefully, they don't run into any trouble," Sophie said with a frown.

"I hope so too."

They stepped onstage to find a circle of chairs set up the way they had been for their initial read through all those weeks ago. Kari waved them over, indicating for Jules to sit to her left. Sophie took a seat on the opposite side of the circle. For the next two hours, they ran through logistics, fine-tuning the afternoon's performance, while Jules tried not to be annoyed by how perky Micki was beside her.

Finally, they broke for lunch, and Jules retreated to her dressing room to force down another protein bar and some water. Her mom texted to say she'd just boarded her flight in Miami, and tears welled in Jules's eyes. She couldn't wait to see her mom and her brothers, although the thought of them watching her onstage in a few hours sent another spasm through her stomach.

Unfortunately, her mom texted again a half hour later to say they'd been delayed at the gate, which meant they'd probably miss tonight's dress rehearsal, but maybe that was for the best, as far as Jules's nerves went.

When the time came, she changed into her robe and went down the hall to have her wig put on. Wigs were fairly standard in this business, to save the performers' hair having to be processed and styled for eight shows a week. They also allowed for quicker hairstyle changes during the show, but she still wasn't overly fond of wearing them. She tended to find them itchy and hot, but she'd gotten used to them over the years.

The team pin curled her hair, covered it with a stocking cap, and then secured the wig. When they'd finished, she wore Bianca's shinier, more polished brown curls. She thanked the hair team and returned to her dressing room to do her makeup.

Thirty minutes later, she slipped into the red dress she would wear for the first segment of the show. Sarah, one of the theater's employees, helped her zip it before leading her up the stairs to take her mark. This was it.

The area beside the stage buzzed with actors and staff, all rushing about as they found their places and took care of last-minute details. From beyond the curtain, Jules heard the murmur of conversation. The audience wasn't empty tonight.

She gulped, swallowing her nerves.

"You're going to *slay*," Sophie whispered in her ear, and Jules jumped, turning toward her. Sophie wore her first costume of the night, a pink dress that showed off plenty of leg. "Also, you look really hot," she told Jules with a wink.

"So do you." She grinned, taking Sophie's hand as she waited for her cue.

Beyond the curtain, the lights dimmed, and the music began to play. Ready or not, here she went. As the curtain lifted, Jules stepped onstage.

18

Sophie sat on the couch in her apartment, script in hand, legs bouncing with nervous energy. It was just past lunchtime on Friday. At seven thirty, *It's in Her Kiss* would open for its first night of previews. She needed to be at the theater by five, but in the meantime, she found herself with a whole lot of empty time to fill, and no one to fill it with.

Nathan and Anthony were out, and although she usually cherished these moments when she had the whole apartment to herself, right now she could use their company. Nathan would be happy to take this script off her hands and run through it with her. Not that she didn't know her lines. She knew every line in the whole show, backward and forward, but she was trying to use this free time to rehearse as Bianca, and then as Melissa...just in case.

Outside her window, a heavy gray sky loomed over Manhattan. Fluffy snowflakes drifted past the window, coating the cars and street below. It was beautiful. Unfortunate timing, but beautiful. Her mom had called earlier to say their flight was delayed. Currently, Sophie had no idea if they'd make it in time for tonight's show, and it was okay if they didn't. She was only a member of the ensemble. She'd give this performance a hundred times over the coming months. If her parents didn't make it tonight, they'd see her perform tomorrow.

Jules's family had flown in yesterday. She'd rushed off after their dress rehearsal in a flurry of nervous excitement, and Sophie hadn't heard from her since. She wanted to call Jules. She wanted to *see* her. She missed her and was a little worried about how Jules was handling her nerves for tonight's performance. Surely her mom was helping to keep her calm, though.

A dull rumble echoed through the room, and Sophie looked up from her script in surprise. Was that...thunder? She pulled up the weather app on her phone, and sure enough, it showed thunderstorms in the area.

Thundersnow.

This felt like an omen, but did it foretell an amazing opening night...or a disastrous one? Sophie opened her messaging app and composed a quick text to Jules.

Thundersnow on opening night! I think Mother Nature is applauding you in advance.

Almost immediately, the little dots began to bounce, telling her that Jules was replying. *Or she's angry. I hope the weather calms down before showtime.*

I think it's supposed to, Sophie told her.

Good. Will your family be able to fly in?

Not sure. They're on hold at the airport in Syracuse right now.

Jules sent a frowning face. *Sorry. Crossing all fingers and toes that they make it!*

Thanks. If they get stuck today, they'll be here tomorrow.

True.

How are you holding up? Sophie asked.

Jules fired off a string of various agitated and emotional emojis.

Oh boy. *Try not to overthink it, because you're ready. You were amazing yesterday, and you will be again tonight. I can't wait to see you at the theater!*

Thanks xxxx

Sophie set down her phone and walked to the window, watching the snow fall. She wrapped her arms around herself, wishing she could speed up the afternoon, hurry the clock until it was time to leave. She was nervous too. No doubt, they all were.

Since she had no one to practice with, she read and sang aloud by herself. Once she'd fully run through both of her understudy roles, she gathered her things, bundled up, and headed to a late lunch with Gia before she went to the theater.

Outside, she tromped through about four inches of fresh snow. Mostly, it had already been trampled by other pedestrians, but she enjoyed finding the deeper spots to sink her boots into. As a child, she'd always loved to play in the snow. She and her brother had competed to see who could build the biggest snowman, make the most perfect snow angel, slide down the sledding hill the fastest.

If she moved back to Syracuse and took the job at the Alton, she could do that again. Not in the same way now that she and Tanner were adults, but it could still be fun to build a snowman, couldn't it? It would sure as hell be fun to have her own space, even if it meant having her own driveway to shovel.

It was hard to imagine that life, especially just hours before her first performance in *It's in Her Kiss*. This kind of excitement was in her blood. It was her lifeblood. But of course, if she worked at the Alton, it still would be. She wouldn't be the one taking the stage each night, but she'd be at the theater. That would still be exciting.

As exciting as this? She frowned, stomping through another untouched patch of snow. Nothing was as exciting as the thrill of taking the stage. It was the most exciting thing in the world.

She ducked into the deli, finding Gia already seated at a table in back. Sophie waved at her friend as she ordered a pastrami sandwich and a coffee, needing both sustenance and caffeine to fuel her through the evening ahead. She had dinner reservations with her parents after the show, but if they didn't make it... Well, maybe she could tag along with one of the other actors for a post-show celebration. Maybe she could tag along with Jules and her family, but that also had the potential to be super awkward.

Would Jules come out this weekend? How would she introduce Sophie?

She was going to do her best not to think about it. She had no control over it, and if she let herself get her hopes up, she would only end up disappointed later. Jules was a nervous wreck right now. Frankly, Sophie couldn't believe how frazzled she'd been yesterday. Coming out was probably the last thing on her mind.

"Oh my God, are you excited?" Gia asked as Sophie joined her at the table.

She felt her lips stretch into a smile. "So excited, you have no idea."

"I can see it on your face," Gia told her. "I'm so bummed I couldn't get tickets for tonight, but did I tell you that Kit's coming with me next week?"

"You did, and I can't wait," Sophie said. "Let's plan to grab drinks after the show."

"Definitely," Gia agreed.

An hour later, Sophie left the deli. She'd be early to the theater, but she didn't care. She was bubbling over with restless energy and counting on some of her castmates being early birds too. Maybe she could borrow a page from Jules's book and take some behind-the-scenes selfies for her Instagram as she got ready.

Actually...

She paused on the street as fresh snowflakes swirled around her. Lifting her phone, she stuck out her tongue as if she was catching a snowflake and snapped a selfie. Then she snapped several more until she got one that looked cute. She uploaded it with a caption about the afternoon's surprise thundersnow and tonight's performance.

She paused outside the theater's back door, stomping the excess snow from her boots and shaking it from her coat and hair before she went in. She headed straight downstairs, disappointed to see Jules's door still closed. Sophie's was open, though. Tabitha was inside, snapping a selfie in front of the mirror.

"Hey," she called as she caught sight of Sophie.

"I see I'm not the only one anxious to get moving today," Sophie told her as she dropped her bag on the couch.

"Nope. Plus, I was worried about how long it would take me to get here in the snow, so I left home super early." Tabitha lived in Queens, and it often took her an hour or more to get to the theater on a good day.

They chatted for a few minutes about travel woes delaying friends and family for the show tonight, and then Sophie's phone buzzed with an incoming text from Jules.

I'm here. Are you?

Yes. Be right over!

Sophie felt almost giddy in anticipation of seeing her.

"I'm going to run down and say hi to Jules before things get crazy. I'll be back in a few minutes."

"Mm-hmm. Better go now before you're wearing any lipstick to smudge," Tabitha said with a knowing smile.

Sophie raised her hands in defeat. She'd never confirmed their relationship to Tab, but she knew their secret was safe with her. Grinning, she jogged down the hall to Jules's dressing room, finding the door ajar. She rapped her knuckles against it as she pushed it open to find Jules pacing in front of the couch.

"Hey," Sophie said.

Jules turned toward her, a wild look in her eyes as she flung herself into Sophie's arms. "I don't know if I can do this."

"Of course you can," Sophie told her, holding her tight. "And you're going to be great."

"I'm a mess," Jules told her. "I've already thrown up twice today."

"Was your mom able to help at all?"

"Oh, she tried," Jules said, pulling back to sit on the couch. "She's been giving me Manzanilla tea and distracting me with endless updates about every member of our extended family."

"What's Manzanilla tea?" Sophie asked as she sat beside her.

"It's, um..." Jules gave her a blank look, and wow, she was really not herself right now. "Chamomile."

"Oh, okay. That's good."

"Mm." Jules glanced at a half-full mug on the table.

"Look at it this way," Sophie said. "You were really nervous last night until you got on stage, and then you were fine as soon as the curtain went up. There's no reason to think it will be different tonight."

"I wasn't this sick yesterday." Jules clutched her stomach, a peaked expression on her face. "I honestly don't know if I can go on. Are you—oh God—are you ready? Just in case?"

"I'm ready," Sophie told her. "But I'm not going on, Jules, *you* are. You've been ready for this for years."

Jules pressed a hand over her mouth, and all the color drained out of her face.

"Listen to me," Sophie said. "Just close your eyes and listen to me for a minute."

Jules obeyed, her body tense beneath Sophie's fingers.

"Slow, deep breaths," Sophie told her quietly. "You've been working toward this moment for what...sixteen years now? You're going to get up there tonight, and you're going to do what you've trained to do. Don't look at the crowd right away. You're going to look for Amir. He'll be there when you take the stage. Look for Amir, and by the end of the first scene, Tab and I will be there. Focus on us until your nerves have settled."

Jules nodded, eyes still closed.

"This isn't that different from the hundreds of other times you've taken the stage. You're just going to be onstage more than you have been in the past, but you've got this, Jules."

She nodded again.

"You need to get out of your head," Sophie told her. "Keep yourself busy until showtime. Once you step onstage, your instincts will take over."

"I hope so," Jules whispered. Her face was alarmingly pale, and a fine sheen of sweat glistened on her brow.

Sophie had never seen her like this, and she was starting to worry. "Are you sure it's just nerves?"

"What else would it be?" Jules asked, squinting at her with one hand resting over her stomach.

"I don't know. Is anyone you know sick?"

Jules's eyes widened. "Not that I know of."

"You could have eaten something bad."

Jules groaned.

"Have you ever gotten sick like this before a performance before?"

Jules looked down at her hands. "Not since high school."

Maybe it was nerves after all. "You'll be okay as soon as you go on stage. I really think so."

"What if I'm not?" Jules lurched from the couch and ran to the bathroom, slamming the door behind her. When she reappeared, she was shakier—and more pale—than ever. "I'm going to call my mom. Can you get Andrew for me... just in case?"

Sophie stood, indecision swirling inside her. Should she leave Jules or keep trying to calm her? Was she *really* ready to go on tonight if Jules couldn't?

"Please," Jules whispered, hunched over as if she might puke again at any moment.

With a nod, Sophie left her dressing room. She stood in the hallway for a moment with her back against the closed door. Beneath her concern for Jules, Sophie felt a sting of rejection that she'd essentially been kicked out so Jules could call her mom. Pushing it away, she hurried upstairs in search of their stage manager.

She found him in his office, talking to Kari. Fighting a sinking feeling about what she was about to set in motion, she rapped her knuckles against the doorframe to get their attention.

"Come in," Andrew said, waving her into his office.

Kari looked at her in surprise. "Sophie? Is everything okay?"

She pushed her hands into the pockets of her jeans to

keep from fidgeting with them. "It's Jules. She's sick...or it might just be nerves. She's afraid she won't be able to go on tonight."

Kari's brows climbed her forehead. "What?"

"Oh dear." Andrew frowned, lurching to his feet.

"I just came from her dressing room," Sophie said. "She asked me to get you."

"How sick is she?" Andrew asked, reaching for his tablet.

"She's throwing up. I think...I think it's nerves, but I can't be sure." Sophie chewed her lip.

Kari sighed. "I've seen her nerves a few times already, but I thought she had things under control. This won't go over well with our patrons if she doesn't go on tonight. I've got people coming specifically to see her."

Sophie flinched, not sure what to say.

"Are *you* ready if she doesn't go on?" Kari's dark eyes locked on Sophie's.

She nodded briskly. "I will be."

"I'll go smooth her out," Andrew said. "Not to worry. I've talked far bigger stars down from far bigger ledges." He hurried out of the room, headed for the stairs.

Sophie turned to leave his office, hating everything about this.

"Do you know why I chose her for Bianca instead of you?" Kari asked from behind her.

"No," Sophie said, not sure she wanted the answer.

"Your audition was extremely impressive," Kari said. "You've got the talent and the charisma to headline a show, but you were too bold for Bianca. She's vulnerable, filled with uncertainty and angst, and Jules captured that part of her perfectly. Maybe tonight, you'll get the chance to show me I was wrong."

"I won't let you down," Sophie murmured.

Kari waved a hand toward the door. "You'd better go start getting ready, then."

"Okay." Sophie nodded as she rushed out of Andrew's office.

A chill ran through her at the idea of headlining tonight's show. What should have been one of the most exciting moments of her life instead left her with a sickening sense of regret that Jules wouldn't get the chance, that she might disappoint Kari and the other industry professionals in attendance tonight. She might even damage her reputation if word got around that she had missed her first performance due to nerves. This wasn't something Broadway performers did, and Sophie could hardly believe it was happening to Jules.

She wished she could hit rewind and try harder to talk Jules through it before she'd gone to get Andrew. No matter how badly Sophie had wanted the chance to take the lead, this wasn't how she'd wanted it to happen. Covering for Jules for a night sometime later in their run was no big deal. It was almost expected. Stepping into her shoes on opening night was wrong. So wrong. And she hated it.

But there was no undoing it now. Sophie rushed to her dressing room, heart pounding in her chest. She stared blankly at Tabitha, who was already in her robe, ready to have her hair done.

"What were you two doing down there? I thought I was going to have to come break up the love fest." Tabitha rolled her eyes good-naturedly.

Sophie shook her head, swallowing over her painfully dry throat. "No...she's..." She gulped. "She's sick, Tab. She might not go on."

Tabitha gaped. "Holy shit. You're her understudy!"

"I know."

Tabitha leaped out of her chair. "Well, we have to get you ready. Oh my God, Soph, this might be your big break. The understudy going on the first night of previews? This is unheard of."

"I know." She grasped the chair in front of her, needing something to hold onto. "It's everything and nothing I wanted."

"Let's focus on the everything part right now," Tabitha said. "You should put on your robe so you're ready for hair and makeup, and then we need to start warming up."

"Okay." Sophie blew out a breath. This was really happening. *Oh, Jules...*

She grabbed her robe and ducked into the bathroom to change. It broke her heart that Jules might miss her big night, that Sophie couldn't be with her right now, helping her through it. But at least Jules was with her mom. Sophie blinked back tears as she knotted the sash of her robe.

She and Tabitha were deep in their scripts, reviewing Bianca's marks and cues, when Andrew poked his head through the door. "You're going on as Bianca tonight."

Sophie stared at him for a moment as a funny sensation rushed through her system, leaving her breathless and cold. She nodded.

He sat with her to run through the schedule for her wig and costume changes as a tech wheeled the rack with Bianca's costumes into her dressing room. "You can do this, Sophie. Let me know if you need anything," he told her before he left, closing the door behind him.

"Holy shit," Tabitha whispered, eyes wide.

Sophie sucked in several deep breaths. "Should I call Jules?"

Tab gave her a sympathetic look. "I think maybe you should just let her be. She's with her mom, right?"

Sophie nodded.

"So she's not alone. You need to focus on yourself right now. This is a big deal for you."

It *was* a big deal. Sophie was going to headline their first performance. Her phone started to ring, and she grabbed it from the counter to see her mom's name on the screen. "Hey. Did you guys make it out of Syracuse?"

"No," her mom said, disappointment heavy in her tone. "The airport has canceled the rest of the flights for today. It's really bad up here. And now it's too late for us to drive or get a train. I'm so sorry, Soph. We'll be there tomorrow night instead."

"That's totally okay," she said, ignoring the biting disappointment that her family would miss seeing her take the lead. Of course, as an understudy, it had always been likely that they would miss it when or if she got that chance, but it had come so close to happening tonight. "I'd rather you be safe in Syracuse than out traveling in this weather."

"I know, but I hate that we won't be there. Take a selfie before you go on and send it to me, okay?"

"Will do, Mom. I've got to run, but I'll text you in a bit, okay?"

"Okay. I love you, sweetie. Break a leg out there tonight."

"Thanks." Sophie ended the call with tears on her cheeks. It took a lot to make Sophie Rindell cry. This night was going to be her undoing.

The next hour was a flurry of activity as she was fitted with Bianca's wig and did her makeup. She couldn't stop thinking about Jules, worrying about her, wishing her star-ring role tonight hadn't come at Jules's expense. She kept trying to sneak away and see her, but there was always something going on, a visit from Kari, and then Micki, and then it was time for vocal warmups. Bianca's red dress hung on the rack in the corner.

This was Sophie's understudy costume, though, not the actual dress Jules would wear. Would have worn. *Oh, Jules...*

Sophie slipped into the red dress and stood in front of the mirror. She looked so different than Jules did wearing it. There were a lot of important people in the audience tonight, people expecting to see Jules make her debut. Would this be a turning point for Sophie? Would it be her big break?

Tabitha took several pictures with Sophie's phone for her to share on social media after the show, and she stared at them with shaking hands. *This is really happening.*

Sophie and Tabitha ran through their vocal warmups together as Sophie started fizzing from the inside out from the anticipation of taking the stage as Bianca. There was a knock at the door, and Tabitha answered it while Sophie looked over her cues one final time.

"Hey, ladies." It was Andrew.

Sophie gave him a steady smile. "I'm ready."

His smile, in return, was apologetic. "I can see that you are, and I have no doubt you would have been magnificent, but Jules is dressed and ready to go. Apparently, her mom worked some kind of last-minute magic with her."

"Oh." Sophie felt an odd sort of embarrassment to be standing here in Bianca's dress, wearing Bianca's hair, thoughts of grandeur in her head when this role had never been hers. And she was so glad that Jules would get her moment. She *really* was. There were those damn tears again. She blinked them back.

"So, we'll see you tonight in the ensemble," Andrew told her, resting a hand on her arm.

Sophie nodded. Then he was gone, and she was rushing

to change. There was no time to think, no time to process. She scrambled into her ensemble costume and held herself still while the hair stylist removed Bianca's wig and gave her the usual sleek ponytail.

Sophie rushed to the stage just in time to see the curtain rise. Jules stepped out wearing the red dress that looked so much better on her, looking every inch the star. She glanced over, and their gazes locked. Sophie blew her a kiss, wishing desperately that this entire day had gone differently. But it had ended the way it was supposed to, because tonight's spotlight had never truly belonged to Sophie.

19

J ules closed her eyes as her lips met Micki's, feeling the heat of the stage lights on her face. Their hands were clasped as they spun slowly toward the audience. Thank goodness her stomach had finally settled, because she'd never particularly enjoyed kissing Micki, and the last thing she needed right now was anything else making her nauseous.

As their kiss ended, the curtain dropped for intermission. Beyond it, Jules heard a respectable amount of applause. She sucked in several slow, deep breaths as she stepped out of Bianca and back into her own shoes, allowing herself to feel the way her muscles shook and the vague sense of dizziness that had plagued her throughout the first act, no doubt a result of the lack of food in her system combined with the adrenaline rush of the show.

Immediately, the stage filled with various staff and theater employees, rushing about to ready things for act two. Andrew stood in the middle of the stage, guiding the action.

"Okay?" Kari asked, materializing beside her, a discerning look on her face.

Jules nodded, well aware she had damaged her director's faith in her earlier that evening. "I'll be ready for act two, promise." And then she headed for her dressing room, doing her best to make it there without stopping for anyone else on the way. She needed a few minutes to collect herself before the curtain rose for act two, because now that intermission had begun, all kinds of emotions were surfacing that she'd held in check for the past hour.

"Great job, Jules!" someone called.

"Thank you." She kept walking.

Once she reached her dressing room, she went straight into the bathroom, although not to be sick this time. Her mom had filled her so full of Manzanilla tea that she desperately needed to pee. While she was in there, she took off the dress she'd finished act one in and slipped into the pantsuit she'd wear for the first half of the second act.

When she came out of the bathroom, Sophie stood in the doorway to her dressing room, also already dressed for act two in black pants and a purple top. "Hey," she said. "How are you holding up?"

Jules was mortified to feel tears brimming in her eyes. "I'm embarrassed mostly, I think. And just...out of sorts."

"It was just nerves, then?" Sophie stepped forward to wrap her arms around Jules.

She closed her eyes, breathing in Sophie's familiar, comforting scent, feeling something unclench deep inside her. "I guess. I mean, I still don't feel great, but that's probably just the aftereffects of being so stressed out, right?"

"Some stomach viruses are really quick too, so who knows?" Sophie held her tight, and Jules sighed in contentment.

"I think it was just nerves," she admitted quietly.

"Doesn't matter now," Sophie told her. "The important thing is that you made it out there and gave a kick-ass performance, and now you'll bring it home in the second act. Ready?"

She nodded, even as a tremor ran through her.

Sophie released her, giving her arms a quick squeeze as she stepped back. "I'll see you onstage, then."

"Yeah." Jules watched her turn to leave. "Hey, Sophie? Thanks."

Sophie glanced over her shoulder. "Any time."

And then she was gone.

Jules sat in the chair at her dressing table, trying to keep her feet from tapping nervously against the floor as she touched up her makeup and adjusted her wig. All the while, she was mentally kicking herself for how close she'd come to buckling under the pressure and the poor impression she'd made on the cast and crew of *It's in Her Kiss* tonight.

The important thing is that you made it out there, Sophie had said.

Jules repeated that to herself as the lights flashed, prompting her that only five minutes remained until curtains went up. She sipped from the—now cold—tea her mom had left for her, letting it soothe her throat and settle her stomach. She sucked in several cleansing breaths, and then she stood, smoothing her hands over the front of her pants.

Here goes nothing...

She headed for the stairs, focused on her breathing as she took her place side stage, waiting for her cue. In this first scene of act two, the ensemble took the stage first, performing a musical number that set the scene for Bianca to enter. There was Sophie at the center of the group, dancing and singing her heart out. She really was mesmerizing to watch. So much so that Jules almost missed her cue.

At the last moment, she snapped to her senses and strolled onto the stage, joining them as they danced their way toward a group of chairs that had been set up for a dinner scene where Bianca would wrestle with the decision to tell her friends about the kiss with Melissa.

Jules's gaze darted to the audience, finding her family in the fifth row, watching her with big smiles on their faces. She looked away before they could distract her, before she could be jarred out of character. Except, as she looked from her family to Bianca's, realization washed over her. There was a parallel here.

Jules's nerves hadn't been about opening night, or not entirely, anyway. She'd been afraid of her family's reaction to seeing her kiss a woman onstage, racked with guilt for the things she hadn't told them at Christmas. She was literally making herself sick the longer she kept lying to her mother about her role in this play and her relationship with Sophie.

And it had to end, as soon as possible.

SOPHIE STOOD in the wings as Jules took her seat at the piano for her big solo. Jules's fingers danced across the keys, and then she began to sing, her rich voice filling the theater. Despite her rocky start, she'd been magnificent tonight.

And even though Sophie had heard her sing this song hundreds of times by now, there was something new tonight, a kind of electricity in the air. Jules's blue dress sparkled beneath the stage lights as she sang. Sophie could feel the energy radiating off her. It rolled over Sophie, making goose bumps rise on her arms.

Presence. That was what they called it. Jules had the kind of stage presence that made it hard to look away from her. Tears stung Sophie's eyes. She was so proud of Jules and everything that had led her to this moment.

When the song ended, Sophie and the rest of the cast joined her on stage for the final group number, as Jules and Micki slow danced together, gazing lovingly into each other's eyes. Sophie didn't give them more than a passing glance, though. She was focused on her own performance. Her routine had been shaken earlier when she'd prepared to play Bianca. It had thrown her off-kilter, and now everything she did tonight seemed to require extra concentration to make sure she got it right.

She and Tabitha locked hands and twirled, grinning at each other as they danced through the final beats of the song. And then it was over. Sophie kept one hand in Tabitha's and took Elena's hand on the other side. Together, they formed a line as they walked downstage to take a bow. Jules stood at their center, flanked by Amir and Micki, with Sophie and the rest of the ensemble fanning out on either side.

The audience applauded generously as they bowed, and then the ensemble stepped back to let Jules, Amir, and Micki have their moment in the spotlight. Last—but definitely not least—Jules took a solo bow, receiving another solid round of applause and several loud whoops from the crowd, probably initiated by her family.

Sophie was so proud of her, she was bursting with it. So proud, her heart ached. As Jules turned to walk upstage and her eyes met Sophie's, she realized that ache in her heart was more than pride. It was love.

She gulped as everything around her seemed to go into slow motion, Tabitha pulling her in for a hug, the crowd clapping, stage lights in her eyes as Jules walked toward her, a triumphant smile illuminating her face. Then Jules's arms were around her, her lips on Sophie's cheek, her familiar scent filling Sophie's lungs.

"We did it," Jules whispered.

"You were fantastic," Sophie told her.

Tears glittered in Jules's eyes when she pulled back. "Thank you."

Arm in arm, they walked off stage. Sophie wanted to kiss her. She wanted to whisk Jules away and show her how much she loved her, how much she needed her. But of course, she couldn't. As soon as they stepped offstage, Jules was surrounded by cast and crew offering praise and congratulations, hugs and kisses from all the people who'd worked with her over the last two months.

Sophie was pushed farther and farther away, like a ripple in the water washing toward the shore while Jules remained at the center. Sophie turned to Tabitha and Elena, sharing more hugs as they celebrated a successful first performance.

The audience would be polled on their way out about what they had and hadn't liked, and various production staff had been in the house tonight, observing which lines got the appropriate laughs and reactions. Tomorrow, the cast would sit for a meeting before their matinee performance where they would implement various tweaks and changes, a process that would continue throughout previews as they perfected the show before opening night. It was exciting to watch the show evolve, and Sophie loved being a part of it.

Slowly, they made their way downstairs toward the dressing rooms as people chatted excitedly about their celebratory plans. Tabitha, Elena, and a few other ensemble members were going out for drinks and invited Sophie to join them.

"Sure," she agreed, knowing she'd back out in a heartbeat if the opportunity presented itself for her to see Jules later.

The crowd in the hallway thickened as friends and family of the actors spilled into the space, joining the celebration. Sophie backed against the wall, knowing no one was here to greet her and not upset about it. Her parents would be here tomorrow night. It was no one's fault that Mother Nature had delayed their arrival.

Since the hallway had become unbearably crowded, Sophie retreated to her dressing room. She ducked into the bathroom to freshen up and change into jeans and the long-sleeved black tee she'd worn here this morning. That felt like a lifetime ago.

Bianca's red dress hung on the rack in the corner, hastily discarded during her frantic costume change right before the curtain went up, a reminder of the night that had almost been. In the end, tonight had belonged to Jules, as it should have. Something heavy settled in Sophie's chest. Would her moment ever come? Or did her future lie behind the scenes?

She stepped out of the bathroom to find Tabitha sprawled across the couch, a celebratory beer already in hand. "God, I love the buzz of a good show."

"Same," Sophie said, dropping onto the couch beside her, but tonight it wasn't quite true. She felt unsettled. Adrift. And helplessly in love.

"Beer?" Tab asked, nudging the mini fridge with her foot.

"Sure."

Tabitha leaned over to grab a beer for Sophie. She popped the cap before handing it to her.

"Thanks." Sophie took a grateful gulp as Tabitha ducked into the bathroom to change.

Sophie stared into the amber depths of her beer. This wasn't like her, brooding after a performance. She set down the bottle and went into the hallway, looking for Jules. Maybe she'd feel better once she'd seen her and made sure she was okay.

She found her in the doorway to her dressing room, still in her floor-length blue dress. Jules was flanked by Kari, Andrew, and several people Sophie didn't recognize but were almost certainly Jules's family. Sophie faltered, unsure whether to interrupt, but Jules glanced over and saw her, breaking immediately into one of her irresistible smiles as she waved Sophie over.

Kari and Andrew excused themselves, congratulating Sophie on her performance as they headed for the stairs, and then Sophie stood facing Jules and her family.

"This is my friend, Sophie," Jules said, turning to fling an arm around Sophie's shoulders. "Soph, this is my mom, Paula." She gestured toward an attractive, petite woman in her fifties with dark hair and a friendly face. "And these are my brothers, Alex and Rob."

Sophie forced a smile, determined not to flinch at being introduced as Jules's friend. She'd been expecting it, but damn, it still hurt. "So nice to meet you." She stepped forward to shake Paula's hand, but Jules's mother pulled her in for a hug instead.

"It's wonderful to meet you, Sophie. I've heard so much about you."

"Have you?" Sophie asked, darting a glance at Jules, whose smile had turned fragile.

"Oh yes," Paula exclaimed, releasing Sophie so that Alex and Rob could each shake her hand. "She's been talking about you since rehearsals started. I'm so glad you two became friends."

"Me too," Sophie said, carefully avoiding Jules's apologetic gaze.

"Maybe you can tell me, Sophie," Paula said conspiratorially. "Who's got my little girl so distracted, making dreamy faces while she sends texts that she won't tell me about? I have my suspicions."

"Mami," Jules said in a pleading tone.

"What?" her mother said with a shrug. "I saw the way Amir looked at you on stage tonight."

Amir. Of course she would think that. Sophie wanted to sink through the floor and disappear.

"He was *acting*," Jules said. "I already told you there's nothing between me and Amir."

"I should go," Sophie said. "I just wanted to say congrats again, Jules. I'll see you tomorrow."

Jules grabbed her hand. "Please stay. Won't you come to dinner with us?"

"Yes," Paula agreed. "I insist. I'd love the chance to get to know you better."

"I wish I could," Sophie said, but as much as it hurt to walk away, she couldn't do this. Not tonight. "But I already made other plans."

Jules's face fell, her expression so wounded that Sophie almost took it back. But she couldn't go to dinner with Jules's family and let her mom grill her about what boy Jules liked. Sophie's emotions were too raw for that tonight. Her pride was dented.

"Please?" Jules asked, holding Sophie's gaze.

"Sorry," Sophie told her, taking a step back. "I'll see you in the morning."

"Okay," Jules whispered, a crease between her brows.

"It was great to meet you," Sophie told her family, and then she turned away, one hand pressed against her heart. As soon as she'd reached her dressing room, she grabbed her coat and bag, making a quick excuse to Tabitha for why she wouldn't be able to join her castmates for drinks after all.

Sophie rushed out of the theater and into the frosty night. Something dark and ugly swelled inside her, building with each step she took. Every fear, every insecurity, every disappointment she'd harbored over the last few years rose to the surface, twisting painfully in her heart.

What if her moment in the spotlight never came? What if she never recaptured the pure, unblemished joy she used to feel at the end of a performance, before she'd allowed this bitterness and resentment to creep in? What if she'd foolishly fallen in love with another woman who'd never be able to acknowledge their relationship publicly?

As she walked down that slushy Brooklyn street, headed for her pull-out couch in the apartment she was about to lose, Sophie feared she was setting herself up for heartbreak, both personally and professionally, and she only knew one way out.

Syracuse.

20

J ules couldn't stop replaying the look on Sophie's face when she'd introduced her as a friend. From there, everything had gone wrong, and Jules was furious with herself for it. In the whirlwind of the day, she hadn't had a chance to anticipate how she should handle the moment, but short of coming out to her family right here in this crowded hallway, she wasn't sure how she could have done it differently.

"I made us a reservation at Fin," her mom said. "I know it's one of your favorites."

Fin, the seafood restaurant where Jules and Sophie had shared their memorable—and memorably interrupted— first date. She forced a smile. "Sounds great."

"You okay, sweetie?" Her mom was nothing if not perceptive.

"Just tired," she said. "And still a little sick." She had hardly felt her stomach during the performance, but it twisted uncomfortably now, reminding her of its presence...and her guilt over the way she'd let Sophie walk away.

"Are you up for dinner?" Paula asked. "Maybe we should celebrate at home."

"Mami," Alex protested. "We're starving, and we promised the girls a fancy dinner if they sat through the show."

"We're going," Jules told him. "Just give me a minute to change." And maybe a quick cry in the bathroom, because she was ridiculously emotional right now. Tonight had been a dream come true, and yet...

"Jules!"

She turned to find Sarah, her assistant from the Sapphire, hurrying down the hall toward her. "Hey, Sarah."

"I just wanted to let you know there are people at the stage door waiting for you. Should I tell them you'll be out?"

Jules blinked. People at the stage door. Waiting for *her*. "Yeah...yes, I'll be right out."

Her mom squealed. "Oh my goodness. You're famous now."

Jules pressed a hand over her eyes, waiting for the room to stop spinning. She really needed to eat something. "There are people who collect signatures after every show they see. They don't know who I am, or they didn't before they walked into the theater tonight."

"Well, they know who you are now, *mija*, and they're waiting for you. Go on and get ready for your fans." Her mom shooed her into her dressing room.

Jules went inside and shut the door softly behind her. Quickly, she slipped out of her costume and into the black knit dress she'd brought to wear tonight. She pulled on her boots and went into the bathroom to freshen up. Then she stared at her phone for a moment, wanting to text Sophie but not quite sure what to say. With a sigh, she tucked her phone into her purse and wrapped up in her coat.

She was about to sign at the stage door. This would be another bucket list item on an already memorable day. The only thing that would make it more perfect would be having Sophie by her side. *Ugh.* She hated the way they'd left things. She stepped into the hallway to find her brothers gone. Only her mother waited for her.

"They've gone ahead to the restaurant," Paula explained. "The girls were getting restless."

"That's fine," Jules told her. "Just give me a minute to do stage door, and then we can walk over too."

"Oh, I'm coming out with you," her mom said, holding up her phone. "I've got to get pictures of my baby girl signing for her fans for the first time."

"Mami," she protested, but truly, she was glad someone would be there to share this moment with her, and if it couldn't be Sophie, her mom was the only other person she'd want to share it with. She led the way down the hall toward the back entrance, hurrying to keep herself from overthinking this. She couldn't handle any more nerves today.

She pushed through the door to find a handful of people standing outside. It had stopped snowing, although the ground was covered in several inches of wet slush. The cold air was a slap to the face, but it did help to clear her head. Someone squealed in excitement, and Jules thought she might be having an actual out-of-body experience, because who would be that excited to see her? But then she saw that it was Josie.

"Oh my God, you were so great!" Josie exclaimed, rushing forward to hug her. Eve stood behind her girlfriend, smiling quietly.

"Thank you," Jules told Josie.

Click. Click. Click.

Her mom, perhaps thinking Josie was a random fan who was super excited to meet her, was snapping away with her phone. Jules wasn't sorry to have the moment documented, though. Later, when she was calm and rested and didn't feel like she'd chugged battery acid all day instead of tea, she would be glad to remember her first stage door experience and the amazing friends who'd come out to support her.

"You really were great," Eve agreed, leaning in for a much more subdued hug after Josie had finally let go of her. "I was very impressed."

"Thanks, you guys. I really appreciate it." Jules swallowed over the lump in her throat. "I'm so glad you came. You totally didn't have to stand out here in the cold snow to wait for me, though."

"Oh yes, we did," Josie told her. "And we've been talking you up to your new fans too." She gestured to a handful of theatergoers Jules actually didn't know, holding *It's in Her Kiss* playbills and smiling politely.

Well, shit. She was really doing this.

"Hang on just a minute, ladies," Jules told Josie and Eve, and she approached the group.

"It was a great show," a woman said, holding her playbill toward Jules. "I really enjoyed it, and it was wonderful to see a lesbian relationship portrayed on stage like that."

"Thank you," Jules said, cheeks burning as she realized she should have brought a sharpie with her to sign with. What an amateur mistake. She felt a tap on her shoulder and turned to find her mom holding a marker toward her. God bless her. Jules honestly didn't know what she would do without her.

Jules signed the playbill, wishing she'd taken the time to practice her signature or think of something meaningful to write. Since she hadn't—and her brain was currently operating at about five percent—she scrawled her name and passed the pamphlet back.

The woman thanked her, and then Jules signed for a handful of other people before returning her attention to Eve and Josie, who were watching with delighted expressions on their faces.

"Someday, we'll get to say 'we knew you when,'" Josie told her, holding out her own playbill.

"Are these friends of yours?" Paula asked, coming to stand beside Jules.

She nodded as she signed. "Josie rescued Pippin and Phantom, and this is her girlfriend, Eve. Actually, Eve is the one who pulled them out of a trash can when they were tiny kittens. Ladies, this is my mom, Paula."

"It's so nice to meet you both," her mom said, smiling widely, although Jules hadn't missed the way she blinked in surprise when Jules introduced them as a couple. "I knew you looked familiar, Josie. I watched a few of your YouTube videos after Jules told me about you and the theater kittens."

"That's me," Josie said with a laugh. "It's so great to meet you, Paula."

"And Eve." Her mom's eyes widened, and she pointed a finger at Eve. "Wait a minute. Jules told me about you too. You're the host of that makeover show!"

Eve nodded, lips twitching, clearly amused that Josie had been recognized before she was, given that Eve was an actual television star. "That's right."

Paula glanced between them. "I didn't realize you two were..."

"We met when Eve found the kittens," Josie told her. If she'd noticed Paula's hesitance over their relationship, she didn't show it. "And then she saved my bar on *Do Over*."

"I think I saw that one, now that you mention it," Paula said. "What a story."

"It is." Josie glanced adoringly at her girlfriend before turning to Jules. "Hey, where's Sophie? We wanted to congratulate her too."

"I think she left already," Jules said, stomach clenching again in fear that Josie would accidentally out her to her mom.

"Oh, bummer." Josie's brows knitted slightly. No doubt, she noticed the incongruity of Jules not knowing where Sophie was, that they weren't spending this important evening together. "Sorry we missed her. Well, we won't keep you. I'm sure you've got important celebrating to do."

"Thanks for coming out tonight to support me," Jules told them. "I really appreciate it."

"We wouldn't have missed it," Eve said with a warm smile.

Jules might never get over how much quieter and more reserved she was in person than she appeared on her TV show. "Thank you."

"It was our absolute pleasure," Josie gushed, giving her another impromptu hug, as bubbly as Eve was reserved. "And you were so good, like *seriously* so good. I'm going to rave about *It's in Her Kiss* to everyone who comes in the bar. I'll send all the lesbians your way. We're all so excited to see good LGBT rep on stage."

Jules blushed. "I am too."

With a wave, Josie and Eve were on their way, and Jules was alone on the sidewalk with her mom. Dampness had started to seep through her boots from the slushy mess on the sidewalk. She looked at her mom, who was scrolling through the pictures she'd taken on her phone.

"Ready?" Jules asked.

"Sure am."

Together, they started walking toward the restaurant, and Jules wished she was in more of a mood to celebrate. Her feet were heavy, and not just from her soggy boots. She was exhausted. The combination of nerves, the performance, her upset stomach, and her worry over Sophie had left her completely drained.

"Josie and Eve seem nice," her mom commented.

"They're the best," Jules agreed.

Paula gave her a questioning look, and Jules sent up a silent prayer that she wouldn't ask, not tonight. Jules wanted desperately to tell her *everything*, and she would—very soon —but she didn't have the energy for it tonight.

"Sure you're up for dinner?" her mom asked instead.

"No," she answered with a small laugh. "But I'm going to come and have some soup and maybe a celebratory flute of champagne, and then I'm going to bed. Tomorrow, we have a production meeting at ten, and then performances at one and seven thirty."

"And I have tickets to both," Paula said, hooking her elbow through Jules's. "I can't wait to see you perform again. I don't even have words for how proud I am of you."

"Thanks, Mami." She leaned into her mom as they walked, taking comfort in her presence, the kind of comfort no one but her mom could ever provide. "I'm so glad you're here."

"Me too, sweetie. Me too."

And so Jules hauled her weary self into the restaurant and enjoyed a celebratory dinner with her family, all the while wishing her dad—and Sophie—could have been here with them, although for very different reasons. She enjoyed a few sips of champagne and a bowl of soup that didn't make her want to throw up, and then she hugged and thanked everyone for coming, and begged off early to sleep.

And boy, did she sleep. She crashed so hard that night, she felt hungover when she woke the next morning. Her eyes were puffy, her brain deliriously sluggish and sore. She stumbled out of bed and managed to fix herself some coffee, which helped to bring her back to her senses. Since her stomach was still off, she ate a banana for breakfast, deciding to ease herself slowly back onto solid food lest she get sick again on what was already going to be a busy and exhausting day.

She glanced at the clock. It was just past eight, and she had to be at the theater at ten. That didn't leave much time for anything else, but she was desperate to see Sophie and apologize for last night. She picked up her phone and dialed.

Sophie answered on the second ring. "Good morning."

"Morning." Jules felt a huge smile spread across her face at the sound of her voice.

"Feeling better today?"

"Definitely better," she said. "But still not a hundred percent."

"I'm sorry," Sophie said.

"It's okay. I'll survive, but...do you think you'd have time to stop by for a few minutes before we head to the Sapphire? I just really need to see you, and today's going to be crazy."

"Yeah, I can do that," Sophie said. "Around nine?"

"Perfect." Jules felt something loosen inside her at the knowledge that she would have at least a few minutes alone with Sophie today. She ended the call to hop in the shower, needing to be ready to go before Sophie arrived. The hot water felt so good, washing away yesterday's sweat and nerves, reviving her for the day ahead.

Afterward, she dried her hair, not bothering with makeup since she'd need to do her stage makeup in a few hours anyway. She'd just finished getting dressed when the buzzer rang, announcing Sophie's arrival. Jules rushed to the door, an entirely different sensation in her belly now, one that had nothing to do with nausea and everything to do with the woman she was about to see.

Sophie stepped through the door with a hesitant smile, holding out a large red cup. "I'm not sure exactly what it is, but the barista promised it would be good for your stomach."

"Thank you." Jules took the cup and pulled Sophie in for a leisurely kiss, the kind of kiss they hadn't shared in too many days. The kind of kiss that Jules had been craving so intensely, she almost cried with relief as her lips finally met Sophie's. "I'm so sorry," Jules told her between kisses. "Last night...everything..."

"It's okay," Sophie said, but it wasn't okay, and they both knew it.

"I missed you so much. I—" Jules pulled back, gasping for breath, reeling because she'd almost said, *I love you,* and before she could even wonder where those words had come from, she knew they were true. She'd never been in love before, not really. She'd never felt anything as intense as what she felt for Sophie, like everything was right when Jules was in her arms and wrong when she wasn't. "I'm going to tell my mom while she's here in town. I am."

"Jules, it's fine," Sophie said. "You've got a lot on your plate right now, and it's obviously stressing you out. It'll happen when the time is right."

She nodded as Sophie stepped out of her arms, leading the way to the couch. Jules lifted the cup Sophie had given her and took a sip. The concoction inside was thick, cold, and fruity, and actually, it was delicious. "This is perfect. Thank you."

"Welcome," Sophie answered. She looked over at Jules, something wistful in her expression.

Despite her earlier words, they weren't okay. Jules could feel it in her bones. "Tell me."

Sophie's eyes widened. "Tell you what?"

"Whatever has you looking at me like that, like something's happened that I don't know about. This probably isn't the best time to get into it, but I'll drive myself crazy wondering in the meantime, so just tell me."

Sophie nodded briskly. "I took the job."

"What?" Jules took another sip of the smoothie, her brain still a little slow on the uptake, and then she almost dropped the cup. "Oh."

"Yeah," Sophie said, looking down at her hands.

Shit. Jules blinked back tears. "Are you sure?" Syracuse was so far away, at least in the sense of maintaining a relationship. Between theater schedules and travel time, they'd be lucky to see each other once a month.

"I'm sure," Sophie said.

"How did you decide? I mean, why now?" They'd just had their first performance last night. How could Sophie have already decided to give that up?

"I've been thinking about it a lot," Sophie said, hands clenched in her lap. "And I think it's the right move for me. Not everyone is destined to play the lead, and maybe my future is behind the scenes. This opportunity is too good to pass up."

"It's a great opportunity," Jules agreed as her tears broke free. "But I'll miss you so much, Soph...I don't even know how...I'm sorry. I'm being selfish." She swiped at her cheeks, setting the cup on the table. Pippin hopped up to sniff at it.

"You're not," Sophie said. "I wish it didn't have to be this way."

"It's not because of me, is it?" she couldn't help asking. "Because I'm still in the closet?"

"No," Sophie said. "But I do feel like our relationship is putting pressure on you to come out before you're ready."

Jules stared at her helplessly. Maybe she was reading too much into this, but she couldn't help feeling like—on some level—Sophie was running away, from Jules, from her frustration with her Broadway career, from all of it. Or maybe she'd really, truly decided she wanted to shift gears and coach youth theater. Either way, Jules felt like her whole world had just tilted, and now she was spinning toward a reality she didn't want to face.

"It's for the best," Sophie said quietly.

Jules turned toward her. "What does this mean for us?"

Sophie's eyes fell. "I won't be leaving the city for a few months, after the show wraps, but...maybe we should just stop here, Jules. I don't think I can date you for a few more months and then let you go."

"Oh God." Jules leaned forward, pressing her face into Sophie's shoulder, tears soaking her shirt. "Dammit."

"I know." Sophie toyed with her hair, sending a shiver of pleasure through Jules that only made the tears come faster. "It's not what I want either."

"Sophie..." Her voice broke, and she just clung to her, at a loss for words.

"Stop it," Sophie whispered. "You're going to make me cry."

"I'm sorry."

"Don't be sorry," Sophie said. "None of this is your fault. It's not anyone's fault. It just...is."

"But we never..." There were so many *nevers* for her and

Sophie. They'd never had a real chance to be together, and the thought of letting her go now was almost more than Jules could bear.

"It's probably better that we never. In the long run, it'll be less painful this way."

21

S ophie fidgeted in her seat during their pre-show production meeting. Across from her, Jules rehearsed with Micki, tweaking dialogue with feedback from last night's performance. Jules's hair was pulled back in a ponytail, her face makeup-free, and it made her look younger than her thirty years, more innocent, impossibly beautiful. She was calm now, nodding in response to something Kari had said, but her tears were still fresh in Sophie's mind.

There had been so many tears. A heartbreaking flood of them. Jules had shed enough for them both, because that was how she lived...heart on her sleeve. Sophie couldn't make herself vulnerable that way. Nor could she keep lying to herself.

If she stayed, if she kept auditioning, coveting her moment in the spotlight, a moment that might never come, her bitterness would grow until it swallowed her whole. She'd seen it happen to other performers, and she refused to become that person. Worse, she feared that eventually, she might even become jealous of Jules, begrudging her success. She couldn't let that happen.

Sophie had an opportunity for a fresh start at the Alton Theater, and she was going to take it. This wasn't the direction she'd expected her life to take, but really, how often did life go according to plan?

Jules glanced in her direction, and their eyes locked for a sizzling moment, until Sophie forced herself to look away. The emotions were still too raw. Surely they'd find a new normal, a friendship that didn't extend beyond the parameters of their time at the Sapphire. But not today. Today, Sophie just wanted to curl up somewhere and lick her wounds.

In retrospect, she probably should have taken the opportunity to shed some tears this morning the way Jules had. Because right now, she felt like she was drowning internally, a heavy, watery feeling that made her afraid to blink lest she open the floodgates. She'd been so certain about her decision last night, so sure when she called Stuart first thing this morning to accept the job. But as she watched Jules rehearse, all she felt was sad. Overwhelmingly, heartbreakingly sad.

Finally, the meeting ended. Sophie had mostly sat and listened. There were only a few minor tweaks for the ensemble. The majority of the work rested on Jules, Micki, and Amir, so Sophie scooted out of her chair and retreated to her dressing room as soon as she could, not wanting to get in Jules's way or distract her from her work.

At least Jules seemed to have regained her footing onstage. When they went on for their one o'clock matinee, she was calm and confident, seamlessly integrating the changes Kari had introduced that morning.

Now it was Sophie's turn to falter, at least on the inside. She'd expected to feel free now that she'd made a decision, knowing she had a plan to move on with her life. Surely that feeling would come once she'd had a chance to grieve the things she was leaving behind. She danced her heart out at the back of the stage, a wide smile plastered on her face. And when she glanced at Jules, shining like a star front and center, Sophie swallowed her heartbreak, for both their sakes.

JULES WOKE on Monday morning feeling like a hollowed-out shell of herself. Four performances in three days with a broken heart and a nervous stomach had taken a toll. She'd shed a lot of tears, both happy and sad. She'd found her confidence as Bianca, had given what she thought to be some of the best performances of her career...and she was just getting started where Bianca was concerned.

But her bed was cold and lonely. She missed Sophie so much, it was a constant ache in her chest, which was ironic since she saw her every day. Every time she turned around at the theater, Sophie was there, and that made it even harder not to touch her, not to kiss her, not to tell her she loved her and beg her not to leave.

But that wasn't for Jules to say. Sophie had made her choice, and Jules had to respect it. She had to live with it. And eventually, it would get easier. Everything got easier in time, even the things that hurt the most. She'd learned to live without her dad, so she could certainly learn to live without Sophie, even if she had to see her every day.

With a sigh, she hauled herself out of bed and stepped into a hot shower. Mondays were her day off, and boy, did she need it. Alex and Rob had flown home already, but her mom was still here, and they were going to spend the day together, which was exactly what Jules needed.

She dressed and fixed two café Cubanos just before her mom rang the buzzer from downstairs. Jules let her in with a smile on her face.

"Morning," her mom said as she huffed up the stairs, a white paper bag containing their breakfast in hand.

"Morning," Jules said as she shut the door behind her. "I've got coffee ready."

"Perfect."

They brought their coffee and pastries to the kitchen table and sat together. Paula chatted as they ate, and Jules was happy just to listen. She was exhausted and emotionally overwrought, but she felt her mood rebounding with every moment she spent with her mom.

"You're quiet this morning," Paula commented.

"Sorry."

"Don't be sorry," her mom said with a laugh. "You've had an exhausting couple of days, and you were sick on top of it. I'd say you deserve to rest today."

Jules nodded, but her smile must have fallen flat, because her mom's eyes narrowed.

"What else aren't you telling me?" she asked, placing a hand on Jules's arm.

She blinked, and two fat tears rolled over her cheeks. She'd known, somewhere in the back of her mind, this was going to happen today. Maybe she'd been anticipating it. Keeping secrets from her mom was eating her alive, and she couldn't bear it another moment. "I have to tell you something, Mami."

Paula gulped, a kind of fear gleaming in her eyes that told Jules she had jumped to a much more serious conclusion than necessary. "Okay. Anything."

Jules laughed through her tears. "It's not anything bad. Well...my heart is a bit broken, but that's the second half of the story."

"Aw, sweetie, you've fallen in love and gotten your heart broken, and this is the first I'm hearing of it?" Paula pulled her in for a warm hug. "Tell me everything."

"I didn't tell you before because there's something else I need to tell you first."

"Okay." Paula pulled back to meet her eyes, her expression searching. "You know you can tell me anything."

Jules nodded. "It's something I've kind of known for a while, but I didn't really figure it out until recently."

Her mom stared at her in confusion, clearly having no idea where this conversation was going.

Jules blew out a breath, heat prickling on her skin. There was nothing else but to just say it. "I'm bisexual."

Paula's eyebrows rose comically. "Bisexual?"

"I'm attracted to both men and women. I always have been, but for a long time, it was just easier to date men and ignore the other side of myself." Jules exhaled, already feeling as if a huge weight had been removed from her chest. Her tears dried. Whatever happened now, Jules was free. No more hiding.

Her mom stared at her blankly for a moment as she processed this news that for her had probably come completely out of the blue. And then her arms were around Jules, holding her tight. "Oh, sweetie. Well, of course you know I love you no matter what." She pulled back to meet her gaze. "You do know that, right?"

Jules pressed a hand to her chest, breathing freely for the first time in weeks. "It's still nice to hear, just to be sure."

"I won't lie, this comes as a total shock to me," Paula said. "So I may need time to process all my thoughts and questions for you, because I want to know *everything*, but I just... wow. I'm so glad you told me."

"Me too," Jules said. "So glad."

Paula tapped a finger thoughtfully against her lips. "So, if you had to tell me this part before...*oh*. You fell in love with a woman."

"Yes." She nodded, and to her surprise, her eyes stayed dry. She was just so glad to have the truth out there, to be able to share her feelings with her mom and get her advice, the way she had always done.

Paula seemed lost in thought for a moment, and then she sat up straight. "Sophie."

Jules exhaled in relief. "You're good at this."

"Well, I like to think I know you pretty well, even if I didn't have a clue you were into women until about five minutes ago."

She gave her mom a grateful smile. "And you're taking it a lot better than I had feared, honestly."

"Oh honey, you didn't think I'd be judgmental, did you?"

Jules shrugged. "I mean...not really, but we're Catholic, you know? All I heard growing up was about marriage being between a man and a woman and all that. I didn't even know bisexuality existed until I was in my twenties and already feeling pretty confused about myself."

"I'm not sure I did either," her mom admitted. "I mean, obviously, I've heard the word, but I've never given it much thought. I definitely didn't think I knew anyone who was bisexual. You'll probably have to be patient with me as I figure it all out."

Jules nodded, leaning in to give her mom another hug.

"If you'd asked me how I felt about gay or bisexual people in an abstract sense yesterday, I probably would have told you that I try to let people live their own lives and keep my nose out of their business. But you're my daughter, Julia, and I love you unconditionally, no matter what. And I will support you in anything. Now tell me more about Sophie."

Jules blew out a breath, so relieved by her mother's words that her broken heart felt temporarily mended. "She's the first woman I've dated. She helped me sort a lot of things out, and it was...it was amazing. I've never felt anything like what I had with her with another person before."

"How do two women..." Her mom's brow furrowed, and she waved her hand in front of her face, cheeks blooming pink. "Never mind. I don't need to know the details."

"Mami!" Jules couldn't contain her laughter. "Use your imagination. It's mostly the same as with a man, except neither of us has a penis."

Paula threw her head back with a laugh. "That belongs on a greeting card. Okay, so what happened with Sophie? You broke up?"

"She's taken a new job working at a theater in Syracuse, so we decided it would be easier to end things now, before we got any more serious."

"A long-distance relationship wasn't a possibility?"

Jules lifted one shoulder half-heartedly. "Realistically, no. It's about a five-hour drive, and between her schedule and mine, when would we ever see each other? Theater schedules are demanding. We only get one night off a week, and I'm usually so exhausted—like today—I can't imagine trying to get to Syracuse and back before I go on stage tomorrow."

"That does seem hard," her mom agreed. "But I also know that I made it work with your father for five years while you were in school here in New York and he was back in Florida with your brothers."

"But you guys had been together almost twenty years

already when you did that. You were married with children, and you knew you'd be together again once I graduated from high school. Sophie and I only dated for a few weeks, and if both of our careers work out the way we want them to, I'll always be here in the city, and she'll always be in Syracuse."

"Okay." Her mom sighed in defeat. "That does sound pretty impossible."

"It is," Jules agreed glumly. "But I still can't be sad for the time we spent together or the way she helped me embrace my sexuality."

"That's my girl, always looking on the bright side," her mom said.

"How do you think Rob and Alex will react?" she asked, voicing the fear that had been rising inside her since she'd gotten over the initial euphoria of her mother's acceptance. "And Abuelita?"

"I think the boys will take it in stride, and if they don't, I'll make them wish they had," she said with the kind of look she'd used in their childhood right before doling out a particularly brutal punishment. "And your *abuelita* may surprise you. You know her friend Alfonso? The one everyone jokingly calls her *novio*?"

"Of course," Jules said. Her grandmother had been attending church and other functions with her "boyfriend" Alfonso for over a decade, since Jules's grandfather passed away. Everyone in the family had been waiting for them to make their relationship official, but they both always waved it off and said they were happy as they were.

"Do you know why they play coy about their relation-ship?" her mom asked.

"I'm guessing I don't," Jules said.

"He's gay," Paula said. "He's in love with a man, but I

guess these things are harder at his age, so he puts on a show with your *abuela*, and they let people think they're dating."

"Whoa," Jules said. "And she knows this?"

"Oh, yes," Paula confirmed. "She knows. She and Alfonso have been friends since they were kids, when they both came here from Cuba."

"I had no idea."

"We've both learned a lot this morning, haven't we?" Paula said.

"We sure have," Jules agreed. "Now can we talk about getting *you* on a date?"

"No. No way," her mom protested, but soon enough, they were swiping through profiles on her phone, giggling as they critiqued Paula's potential suitors.

Jules and her mom spent the rest of the morning in her apartment. It was something she had always treasured about their relationship, the way they could pass seemingly endless hours talking about anything and everything. Paula had so many questions about her sexuality, and Jules was relieved to be able to share it all with her.

They went out to lunch together and then to a movie, wanting to soak in all the mother-daughter time they had today, although Jules was too exhausted to do much more than that. She needed to conserve her energy for the week ahead. At least her stomach had finally recovered. Coming out to her mother had been an immediate cure, confirming her suspicion that it was her own conscience all along. Damn that Catholic guilt.

If only she'd been able to sort herself out in time to introduce Sophie to her mom the way she'd wanted to, as her girlfriend...

On Tuesday, she slept in again and had lunch with her

mom before she headed to the airport to fly home. She'd be back in a few weeks for their official opening night, and Jules already couldn't wait to see her again.

When she got to the theater that evening, she almost closed the door to her dressing room, feeling an uncharacteristic urge to be alone. Or maybe it was a desire to avoid Sophie, not that she didn't want to see her. On the contrary, she wanted her more than ever. But seeing her in passing, pretending she wasn't helplessly in love with her...it was torture.

Jules left her door open.

And when she looked up from her phone a few minutes later and saw Sophie standing in the doorway, she couldn't help the way her heart leaped, no matter how foolish it was.

22

"Hi," Sophie said, shoving her hands into her pockets to keep from reaching for Jules. This was torture. Avoiding her was torture. Talking to her was torture. When would it get easier?

"Hi," Jules said with an awkward smile that said she felt the same way. She looked good, though. The color was back in her cheeks, and there was a sparkle in her eyes that had been missing last week when she was sick. And then there was the way she was staring at Sophie, like she was some kind of forbidden treat, one Jules really wished she could indulge in.

Sophie cleared her throat. "You look like you're feeling better."

"I am," Jules said with a nod. "All better."

"I'm glad."

They stared at each other for a few seconds of uncomfortable silence. Sophie's feet seemed rooted to the floor, her tongue glued to the roof of her mouth. Was this what it would be like for them now? If so, she hated it. She hated it so much, but she was determined to do what she could to keep things friendly between them.

"How was your visit with your mom?" she asked.

Jules's expression softened. "It was great. Thanks for asking."

Another lengthy pause descended between them. They seemed to have lost their ability to engage in casual conversation, and maybe that was the saddest thing of all.

"Well, I'll see you on stage, then," Sophie said, backing out of her dressing room.

"See you." Jules crossed the room to sit at her makeup table.

Sophie walked down the hall feeling like she'd been punched in the gut. She wanted to ask Jules everything. She wanted to know how it felt to sing her solo up there in front of a sold-out crowd, what it was like to sign playbills at the stage door. Was it everything she'd dreamed of? Sophie wanted to catch up on everything she'd missed. She wanted to lose herself in the welcome warmth of Jules's body. Oh God, how she wanted...

"Earth to Sophie."

She looked up to see Tabitha standing in front of her. "Sorry."

"Daydreaming about your new job?" Tabitha asked. "Can't say I'm not jealous."

"More like...thinking about Jules." She closed the door to their dressing room behind her and dropped onto the couch with her face in her hands.

"Uh-oh." Tab sat on the couch beside her. "What happened?"

"We broke up, since I'm moving to Syracuse."

"Ah, shit. That sucks. I'm sorry."

"Now everything is awkward, and I hate it." Sophie made a face.

"That's the problem with dating someone you work with," Tabitha said sympathetically. "But it sounds like you did the right thing, breaking it off now rather than later."

"I hope so."

Tabitha gave her a quick hug. "Things will get easier."

But as the week progressed, that began to seem less likely. Sophie and Jules shared some of the most painfully polite yet unbearably awkward interactions she'd ever endured. They were both trying so damn hard to act like everything was fine, when it plainly wasn't.

At least things were going smoothly with the show. Jules delivered one flawless performance after another. If it was possible, she got more impressive every night. Sophie found her own rhythm in the ensemble. She had a great rapport with the other dancers, and they had a lot of fun, both backstage and in front of the audience. Every night, as she stepped off the stage, she wondered how she was going to give this up. As frustrated as she'd become with her journey, she was going to miss performing so much.

And she was going to miss Jules. Maybe even more than she would miss the stage.

The following Thursday, two weeks into previews, Sophie arrived at the theater before lunchtime. Thursdays and Saturdays were their two show days, with both an afternoon matinee and an evening performance. They were tiring, but Sophie liked the challenge of trying to top her afternoon performance for the evening crowd.

As she scrolled through the photo roll on her phone, looking for something to share on her social media, she stumbled across the photos of herself in Bianca's red dress from the first night of previews. She felt a funny twinge in her chest. What would it have been like to perform as Bianca? Hopefully, she'd never get the chance to find out, because it would mean Jules missing a performance. And even more than she'd wanted her own moment in the spotlight, she wanted Jules to succeed.

Tabitha arrived, and she and Sophie got ready for the show together. When they made it upstairs to the stage, Jules was already there, wearing the red dress. God, it looked good on her, perfectly hugging all her perfect curves. She looked at Sophie, and she felt it in the pit of her stomach, a zap of awareness and longing. Then Jules turned away, leaving Sophie to stare at her equally lovely ass and wishing like hell she could rewind the last few weeks to have even one more night with her.

The house lights dropped, and Jules took her place onstage, while Sophie stood with the other ensemble members. The music swelled. Jules stepped into the spotlight, soon followed by Sophie and the rest of the dancers. They gave their all at every performance, but the matinee seemed to draw extra energy from the cast, maybe because it was the middle of the afternoon.

After the show, Sophie and Tabitha went out for a late lunch, and then she spent the rest of the afternoon in her dressing room, looking at apartment listings in Syracuse. This had become her new favorite hobby and a good way to keep up her excitement about moving, because there were some really cute and affordable apartments out there. She could hardly wait to have her own space.

Soon, it was time to get ready for the evening performance, and she went through the routine of hair, makeup, and costume for the second time that day. Sometimes, it felt repetitive, but most days—including today—she wished they had two shows every day. Already, she was excited to get back on stage and perform again.

By the time the curtain dropped at the end of the evening performance, Sophie was ready for a beer. She walked offstage, wondering if she should text Gia and Kit to see if they wanted to go for a drink when she caught sight of Jules and Micki in a back corner.

They were leaned in close, and...Sophie's scalp felt like it had caught fire. She had the irrational urge to leap at them and start the kind of cat fight she might have engaged in back in high school. Instead, she forced herself to keep walking toward the stairs. It was none of her business if Jules wanted to kiss Micki. She was free to kiss anyone she wanted to. It wasn't the first time she'd noticed Micki's interest in Jules, but she'd never imagined Jules returned the feeling.

Sophie wanted to scream at the thought. But on second glance, she noticed the way Micki was gripping Jules's arm and heard the hiss of angry voices. What in the world? She paused, unsure whether she should intervene. Before she could decide, Jules yanked free from Micki's grasp.

"Stay the hell away from me," she spat as she stalked toward the stairs.

Whoa. Unable to help herself, Sophie hurried after her. "What was that about?"

Jules wheeled on her, cheeks pink, fists clenched. "Nothing." She strode toward the stairs, waving a hand over her shoulder as if she were too angry—or upset—to speak.

And maybe Sophie should take a hint and leave her alone, but something had her following Jules, hurrying down the stairs, half jogging to keep up with her. Jules ignored her, heels clicking against the tiles, moving as fast as she could within the confines of her blue dress, the one that had been driving Sophie crazy ever since the first time she'd seen her in it...during the photo shoot where she'd been kissing Micki.

"Jules..." she called.

"Leave me alone, Sophie," Jules warned as she stormed into her dressing room, attempting to close the door behind her.

Sophie wedged herself through it, wincing as it slammed shut behind her. "Are you okay?"

"No." Jules's eyes snapped with a fierceness Sophie had never seen from her. "I'm pissed, and I just..." She turned away, yanking off her wig. She tossed it on her makeup table and began tugging the pins out of her hair. "You should go."

Sophie hesitated, wishing she could help. What had Micki done to get Jules this worked up? But Jules had asked her to leave, so she stepped toward the door. At the same time, Jules moved to open it for her, and they collided, bodies bumping solidly into each other.

Before Sophie had even realized what was happening, they were kissing. Jules pressed her against the door, flattening her body against Sophie's as her tongue swept into Sophie's mouth. Sophie melted beneath the heat of her kiss, overwhelmed with the need to touch her, to tangle her hands in Jules's hair and pretend she still had a right to do so after she'd decided to chase her career in the opposite direction of their relationship.

Jules groaned as her hips rubbed against Sophie's, desperation evident in every frantic movement of her body. Her fingers slid beneath the waistband of Sophie's pants, fumbling with the clasp at the top of the zipper.

"Jules..." Sophie tried to find some sense in her brain, a reason why she shouldn't give in to the almost overwhelming need building inside her.

"Shut up," Jules panted, pulling her closer. "Just fuck me, Sophie. Please."

It was the plea that did it. Or maybe it was the word *fuck* on Jules's lips, because she so rarely used it. Maybe it was just that Sophie was starved for release, not having been touched since her last night with Jules weeks ago. But really, it came down to the simple fact that she needed Jules, needed her more than she could put into words, and so she reached for the zipper on the back of her dress, dragging it down her back with a hiss of metal that had them both gasping with anticipation.

She pushed the dress over Jules's shoulders, revealing the flesh-toned bra and seamless panties she wore beneath. With trembling fingers, she lay the dress over the back of Jules's chair, aware it was a costume despite the frantic need racing through her veins and sparking in the air between them.

Sophie stepped out of her costume, tossing her top and pants over Jules's dress. Jules reached behind her to flip the lock on the door, and then they were pushing at each other's underwear, stripping as fast as they could, the dressing room filled with the sounds of sex—Sophie's gasp and Jules's sharp inhale as Sophie's fingers slipped between her thighs.

They tumbled onto the couch, kissing desperately. Jules straddled Sophie's thigh, grinding against her as she stroked Sophie with her fingers. Tears streamed over Jules's cheeks as she whimpered with pleasure. Sophie was too in love with her to see straight, too aroused to do anything but attempt to keep herself quiet as a cry rose in her throat.

Her eyes met Jules's as she came, release rushing through her in a scorching wave. Jules stilled her hips with a frustrated sob, as if she was too upset to succumb to her own release, tension vibrating from every inch of her.

"Come for me," Sophie said, sliding a hand between them to touch Jules's swollen clit.

Jules whimpered. "I can't. I'm too—"

"No, you're not." Sophie flicked the hardened bud, swirling her fingers the way she knew Jules loved.

"Please," Jules gasped, moving against Sophie's hand.

She increased her rhythm, stroking harder and faster, and then Jules was coming, her pussy fluttering against Sophie's hand as she flung her head back in soundless pleasure. Sophie pulled her close, their bodies hot and damp with sweat, entwined in the most intimate way, and for a moment, Jules lay against her, clinging to Sophie just as tightly as Sophie clung to her.

Then Jules sat up. She wiped the tears from her cheeks and stood, wrapping herself in the black-and-white patterned robe that hung from a hook in the corner. She turned her back to Sophie.

"Are you going to tell me what happened with Micki?" Sophie asked quietly.

"She was threatening to make trouble with Kari about our relationship." Jules shook her head. "It doesn't matter. I told her we weren't together, and it was none of her damn business."

"I'm sorry," Sophie said, sitting up. "That was really shitty of her."

Jules huffed in anger. "I don't know why she even cares."

"I think she's probably jealous." Sophie wished she had something to wear other than her slightly rumpled stage costume, but since she didn't, she stood and started redressing.

"Jealous of what?" Jules asked, tugging the last pins from

her hair. It hung over her shoulders in unruly curls, and it was all Sophie could do not to touch them.

"Of us," she told Jules. "I've seen her looking at you."

Jules's eyes widened. "I...well, *shit*."

"Yeah, you might want to watch your back around her."

Jules finger-combed her hair, yanking angrily at an overlooked pin. "I will."

"Jules..."

"Look, I'm sorry about that." She gestured toward the couch where they'd just had sex. "But I can't do this with you. It's too painful."

Sophie tugged her top over her head, wishing for a shower in her dressing room like the one she'd seen in Jules's bathroom. "I'm sorry for a lot of things, but I'm not sorry for this." She drew her in for one last kiss. "I just wish it could have ended differently."

Jules turned away, but not before Sophie saw the tears swimming in her eyes. "It never would have worked for us anyway."

Sophie paused, one hand on the door. "What's that supposed to mean?"

"A lifetime of competing for the same roles, you getting jealous if I land a better part than you? It would have destroyed us." Jules didn't sound angry anymore, just tired, as if she'd fought a battle and lost, and somehow, that hurt even worse.

Sophie's skin burned with shame as Jules voiced her deepest, darkest fear. "I wouldn't..."

"I've been doing a lot of thinking these last few weeks," Jules said. "And I keep coming back to that first day of rehearsals, how bitter you were."

"I didn't know you then."

Jules's expression hardened. "And that made it okay?"

"No," Sophie admitted. "And for what it's worth, that's one of the things I'm most sorry for."

Jules just shook her head, opening the door to her dressing room.

And then, since there was nothing else for her to do—or say—Sophie left.

23

J ules was sure there would be no one left at the stage door by the time she made it out, dressed now in jeans and a sweater beneath her wool coat, all remnants of sex and tears scrubbed from her skin. But a pair of women stood waiting, playbills in hand, and honestly, how was this her life now?

"Hi," Jules said as she approached them.

"Hi," they echoed, holding out their playbills for her to sign.

"You were great," one of them said. "As a queer woman and a Latina, I can't tell you how much it meant to see myself represented on stage like that."

"I'm so glad," Jules told her as she took the playbill—thankful she'd been doing this long enough to remember to bring a marker outside with her—and signed her name with shaking fingers. She signed both playbills, thanked the women for their support, and started walking home. Except she wasn't quite ready to go home.

She had some emotional steam to burn before she could relax and sleep. Maybe she ought to stop by Dragonfly for a drink. Alcohol sounded like an excellent idea, a necessary one, even, but she wasn't in the mood to see Josie or anyone else she knew. Tonight, she wanted to be a nameless face in a crowded room.

So she stopped in a random bar she walked past. She sat at a small table by herself and ordered a burger and a beer, watching the other patrons as they laughed and conversed around her, blanketing her in the comforting buzz of conversation.

She was halfway through her second beer when the emotions that had been churning relentlessly inside her all evening finally began to sort themselves into her thoughts. Her life had been in limbo the last few weeks, ever since she broke up with Sophie. She'd been focused on the show, but maybe she'd also been using that as an excuse to avoid dealing with the fallout from their breakup.

And now, the time had come. She had to accept that her relationship with Sophie was over. No more pathetic attempts at friendship, and certainly no more angry sex in her dressing room. It was too painful to keep doing this to herself. She had to move on, for her own sake, and probably for Sophie's too.

She also had to finish what she'd started when she took the role in *It's in Her Kiss*. Her personal journey had come full circle, and it was time to call her agent and make it official. Pierce had been booking interviews for her as opening night approached, so the timing couldn't be more perfect.

She was ready to share the way playing Bianca had mirrored her personal experience. She'd met so many people at the stage door who'd told her how Bianca resonated with them, how much it meant to see themselves represented on stage, and Jules was ready to add herself to that conversation.

∾

SOPHIE BARELY SAW Jules after that night. Obviously, it wasn't an accident that Jules always managed to be somewhere else when they weren't onstage. It wasn't a coincidence that her dressing room door—which she had always kept open in the past—now remained closed. And if it was killing Sophie a little bit more each day, it was nothing less than she deserved. She'd brought this on herself, and now she had to deal with the consequences.

Night after night, they took the stage. They danced, sang, and acted their hearts out, and Sophie wished it could last forever. They'd ironed out all the kinks during previews, and now, their official opening night was almost upon them. *It's in Her Kiss* seemed poised for off-Broadway success. Early buzz had all been positive, largely due to Jules's performance as Bianca, but Micki and Amir had received positive reviews as well.

On the last Wednesday in January, Sophie woke as usual on her sofa bed. In just a few weeks, she'd be moving out of this apartment, but she'd coordinated with several of her friends to couch surf until the show had wrapped and she'd left the city.

She got up and folded her bed away the same as she did every morning, then stepped into a quick shower before her roommates were up. Oh, how she missed the luxury of sleeping in, but that wasn't an option when she slept in the living room. She packed a bag and headed to the coffee shop down the street.

The frigid morning air nipped at her exposed skin, and she tugged her scarf up to cover more of her face. At the coffee shop, she ordered her usual vanilla roast and a muffin, snagging an empty table to eat her breakfast. Then she walked home to relax until it was time to head to the theater that evening. She hoped to spend the majority of her day bingeing Netflix.

She'd just let herself into her apartment when her phone rang. Andrew's name showed on the screen, and *oh God*. She could only think of one reason her stage manager would be calling. She connected the call, trying to contain her racing thoughts, because no matter how comfortable she'd gotten with her role in the ensemble, it was never far from her mind that she was also an understudy. *Is Jules okay?* "Hello."

"Hi, Sophie, it's Andrew," he said. "You've probably guessed why I'm calling."

"Probably," Sophie echoed, her chest squeezing uncomfortably. She couldn't bear the thought of anything happening to Jules this close to opening night.

"Micki's had to go out of town for a family emergency, so you'll be going on as Melissa tonight, and for both of tomorrow's performances."

Micki.

Sophie exhaled. She'd spent so much time thinking about her almost-performance as Bianca on the first night of previews, she'd barely considered the possibility of taking the stage as Melissa. "Oh no. I hope everything's okay."

"Her grandmother broke her hip, so Micki's staying with her for her surgery."

"Oh damn," Sophie said.

"Yep," Andrew agreed. "At any rate, you've got the afternoon to prepare."

Sophie's brain was still catching up to speed. "These are the last two days of previews." Early reviewers would likely be in the audience, and the production team would be solid-

ifying any last-minute tweaks before opening night on
Friday.

"The timing is unfortunate," Andrew agreed. "But I'm
sure you'll do us proud. I'll see you at the theater in a few
hours."

"I'll be there," Sophie told him. She hung up the phone
as a funny tingle spread through her system. She would be
going on tonight as Melissa. Unlike what happened with
Jules, this was definitely happening.

Sophie dropped onto the couch, fingers tapping against
her thighs. She needed to practice, since she had this extra
time to make sure she knew Melissa's part backward and
forward. Oh, how she wanted to call Jules. The majority of
Melissa's lines were with Bianca, after all. A few weeks ago,
Jules would have come over to rehearse with her, but now...

Oh shit.

Sophie would kiss Jules onstage tonight. And twice
tomorrow. She pressed a hand to her lips. This was something she'd never really considered, or at least not since they
had broken up.

No doubt Andrew was calling Jules right now to let her
know about the change in tonight's lineup. Would she call
Sophie once she knew? But Sophie already knew she
wouldn't. They hadn't spoken since that night in her
dressing room, despite seeing each other every day. Tonight
would be awkward, but they were both professionals.
They'd get through it.

Sophie picked up her phone and dialed Tabitha.

"I just heard!" Tab said in lieu of hello. "Oh my God, are
you freaking out right now?"

"That was fast," Sophie said with a laugh. "And maybe a
little bit."

"Andrew texted to let us know," Tabitha explained. "I

heard that Micki was raised by her grandma, so it's not surprising she flew up to be with her."

"Oh wow. I didn't know that." Sophie didn't have much love for this particular costar, for any number of reasons, but she certainly wished her grandma a full and speedy recovery.

"Yep. So are you ready?"

"Actually, I was wondering, if you weren't busy this afternoon, if you wanted to come over and run lines with me? I could order lunch. Your choice."

"Make it subs from that amazing place down the street from you, and I'm in," Tabitha said.

"Sold," Sophie told her gratefully. "Come over anytime."

"Be there in an hour or so."

In the meantime, Sophie paced her apartment. This would be the biggest role she'd ever played, on or off Broadway, and she'd be performing as Melissa three times over the next two days. She stared at her phone, debating whether or not to text Jules. But what would she say? So in the end, she didn't say anything.

Tabitha arrived, and they spent the next few hours rehearsing together. Tab read for both Bianca and Trevor, allowing Sophie to run through the whole show as Melissa.

"You're ready," Tabitha told her as they stood across from each other after finishing the final song. "You've got this."

"Thanks." Objectively, Sophie knew she was right. She knew the lines and her cues. Even if she screwed up, most people wouldn't know the difference. She would be fine. But this was still a big deal—especially with these being the final preview performances—and she was practically vibrating with anticipation and nervous excitement.

"Have you talked to Jules?" Tabitha asked.

Sophie shook her head, bottom lip pinched between her teeth.

"I can't believe you guys aren't even speaking anymore." Tabitha swiped a chip from the bag on the table. "It's so sad."

"I know."

"Think it will be awkward tonight?"

"Probably," Sophie said with a resigned sigh.

When the time came, she and Tabitha packed up and walked to the theater together. It felt like a lifetime ago when Sophie had walked home every night with Jules, the evenings when they would stop by Dragonfly for a drink or head to Jules's apartment for a sizzling night in her bed.

Once they'd reached the Sapphire, she and Tabitha headed down to their dressing room. Jules's door was closed, and Sophie resisted the urge to knock. Instead, she entered her own dressing room to find that the rack in the corner already displayed Melissa's outfits. A thrill raced through her system. This was really happening.

Andrew popped his head in a few minutes later to run through last-minute details and make sure Sophie was ready to go. The next hour was a flurry of hair and makeup, punctuated by various castmates dropping by to wish Sophie well on her performance tonight. Without doing an official count, she was pretty sure everyone had popped in... except Jules.

Soon, Sophie was wearing Melissa's purple-and-black opening outfit, a swarm of butterflies in her stomach. She pressed a hand against it, remembering Jules's nerves before their first performance. She had a new appreciation now for what Jules had felt that day.

"Ready?" Tabitha said.

Sophie nodded. Together, they walked upstairs to the

stage. As Melissa, Sophie would enter from stage right, the opposite of Jules. Across the darkened stage, she caught a glimpse of red, and the butterflies in her stomach gave another nervous flutter.

The house lights dropped, and the curtain rose. Jules stepped on stage, talking into a cell phone as she walked toward Amir. Soon after, the ensemble joined her, running onto the stage for the first musical number. Sophie felt so out of place here on the other side of the stage, watching a swing performer take her place.

"I'm just not sure," Jules said, turning away from the other performers, and that was Sophie's cue.

She stepped out as a surge of adrenaline rushed through her system, making her whole body shake. "Anything I can do to persuade you?"

Jules spun to face her, brown eyes snapping. "And who are you?"

"Melissa Barrett." She extended her right hand.

Slowly, methodically, Jules stepped forward to take it. The moment was supposed to be loaded, as Bianca met the woman she would eventually fall in love with, but the electrical current that raced up Sophie's arm when Jules's fingers closed over hers had nothing to do with Melissa and Bianca and everything to do with Sophie and Jules.

Sophie's confidence grew with each line that she delivered, especially the lines that drew a response from the crowd. She hadn't dared look out there yet, not wanting to break character or distract herself. By the end of the first act, she was fully immersed in Melissa, as if she'd been performing this role for weeks, as if she'd never *not* been Melissa.

She and Jules sparred effortlessly as Melissa and Bianca fought their attraction, with Amir providing the chink in their wheel, the man Bianca was assumed to have feelings for. And then it was just the two of them at the center of the stage, hands clasped, staring into each other's eyes.

"It wasn't supposed to be you," Jules said, her voice projecting across the theater. "And yet, you're the only one I can think about."

"And for me, it's only ever been you," Sophie replied, her fingers squeezing Jules's.

Jules leaned in, and Sophie met her halfway, holding her gaze as their lips met. It was a closed-mouthed kiss, a stage kiss, and yet it consumed Sophie from head to toe, as if the spotlight illuminating them was shining out from inside her, burning her with its intensity.

Jules's lips trembled against hers, but her grip was steady, her eyes glittering with the reflection of the stage lights. They spun slowly—the way they'd done that time Jules had helped her with her understudy rehearsal—turning to face the crowd as their lips parted, hands still clasped between them. Jules smiled, chest heaving as she sucked in a deep breath.

The crowd burst into an enthusiastic round of applause as the curtain began to drop. Sophie darted a quick glance into the audience, taking in a brief impression of the rows of seats, filled with patrons all watching them with rapt attention. She returned her gaze to Jules, grinning at her until the curtain was down.

Sophie's head was spinning. The adrenaline rush of the crowd, that kiss, and her proximity to Jules had her half-drunk on its power. The stage lights dimmed, and Jules gave Sophie's hands a quick squeeze before releasing them.

"You did great," she whispered, and then she turned and walked off the stage without another word.

Sophie stood there for a long moment, one hand pressed

against her lips. Around her, the stage filled with various members of the crew, rushing about to prepare for the second act. On the other side of the curtain, a buzz of conversation grew as the audience rose to stretch their legs during the intermission. Sophie shook herself out of her trance and hurried off stage.

"Girl, you were amazing." Tabitha materialized at her side, hooking her arm through Sophie's as they walked to their dressing room.

"It felt amazing," Sophie admitted. Her whole body felt fuzzy and light, like she'd swallowed helium. All she could think about was getting back out there for the second act.

"And how was the kiss?" Tabitha asked once they'd closed the door behind them.

"More electric than it probably should have been, all things considered."

"You two *are* electric together. I think the whole crowd saw that tonight. I know I sure as hell did, and I'm pretty sure Kari did too."

Sophie rolled her eyes, trying to play it off. "So we still have chemistry."

"You're combustible."

"Good thing we can use it to our advantage." Sophie reached for her next costume. She freshened up, got changed, and then it was time to take the stage again.

The second act was a whirlwind, with both Sophie and Jules on stage the majority of the time. They shared a synchronized dance as they sang about their blossoming romance, and although they'd never practiced it together before—this number having been significantly reworked for Jules and Micki during previews—they were almost effortlessly in sync.

Before Sophie had realized it, Jules was taking her seat at

the piano for her big solo, and then they were dancing their way through the final number. As they approached the front of the stage during curtain call, Sophie stood next to Jules, hands clasped, remaining up front with Jules and Amir for a second bow.

This time, she let herself *really* look into the crowd, memorizing the sea of faces smiling back at her. Many of the audience members were on their feet. The cheers and applause were deafening. This happened at the end of every performance, but it felt louder tonight, standing beside Jules. The crowd didn't always give a standing ovation, especially not on a Wednesday. Some audiences were more enthusiastic than others.

When it was time for Jules to take her solo bow, she clung to Sophie's hand for an extra moment. Sophie turned to her in surprise, and Jules winked at her with a dazzling smile, the kind of smile that sent Sophie's pulse whirling and had heat spreading over her skin. She grinned back, even as she dropped Jules's hand and retreated, leaving her to take her solo bow.

As Sophie walked off stage, Kari caught up to her in the wings. "You were brilliant tonight, Sophie. Absolutely wonderful."

"Thank you." Her voice sounded breathless, her pulse still racing from that loaded moment with Jules.

"I don't really have any notes for you," Kari said. "Just do what you did tonight again tomorrow, and we'll be in great shape."

"Thanks," she whispered, one hand pressed against her heart. "I really appreciate that." She jogged down the stairs to her dressing room like she was floating, and then she stood there for a moment, eyes closed, wanting to remember this moment, wanting to seal the entire evening in a vault inside her brain and live there forever.

And the realization that had been rising steadily inside her over the last few weeks—ever since she'd decided to leave—finally broke through her consciousness.

I can't give this up.

She couldn't quit. She couldn't leave Broadway. Performing was in her blood. *Jules* was in her blood. She had to stay. She had to fight for her career, the only career she'd ever wanted. And she had to fight for the woman she loved.

24

J ules sat in the solitude of her dressing room. She'd never been a woman who enjoyed that sort of thing. Solitude was for others. Jules preferred to be surrounded by friends and family, laugher and hugs and conversation. Lately, though, she enjoyed taking time for herself, time she'd tried not to spend nursing her broken heart, but then again, wasn't that the whole point? Obviously, it was the reason she no longer felt like celebrating with her friends.

Performing with Sophie tonight had been...hard. Sophie had been amazing, just as Jules expected her to be, and the energy between them was electric. But now Jules was paying the emotional toll. All she wanted to do was sit here in her dressing room and indulge in a good long cry, but she didn't have time for that. Sarah had already been by to let her know people were waiting outside the stage door, not that she really needed to at this point. It had become a nightly event, a highlight of Jules's day.

So, she stood, wrapped up in her coat, and grabbed her bag. She picked up two markers from the pile on her dressing table and went down the hall to Sophie and Tabitha's dressing room, wishing like hell that her heart wasn't already trying to beat its way out of her chest at the thought of speaking to her.

Sophie was on the couch, deep in conversation with Tabitha, hands waving in the air as she spoke, and Jules saw the moment she spotted her, because she froze, mouth hanging open, eyes widening just slightly.

"Want to join me?" Jules asked, holding out a black sharpie.

Sophie's eyes got even bigger. "What?"

"Micki and Amir come out every night. This time, it's your turn."

"Oh shit," Sophie said, confirming Jules's suspicion that it wouldn't have occurred to her to sign at the stage door otherwise.

Tabitha squealed, giving her a playful shove off the couch. "Go, go! Sign for your fans."

"Come on," Jules said, glad for her coat and scarf to hide the pounding of her heart and the way she couldn't quite seem to catch her breath whenever she stood this close to Sophie. She'd hoped by now it would have gotten easier, but of course, it hadn't.

Sophie was oddly quiet as she stood and started putting on her coat. She picked up her bag and said good night to Tabitha before following Jules into the hall.

"Here." Jules handed her the sharpie, making sure their fingers didn't brush in the process. "You were really great tonight."

"Thanks," Sophie said. "Helps when I'm performing with the best."

They smiled at each other, and Jules felt something inside her loosen. Maybe it would be easier if they just acted normal with each other. Maybe she was making things more difficult by avoiding Sophie. Then she felt her gaze drawn to Sophie's pink lips, and just like that, her heart was racing all over again. She held in a sigh as she pushed through the door to reveal a handful of people standing outside in the cold, playbills in hand.

Amir was already out there, chatting with the theater-goers as he signed their playbills, and Jules and Sophie joined him. They weren't a talkative crowd tonight, thanking Amir, Jules, and Sophie politely for their time before they headed off into the night. With a wave, Amir headed toward the subway, leaving Jules and Sophie standing there alone with no choice but to walk home together the way they'd done before everything had fallen apart.

They were quiet as they started to walk, and Jules wished she could say it was a comfortable silence, but it wasn't. It was the kind of loaded silence shared by two people who no longer knew what to say to each other, heavy with unspoken words and hurt feelings. Several times, Sophie looked over at her like she had something to say, but she never spoke, and neither did Jules. They reached the corner where they would part ways without having said a word.

"Jules..." Sophie gave her a beseeching look.

"I know." She rubbed a hand over her face. "I'm sorry. I'm doing my best."

"If I stayed, would that change things?" Sophie asked hesitantly.

Jules felt her stomach plummet to her toes. "That is such an unfair thing to ask of me, Sophie. You made the decision to leave. You accepted the job in Syracuse. You ended our relationship. You don't get to just change your mind because you went on for Micki tonight."

Sophie bowed her head. "What if I made a mistake?"

"Sophie!" Her voice came out sharper than she'd intended. "I'm not a puppet. You can't yank me back and forth depending on whether you had a good night on stage or not."

Sophie flinched. "I'm sorry. That's the last thing I meant to do."

Jules tugged at her scarf, unsure what to say.

"Did you mean those things you said?" Sophie asked. "About how it never would have worked between us, always competing for roles?"

"I don't know." She looked at her hands as the icy night air stung the tears on her cheeks. "I want to say we're better than that. If the tables were turned, I would have been thrilled for you if you'd been cast as Bianca, but can you honestly say the same?"

Sophie's bottom lip trembled, her eyes glossy, and unlike Jules, Sophie was not a crier. "I know I was bitter at first, and I shouldn't have been. Honestly, that's part of the reason I decided to leave, because I don't want to be that person."

"And that's a problem I don't know how to fix," Jules said quietly.

"I..." Sophie faltered.

Jules sighed. "This was always about more than your job in Syracuse. I think you were running away. You got frustrated or scared or whatever, and you decided to run."

"I did," Sophie whispered. "I know I did."

"Then you need to sort yourself out, *really* sort yourself out, before you ask me the things you asked me tonight."

Sophie gulped, nodding. "Okay."

"Good night, Sophie." She turned to walk away, wishing her heart didn't feel like it was breaking all over again. It would have been so easy to fling herself into Sophie's arms tonight. She could have done it, could be there even now, but at what cost?

SOPHIE CLOSED her eyes as her lips met Jules's, absorbing the moment, soaking it in. But she wasn't herself, not right now. She was Melissa, and Melissa was kissing Bianca. She opened her eyes, centering herself in her character, in the scene, in the show, for the final moments until the intermission.

As soon as the curtain was down, Jules dropped her hands, although Sophie saw the apology in her eyes before she walked away. They'd gone back to ignoring each other after their confrontation on the street last night. That was going to change, though, at least on Sophie's part. She'd been up most of the night tossing and turning, racking her mind and her soul for the answers Jules had asked for last night.

And now she had them. She just had to tell her. But not during intermission.

She rushed to her dressing room to change into her costume for act two. Tabitha strolled in a minute later, giving her a funny look. "In a hurry?"

"Yes," she answered as she buttoned her pants.

"For what?"

"To finish the show."

"You realize intermission is the same length regardless of how quickly you get dressed?"

"I know." Sophie grabbed a bottle of water out of the fridge and began to pace with it.

"Big plans?" Tabitha asked with a raised eyebrow.

"No...I don't know...I hope so." She drank half the bottle.

Tabitha took her costume off the rack. "Does this have anything to do with Jules?"

"I have to talk to her, and I can't wait until tonight. We've got hours to kill between the matinee and the evening performance."

"Whoa." Tabitha raised her eyebrows at Sophie's rushed response. "And you think this will go well? Because if you piss her off, you could throw off tonight's performance."

Sophie paused, then shook her head. "I can't wait, Tab."

Tabitha threw her hands up. "Okay, then."

So Sophie paced through the rest of intermission, drank way too much water, and then had to make a last-minute trip to the bathroom before she went onstage so her bladder didn't burst before the end of the second act.

Jules was polite when they passed each other in the hall, but she kept walking without a single word. Sophie had a *lot* of words to say to her in a little while. The curtain rose, and they fell into character, portraying Bianca and Melissa's angst for another packed theater.

There was definitely an energy between them when they interacted on stage that she'd never sensed when Jules did these same scenes with Micki. It seemed to resonate with the crowd too, because they received another standing ovation during curtain call, and the Thursday matinee crowd almost never gave standing ovations.

Sophie watched with tears in her eyes as Jules took her final bow. God, she was beautiful. Talented. Wonderful. The total package. And Sophie loved her so much, her heart ached with it.

Jules turned to leave the stage, passing Sophie without a glance in her direction, striding toward the stairs at a speed that left Sophie scurrying frantically in her wake. She was breathless by the time she reached the doorway to Jules's dressing room, positioning herself in it before Jules could shut it in her face.

She stood there facing Sophie in that blue dress, eyes glinting, tension palpable, and it was so much like that other time Sophie had chased her to her dressing room, the night they'd had angry sex on her couch. Sophie's body tingled at the memory, and Jules sucked in a breath, following her gaze to the couch.

Yeah, so they were both thinking about that. Okay, maybe this could work to her advantage.

"I need to talk to you," Sophie said.

Jules shook her head. "Not now."

"Yes." Sophie clasped her hands in front of herself. "Please."

Jules exhaled, stepping back to let Sophie into her dressing room. She closed the door after her, and then she just stood there, watching Sophie, arms clasped over her chest. That dress...

Sophie longed to reach out and touch it, touch *her*. "You were right," she said. "About everything you said last night."

Jules gave her a loaded look—so much emotion there, frustration, sadness, affection.

"I was running away," Sophie said, needing to get it off her chest. "Because I felt myself getting bitter about my career, and also, I was afraid of where our relationship was going. You introduced me to your family as a friend, and I know why, I *do*, but I panicked."

"Sophie..."

She held a hand up. "No, just let me finish. I told you my last serious girlfriend was still in the closet, but maybe I didn't tell you she broke my heart. I was in love with her, and she broke up with me because she couldn't be truthful about herself. And I guess I still have some issues from it, because I felt myself falling in love with you, Jules, and I fucked it up because I was afraid."

Jules slapped a hand over her mouth, tears rising in her eyes. "What?"

"Yes. I fell in love with you. There, I said it." She laughed, but she was shaking now, talking over herself to get it all out. "The first night of previews was...well, it was a tough night for me...for both of us. You were sick, and I almost went on as Bianca, and it felt like you were pushing me away to be with your family, and I just...I acted like an idiot."

Tears rolled over Jules's cheeks, and she swiped at them, smudging her mascara, which was a shame since they had another performance in a few hours.

"That night, it felt like the universe was telling me to go to Syracuse, but almost as soon as I said yes to the job, it felt wrong. All I could think about was how much I would miss being a part of this world, being on stage, being with *you*. It's been absolute torture having to stay away from you, Jules. This is the world I'm meant for. I can't leave Broadway, and I need you, if you'll still have me."

"But what about what you said before, about feeling bitter?" Jules asked. "I can't help feeling like this surge of courage came because you got your chance to go on as Melissa."

"It definitely did," Sophie agreed. "When I took the stage as Melissa yesterday, it reminded me why I love this so much. I think it shook me out of my denial about what I was doing and why I was leaving."

"And you're not worried you'll be bitter about it all again tomorrow?" Jules asked, impossibly sensible despite the tears streaming over her cheeks.

"No," Sophie told her. "I know it doesn't make sense, but these last few weeks, when I was preparing to give it all up, it changed my view. It reminded me that I'm a performer at heart. This is what I do. It's what I love. After tonight, I'll go back to the ensemble, but I'm not upset about it. I'd rather dance in the ensemble than leave New York—or you—any damn day. And after *It's in Her Kiss* wraps, I'm ready to get back out there and audition again."

"I don't know what to say," Jules whispered.

"You don't have to say anything. I just needed to get this off my chest so you knew how I felt."

"Sophie..." Jules reached for her, pulling her into the warmth of her arms, and for a moment, they just clung to each other. "I have some things to tell you too, but my mom is going to be here any minute with my grandma. They flew in this afternoon."

"Oh," Sophie said. "Well, shit."

"Can we finish this conversation later?" Jules asked, her arms tightening around Sophie. "I wish I could say tonight, but I've promised my *abuelita* a night out in the city."

"Oh my God, that's like the sweetest thing I've ever heard." And then they were kissing, holding on to each other with a desperation born out of weeks of pent-up emotion and desire. Sophie gripped Jules's ass through that blue dress, hips pressed so tightly together, she could hardly breathe. "I wish I could lock that door and—"

There was a knock, and they froze. Jules's eyes crinkled in laughter as she pulled away, rubbing her hands over her dress. "Who is it?" she called.

"It's Kari."

"Oh shit," Sophie whispered.

"Just a second," Jules said, turning to face the mirror. She rubbed away her smudged mascara and straightened her wig while Sophie checked her own appearance, but there was no hiding the flush on either of their cheeks or the way Jules's nipples poked against the thin satin fabric of her dress. She tugged at it self-consciously, giving Sophie a helpless look as she opened the door.

Kari glanced between them and shook her head. "I'm not even going to ask. I was actually looking for you, Sophie. Tabitha told me I might find you here."

She felt like her cheeks might catch fire. "We were just—"

Kari held up a hand. "I don't need to know, but I do have some news for you. Actually, it affects you both."

"Okay," Jules said, brows knitted, concern evident in her tone.

"Micki's grandmother came through surgery well, but the rehab for her hip will take weeks, if not months, and Micki has decided to stay with her for that," Kari told them.

"Oh," Sophie said, but she could hardly hear her own voice.

"You've been phenomenal as Melissa, Sophie, and there's no denying your onstage chemistry with Jules. We've had more buzz off our last two performances than we had during the last three weeks combined." Kari raised her eyebrows for emphasis. "So, you're our new Melissa for the remainder of the run. Tabitha is going to step into your former role as understudy."

"Oh my God." Sophie slapped a hand over her mouth. She was going to be Melissa for the next three months. It was almost too good to be true.

Jules beamed at her. "Congratulations."

Kari pointed a finger in their direction. "Whatever is going on between you two, do *not* let it affect your performance. Are we clear?"

Jules's smile widened as she nodded. "Absolutely."

Sophie almost laughed at the vehemence in that one

word, but seriously, if they could get to this point while fighting pretty much since the first night of previews, nothing was going to stop them now. "You have my word," she told Kari.

Kari nodded, and then she left, heels clicking down the hallway as she headed for the stairs.

Jules and Sophie stared at each other for a few seconds in shocked silence. Sophie was at a loss for words, and before she'd found them, two women appeared in the doorway to Jules's dressing room. One of them, Sophie recognized as Jules's mom, Paula. The older woman was clearly her grandma, leaning heavily on a cane.

Jules let out a little squeal, flinging herself into her mother's arms before turning to her grandma and hugging her much more gently. "Abuelita," she whispered. "I'm so glad you're here."

Her grandmother muttered something in Spanish, and Jules half laughed, half cried as her arms tightened around her. She responded to her grandmother in rapid Spanish, and Sophie edged toward the door, feeling like an intruder on this family reunion.

"It's good to see you again, Sophie," Jules's mom said warmly.

"You too, Mrs. Vega," Sophie told her.

"Paula, please," she said with a laugh, looking on fondly as Jules and her grandma laughed and joked with each other, and Sophie wished desperately that she'd taken Spanish instead of French in high school.

Jules looked over and caught her eye. "Sophie, this is my grandma, Beatriz. Abuelita, this is Sophie."

Her grandmother extended a hand. "Pleasure to meet you, Sophie."

"Likewise," Sophie told her. "I hope to see you both again later." She edged toward the door.

"I hope we do too," Paula told her with a look that made Sophie think she knew a lot more than she had the last time they'd met.

Sophie darted a glance at Jules, who shrugged slightly, still smiling.

"I'll catch up with you later, Soph," she said.

"Yep." Sophie waved as she stepped into the hallway, feeling like her whole world had shifted in the last half hour. She'd said what she needed to say, but Jules hadn't gotten the chance to say any of it back. Sophie wouldn't be able to breathe easy until they'd finished that conversation, because even her new role as Melissa felt like a hollow victory without Jules by her side.

25

J ules glanced sideways at Sophie as she bowed. Before them, the audience cheered, rising to their feet. Opening night had gone almost impossibly well. A few early reviews had posted today, all of them positive. Last night, over a round of Broadway Bubbles at Dragonfly, Jules had come out to her grandmother, receiving the reaction her mom had predicted. Her family really was the best.

She hadn't been able to talk to Sophie alone since that frantic meeting in her dressing room yesterday afternoon, but the air between them felt more electric than ever. Jules had lain awake for hours last night, thinking about the things Sophie had told her, and now, she was ready to make their reunion official.

She walked to the front of the stage for her solo bow. Before her, row after row of people stood clapping. Happy tears welled in her eyes, blurring her vision, and before she knew it, they were spilling over her cheeks. She bent for one final bow, and as she straightened, her gaze found her mom and grandma in the fifth row, clapping enthusiastically.

Jules blew them a kiss before she turned to join the rest of the cast. Sophie stood a few feet away, and Jules couldn't help it. She gave Sophie a quick kiss before taking her hand as they walked off stage. The first of several interviews Jules had given, where she talked about how her role as Bianca helped her embrace her own sexuality, had posted that morning.

She was officially out, and it felt good. Freeing.

She and Sophie stepped offstage, grinning at each other.

"That was...something," Sophie said.

Jules nodded. "I have so many things to tell you later. Hopefully, we can steal away from the party." Because right now, they had to get changed and head to the *It's in Her Kiss* opening-night celebration.

"I bet we can." Sophie gave her hand a squeeze as they parted at Jules's dressing room.

Jules ducked inside. She took off her wig and tugged the pins out of her hair before changing into the dress she'd chosen for tonight. Then she styled her hair and touched up her lipstick before joining the crowd in the hallway. Everyone was hugging and celebrating as they prepared to head down the street to the restaurant they'd rented out for the night.

"Boo," Sophie whispered in her ear, and Jules turned with a smile.

"Ready for this?" she asked.

"So ready." Sophie wore red pants and a black sequined top, and it was all Jules could do to keep her hands to herself. Since she had no choice, she let herself and Sophie get caught up in the tide of people surging toward the back door. Her mom and grandma would be taking an Uber down the street since her grandma's ankle still wasn't one hundred percent.

She tightened her grip on Sophie's hand as they stepped outside into the frigid night. They walked quickly to the restaurant, eager to get out of the cold. She desperately wanted to whisk Sophie off to a dark corner somewhere, but almost as soon as she'd hung up her coat, Jules found herself surrounded by castmates, members of the production company, and the press. Everyone wanted to talk to her, and she lost sight of Sophie after they got their first round of drinks from a waiter passing by with a tray of champagne flutes.

Jules had polished off three flutes by the time she made it over to her mom and grandma, who were seated against the wall. She felt those bubbles in her stomach as she bent to hug them both. They made her feel light and airy, like she could take on the world. Maybe she already had.

"Where's Sophie?" her mom asked.

"I don't know, but I need to find her."

"*Por ahí*," her grandma said, nodding toward the far side of the room, where Sophie stood with an older couple who were almost certainly her parents.

"Ahh, thank you. I'll be right back, okay?"

"Take all the time you need," her mom told her.

Jules squeezed her hand before she made her way across the room. She stopped in front of Sophie, catching her eye with a smile.

Sophie beamed, moving to stand beside her as she turned to her parents. "Mom, Dad, this is Jules. Jules, these are my parents, Donna and Rick."

"Oh, it's so nice to finally meet you, Jules," Donna said warmly. "Sophie told us all about you at Christmas."

"Likewise," Rick said, extending a hand.

Jules took it and shook. "It's great to meet you both."

"Will you be able to join us for lunch tomorrow?" Donna

asked, darting a worried look at Sophie, as if she wasn't sure whether or not they were back together.

Jules was dying to answer that question, if only she could get Sophie alone for a few minutes. "I'd love to, but I've got my mom and grandma in town this weekend too," she told Sophie's mom apologetically.

"Oh, bring them," Rick said. "We can easily change the reservations, can't we, Donna?"

"Absolutely," Sophie's mom said, looking thrilled.

Sophie gave Jules a slightly panicked look before turning back to her parents. "Can you excuse us for a minute?"

"Of course," her mom said, waving them off as she turned toward a passing waiter.

"Thank you," Jules whispered to Sophie as she led the way out of the main dining room in search of somewhere more private. The restaurant was overflowing with partygoers, but she found an empty hallway near the kitchen that would have to do.

"Been waiting all day to do this," she said as she brushed her lips against Sophie's.

Sophie arched her back, pressing closer. "Been waiting all day for you too."

For a minute, they just kissed, and Jules could get lost here so easily, but she had things to say, so she forced herself to pull back, hands on Sophie's hips, heart jumping erratically in her chest. "I did some pretty big things during those weeks when we were apart."

"I saw," Sophie said breathlessly. "Tab showed me the article where you came out. I had no idea, and I'm so friggin' proud of you."

Jules nodded. "It was something I needed to do for myself, like you said, but I hope it also alleviates your fears that I'll treat you like your last girlfriend did."

Sophie shook her head, a brown curl falling across her eyes. "It was wrong of me to ever put that on you, Jules. That was definitely my issue, not yours."

"Well, regardless, you inspired me to embrace my sexuality, you and Josie and Eve and all the people I've met at the stage door. I had no idea when I auditioned for *It's in Her Kiss* what a personal journey it would become, but it's changed my whole life."

"That it has," Sophie agreed. "And mine too."

Jules closed her eyes, kissing Sophie deeply and thoroughly. "Want to say those three words again? The ones you said yesterday?"

"I love you," Sophie murmured against her lips, spreading warmth though Jules's body.

"I love you too," she said, tears spilling over her cheeks. "So much that my heart hurts when we're not together."

Sophie lifted a hand to brush away Jules's tears. "Then we'd better stay together, hadn't we?"

"Yes." Jules melted into her, forehead resting against Sophie's, bodies pressed together everywhere. God, she could hardly wait to get her alone later, but a waiter pushed past them, giving them an annoyed look and reminding her of her surroundings. "Ready for me to reintroduce you to my mom and grandma? Because they're dying to welcome you to the family."

"Oh God," Sophie said, grinning. "Yes, I'm ready."

"And then we'd better introduce them to your parents, so we can officially agree to that family lunch tomorrow."

Sophie nodded. "Yes."

Jules brought her lips to Sophie's, capturing her mouth for another searing kiss. "I'm going to show you just how much I love you later tonight."

Sophie gasped. "Counting on it."

Before they could get carried away—because they were standing in a cramped hallway outside the kitchen, after all —Jules pulled back, threading her fingers through Sophie's as she led her into the dining room packed with cast, crew, and family members. Her mom and grandma rose from their chairs as they approached.

"Mami," Jules said. "Abuelita, you've already met Sophie, but I haven't been able to introduce you properly, because I really want you to meet the woman I love."

As her mom and grandma threw their arms around Sophie, Jules saw her past collide with her future. She joined them for a group hug, her whole life wrapped up in that embrace, with Sophie's warm eyes and soft lips at the center.

"I love you," she murmured. "I love all of you so much."

EPILOGUE

S ophie woke in the red-tinted refuge of Jules's bed —*their* bed. And then she snuggled against the woman behind her, because it was Monday, which meant it was their day off. No show tonight. There was a warm, furry presence against her stomach, and she knew before she opened her eyes that it would be Pippin. He'd cuddled with her almost every night since she moved in with Jules a few months ago.

Smiling, she pushed back the curtain to peek outside. The April morning shone through the window, spilling warm sunshine across her pillow.

"Bright," Jules mumbled as her arm came around Sophie's waist, drawing her close.

"Do we really have to go to that party tonight, or can we just stay in bed all day?" Sophie asked, rolling to face her.

"Both," Jules said, one hand toying with the hem of Sophie's sleep shirt, grazing the skin beneath. "The party doesn't start until seven. That leaves us hours and hours to stay in bed. A whole day's worth, really."

"Mm, I like the way you think." She liked it even more

when Jules's nimble fingers slipped between her thighs, lighting her up as brightly as the sun outside the window. Sophie rolled to her back so Jules could ride her thigh, a position that had always been her favorite.

"Together," Jules had said that first time, and it was a concept they'd embraced in every aspect of their relationship since their reunion on opening night. She rolled her hips against Sophie, a soft whimper of pleasure escaping her throat as her fingers brought Sophie ever closer to her own release.

They lived together now, sharing what had been Jules's studio apartment. They performed together every night at the Sapphire Theater, portraying Bianca and Melissa's love story for one sold-out audience after another. And right here, in their red-curtained bed, they came together, hands clutching at each other as they rode out their release.

"I want to do that a few more times before we get out of bed," Jules said, her voice soft and breathless.

"I like the way you think." Sophie tugged at a caramel-brown strand of Jules's hair.

One thing would be changing soon, though. While *It's in Her Kiss*'s initial run had been extended and Jules had recently signed a new contract as Bianca, Sophie had begun auditioning again. She was ready to spread her wings, eager to see what else Broadway held in store for her. With the role of Melissa under her belt, a door seemed to have opened, and she'd already auditioned for several parts she would be absolutely thrilled for the opportunity to play.

Despite their plans to spend the day in bed, eventually their empty stomachs—and an equally empty pantry—drove them outside. They got breakfast at a place down the street and wandered through Prospect Park together, enjoying the sunshine. Jules was texting with her grandma, which Sophie found endlessly adorable, and when she sent her a selfie of the two of them, Sophie decided to send one to her parents too. They were happy, and she wanted to share it with the world.

Before she got the chance to hit Send, her phone rang with a call from Estelle. A thrill raced down Sophie's spine as she pointed to her agent's name, catching Jules's attention before she connected the call. Jules beamed at her, holding up two fingers crossed for good luck.

"Hi, Estelle," Sophie said.

"Hello, my dear," her agent said in her scratchy voice. "I'm calling with some good news."

"Oh yeah?" Sophie tried to keep her voice level, tried not to bounce on the balls of her feet like an excited child.

"I've just gotten off the phone with Phil Martinez."

Sophie's excitement further soared. Phil Martinez was going to be directing an exciting, modern new production of *Chicago* that was already generating a lot of buzz.

"And he's cast you as Roxie Hart," Estelle finished.

Roxie Hart. The lead. Her first starring role.

Sophie's feet left the ground.

JULES DIDN'T THINK the day could get any better, but as she pushed through Dragonfly's heavy wooden door, she had a feeling it might. The bar was usually closed on Mondays, which—since *It's in Her Kiss* was also dark on Mondays—had allowed Jules, Sophie, Josie, and Eve to finally have that double date they'd been talking about...several of them, in fact.

But tonight Josie was opening her doors to friends and family for a special party to celebrate...well, Jules wasn't quite sure what they were celebrating, but as she took in the fairy lights twinkling overhead, she knew it was going to be a good night.

Eve stood near the bar, talking on her cell phone. She wore a knee-length white sheath dress with silver strands woven into the fabric that winked in the light, her dark hair swept back from her face, looking every bit the glamorous television star.

"Jules! Sophie!"

They turned to see Josie hurrying toward them, a wide smile on her face. She'd dyed her hair lavender, and it hung in loose waves around her face.

"I'm so glad you guys could make it."

"We wouldn't miss a party at our favorite bar, with some of our favorite people," Jules told her as Josie pulled her in for a quick hug.

"Aw, you're sweet," Josie said. "Want a drink? Midnight in Manhattans are on the house tonight."

"We can't say no to that," Sophie said, and they followed Josie to the bar, where a bartender Jules didn't recognize was mixing drinks.

Josie's friends Adam and Kaia sat on bar stools nearby, drinks in hand, and about a dozen other people in cocktail attire milled around, filling the room with a pleasant hum of conversation. The bartender handed matching glasses to Jules and Sophie, and they tapped them together before they drank.

"To the new Roxie Hart," Jules said.

Sophie beamed. "And your next season as Bianca."

"It's going to be a good year," Jules said.

"The best."

They sipped their drinks before leaning in for a kiss.

"It's in her kiss," Sophie whispered. "Or maybe it's in the

drink. Remember the rumor about this one?" She lifted her Midnight in Manhattan.

Jules grinned. "I had forgotten about that. Drink one at midnight, and you'll fall in love, right?"

"That's right," Sophie confirmed.

"I never drank one at midnight," Jules protested.

"Must have been close enough," Sophie said with a shrug. "Right?"

"It might have been the drink," Jules said, remembering that afternoon in her dressing room, the "practice kiss" that had been so much more. "But I think it was the kiss."

"Between the two, we never stood a chance."

"Nope." Jules leaned in for another kiss. They'd come to this bar together the day they met. It was almost as much a part of their journey as the show, so it seemed only fitting that they'd celebrate Sophie's new role here tonight.

"Hey, Jules," Sophie said, eyes widening. "Do you see what I see?"

Jules followed her gaze to the bar, where Josie was putting on a white blazer over her lavender blouse. Now she was wearing a white suit, standing next to Eve...in her white dress.

"Oh my God," Jules whispered. "Are they...?"

"I think they are," Sophie said, her voice slipping up a notch in excitement.

As they watched, Josie clapped her hands together, drawing the attention of everyone in the room. "Thank you all so much for coming tonight," she said. "I know you're probably wondering why you're here, and I hope you're not upset when you find out, but we didn't want to make a fuss, so...Eve, you tell them."

Eve gazed lovingly at Josie before turning to face their guests. "We're getting married tonight."

A ripple of surprise spread around the room, gasps and squeals followed by cheers and applause. Sophie brought her fingers to her lips and whistled while Jules clapped and whooped her excitement. Oh, this was definitely going to be an unforgettable night.

"So, if you'll just follow us..." Josie led the way toward the back hall and into the stairwell.

"This is so exciting," Sophie whispered, giving Jules's hand a squeeze.

They came out on the rooftop, which had been strung with yet more fairy lights and set with white chairs facing a flower-laden arbor against the railing, with Manhattan twinkling as a backdrop.

"Wow," Jules gasped, pressing a hand over her mouth.

"Wedding goals," Sophie agreed. "These ladies have really outdone themselves tonight."

They found seats next to a couple Jules didn't know but had seen in the bar before. Josie and Eve lingered in the doorway, watching as their guests all took their seats. An older woman walked out and stood beneath the arbor, note-book in hand, presumably there to officiate the ceremony.

An instrumental song began to play over the sound system. It wasn't "Here Comes the Bride," and Jules didn't know its name, but it was a familiar tune that invoked wedding scenes in her head. Josie and Eve linked elbows, gazing adoringly at each other before they began to walk down the aisle.

"Oh," Jules whispered, swiping at the tears on her cheeks.

"I knew you were the type to cry at weddings," Sophie teased, but her eyes were glossy too.

Josie and Eve took their places in front of the arbor as sunset streaked the sky behind them, spreading pink and purple hues over the Manhattan skyline. It was a breath-taking moment, and Jules heard the clicking of a camera somewhere behind her as their wedding photographer documented the moment.

"Good evening, friends," the officiant spoke. "We're gathered here today to join Eve and Josie in marriage."

Josie grinned, tears glistening on her cheeks, and Eve swallowed hard, her chin quivering as she fought her own tears. Jules pressed a hand to her chest, the other clasped tightly between Sophie's. She knew Eve was a widow, that it had been a struggle for her to open her heart again to Josie, and somehow, it made this moment even more beautiful.

Josie and Eve exchanged heartfelt vows, their eyes never leaving each other as they said their "I do's."

"By the power vested in me by the great State of New York, it's my absolute pleasure to pronounce you married," the officiant announced. "Eve and Josie, you may now kiss your bride."

A lone tear rolled over Eve's cheek as she leaned forward, pressing her lips against Josie's. The rooftop erupted in applause, friends and family rising to their feet to celebrate the new couple as they made their way back down the aisle, hand in hand, beaming with joy.

"Come on downstairs," Josie called over her shoulder as she and Eve entered the stairwell. "There's food...and cake!"

Jules turned to look at Sophie. *Someday, that will be us.* She saw the same sentiment reflected back at her in the chocolate depths of Sophie's eyes. They leaned in, sealing the moment with a kiss.

ACKNOWLEDGMENTS

I hope you enjoyed *It's in Her Kiss*! This is the second book in my Midnight in Manhattan series. The first book, *Don't Cry for Me*, came out in April. It's where we first met Josie and Eve and the theater kittens. The third book in the series, *Come Away with Me*, is out now. Keep reading for a look at the first chapter.

Please know that I never intended to release a Broadway book while Broadway—and indeed much of the world— was shut down. We hadn't yet heard of COVID-19 when I wrote *It's In Her Kiss*. I hope you've been able to stay safe and healthy, and I certainly hope life starts to get back to normal soon. In the meantime, I hope this book was able to provide a brief escape from reality.

Thanks as always to my family for your support. I edited this book during a global pandemic, which made it extra challenging for a number of reasons, most notably that we were all trapped at home together. Thank you for helping me find time to meet my deadlines when the world is upside down.

Thank you to my editor, Linda Ingmanson, for making

this book shine. And as always, a huge thank you to my critique partner, Annie Rains. Special thanks to Heather Siebert for answering all of my (many) questions about Broadway. All mistakes are my own.

A huge thank you to all the readers, bloggers, and reviewers who've read my books and supported me along the way. Love you all!

xoxo

Rachel

KEEP READING

If you enjoyed *It's in Her Kiss*, turn the page to read the first chapter of *Come Away with Me*, the third book in the Midnight in Manhattan series.

COME AWAY WITH ME

CHAPTER ONE

P iper Sheridan stood on a darkened Brooklyn sidewalk, staring at the bar on the opposite side of the street. A lavender, dragonfly shaped logo gleamed above the door, announcing the bar's name. Inside, Piper could see a handful of people on stools, laughing and sharing conversation, out for a drink with friends after work. Maybe a date. Piper used to be one of those people.

Now she was standing outside, heart pounding, palms damp as she summoned the courage to cross the street and go inside. It had been over a year since she'd gone out in public like this, but she was going to change that statistic tonight. She and her therapist had talked through all the details ahead of time. They'd covered every possible scenario and how Piper would handle it. She was doing this.

One step at the time. That's what Dr. Jorgensen said. Piper glanced both ways to ensure the street was clear, and then she took that first step. And the second. She crossed the street, gaining speed with each stride. With a quick tug at the black wig covering her distinctive auburn locks, she grasped the bar's heavy wooden door and pulled it open.

Immediately, she was enveloped in the murmur of conversation undercut by strains of jazz music. A pink-haired bartender waved in her direction with a friendly smile. Piper spotted an empty stool against the back wall, and she made her way to it before she could lose her nerve and bolt back out the door. She took off her jacket and hung it on the hook under the bar before sliding onto the stool. Then she reached for a lavender drink card on the lacquered bar top in front of her, not because she didn't know what she wanted to drink, but because she wanted something to do with her hands, something to focus on. If she fidgeted, she'd only draw unwanted attention to herself.

Piper wasn't exactly a household name—not yet anyway —but after four seasons as Samantha Whitaker on the legal drama *In Her Defense*, she was fairly recognizable here in New York, and for tonight, anonymity was key. If she made it through the evening without a panic attack, she'd be one step closer to going out in public as herself again.

She wanted to reclaim that freedom, but even more urgently, she needed to get her panic attacks under control before her audition next month. This movie could launch her career, and it was ultimately what had driven her out of her apartment on this Thursday night.

"Welcome to Dragonfly," a cheerful female voice said. "I'm Josie."

Piper looked up to see the pink-haired bartender standing in front of her. "Hi."

"Know what you're having?" Josie asked.

"A negroni, please." She'd chosen her drink before she left her apartment. Tonight, she was following her own script, no unnecessary decisions to elevate her anxiety.

"You got it." The bartender turned around to mix the drink.

Piper darted a quick glance around the bar, relieved to find that no one was paying her any attention. Her chest was tight, and claustrophobia pressed over her, the feeling that everyone was just *too close*, even though she had the wall to her left and an empty stool to her right. She had to recondition herself not to react this way in public places, and tonight was a first step toward achieving her goal. She blew out a slow, measured breath.

The door to the bar opened, and a petite brunette entered. Piper tugged a strand of black hair into her face as recognition dawned. That was Eve Marlow, the host of *Do Over*, a popular makeover show on the *Life & Leisure* channel. She and Piper didn't exactly know each other, but they'd met in passing at industry events, and Piper didn't want to be recognized tonight. Her entire strategy for the evening hinged on remaining anonymous.

"I see who you're looking at, but don't get any ideas," Josie said playfully as she placed a glass tumbler on the bar in front of Piper. "She's married."

"She is?" Piper was genuinely surprised at this news. She hadn't heard anything about Eve getting married, but sure enough, as her eyes tracked to Eve's left hand, she saw a gold band glinting there.

"I'm her wife," the bartender said with a wink, and Piper wasn't sure whether or not she was joking. "It was a small, private event."

"No shit?" Piper said as she spotted a matching ring on Josie's finger. "You're married to Eve Marlow?"

"I am," Josie confirmed as she moved down the bar. Perhaps to make her point, she leaned across the counter and kissed Eve.

Well, that was interesting, and Piper was glad to have

Eve's attention elsewhere tonight. She lifted her drink and sipped, feeling the burn of liquor all the way to her stomach. She blew out another breath, and some of the rigidity left her spine. This was okay. She was okay. She'd finish her drink, maybe have another, stay long enough to be able to report tonight as a success to Dr. Jorgensen, and then she'd go home.

"Is this stool open?" a woman's voice asked, and Piper became aware of someone standing beside her, uncomfortably close.

Her muscles stiffened, tension prickling across her scalp. She kept her eyes on her drink, watching the reddish liquid as it glistened beneath the bar's track lighting. "Yep."

"Thanks," the woman said cheerily as she slid onto the stool.

Piper caught a glimpse of jean-clad legs and knee-high black boots. She lifted her drink for another sip. Maybe she'd only stay for one drink after all. A hand strayed across her vision as her new neighbor reached for the drink card.

"These specialty drinks sound so good," the woman said after a moment. "What did you get?"

Piper darted a glance in her direction to see if that question was meant for her. The woman sitting beside her had shoulder length blonde hair and hazel eyes, which were crinkled at the corners as she smiled at Piper. "Mine's a negroni," she said, answering the woman's question, grateful that she found no hint of recognition in her neighbor's eyes.

"Oh," the woman said, lips pinching. "Too bitter for me."

Piper hummed noncommittally as she returned her gaze to her drink.

The bartender approached. "Welcome to Dragonfly. I'm Josie. Do you know what you'd like to drink?"

"Hm," the blonde said. "I'm torn between the Midnight in Manhattan and the Broadway Bubbles."

"They're both really good," Josie told her. "The Midnight in Manhattan is cooler because of the mint, where the Broadway Bubbles has a bit of a bite."

"Let's go with the Midnight in Manhattan," the blonde said. "Lemon and mint sound like a winning combination to me."

"Perfect," Josie said. "I'll be right back with that."

The blonde sighed as she settled on her stool. "Come here often?"

Piper glanced to her right, and yep, her neighbor was making another attempt at starting a conversation with her. Maybe she'd come in looking for a hook up. This was a gay bar, after all. "No. You?" She surprised herself by tacking on that little question, since she really wasn't trying to get into a conversation.

"First time," the blonde said. "I'm a flight attendant, just in town for the night. One of my coworkers recommended this place, so I decided to pop in for a drink."

Did she even know it was a gay bar? Maybe she was just talkative. That was probably part of her job description. And maybe Piper should indulge her to keep from focusing on the fact that she was in a room full of strangers. Actually, this was one of the scenarios she and Dr. Jorgensen had rehearsed. "Seems like a nice place," Piper said.

"And bonus, I don't have to worry about being hit on by any of the men in the room," the blonde said with a sly wink. Okay, so she did know.

Piper let out a soft laugh. "That *is* a nice bonus."

Josie reappeared in front of them, setting a glass containing an opaque liquid on the bar.

"Thank you," the blonde said, tapping her finger

thoughtfully against the drink menu. "So, what's the deal with this rumor about the Midnight in Manhattan? Did you make that up?"

Intrigued, Piper peeked at the menu, noticing the italicized line beneath the blonde's finger: *Rumor has it, it you drink one at midnight, you'll fall in love before the end of the year.*

Josie laughed. "I could tell you I made it up, but I could also tell you that it worked on me and several of my friends, so I wouldn't discount the rumor." With a wink, she walked off.

"There's no way a drink could make me fall in love," the blonde said, "but I guess it can't hurt, right?"

"You want to fall in love?" Piper asked.

"Well, not tonight, obviously, since I don't live here, but I'm a romantic at heart, so I wouldn't complain if the right woman were to come along and sweep me off my feet."

"Where are you from?" Piper asked, because it seemed the only safe part of that statement to respond to.

"North Carolina," the blonde said as she sipped her drink. "Mm, this is delicious. Ever been?"

"Once," Piper told her. She'd filmed a bit part in a movie there a few years ago. "The mountains are beautiful, although I only got to see them in passing."

"Oh, that's where I live," the blonde said. "My family's just outside Asheville. I love it there, even though I'm hardly ever home."

"Do you fly somewhere new every day?"

"Almost. I'm a long-range flight attendant, so I typically travel for four or five days at the time, then go home for two to three days, and then I'm off again."

"That sounds exciting but exhausting," Piper commented.

"It is both of those things," the blonde agreed with a laugh.

"How did you get into that line of work?"

The blonde swirled her drink, staring into its opaque depths. "I'd always wanted to see the world, and since I was young and on a budget, this seemed like a good way to make it happen. It's been amazing, but I'm actually moving on at the end of next month."

"You're quitting?" Piper asked.

"Yep. I think it's finally time to stay in North Carolina long enough get my own place and put my interior design degree to good use."

"Ah," Piper said, intrigued by this woman who'd spent however many years flying around the world, traveling so often she had no home of her own. "Where do you live now?"

"With my parents," she said, scrunching her nose. "I know that sounds super lame for a woman my age, but I couldn't justify paying rent when I'm only home two days a week."

"It's not lame," Piper said. "It sounds practical."

"I guess it is." The blonde smiled, drawing Piper's attention to her lips, soft and full and glistening with a combination of lipstick and her drink. "I'm Chloe, by the way."

Piper dropped her gaze to her negroni. *This* was why she'd intended to keep to herself tonight. She could give Chloe a fake name, but somehow that felt disingenuous. They'd only just met, but Chloe seemed so open, so honest, so *real*. It was refreshing. "I'm...trying to be anonymous tonight. Sorry."

～

CHLOE CARSON SIPPED HER DRINK, cheeks puckering slightly from its tart flavor as she watched the mysterious woman sitting beside her. She was about Chloe's age, probably late twenties or early thirties, with striking blue eyes. A cascade of shiny black hair tumbled over her shoulders, but it was a bit *too* shiny, and it didn't match her eyebrows, leading Chloe to think it was a wig. What kind of woman came to a bar in disguise and unwilling to share her name?

The kind Chloe wanted to get to know, apparently.

"Why didn't you just give me a fake name?" she couldn't help asking.

"Good question," the woman said with a shrug. "That would have been easier, wouldn't it?"

"Yep," Chloe told her. "But this way is more intriguing. So, tell me something less revealing. What brings you to this bar tonight?"

"Trying to prove something to myself," she said as she sipped the reddish liquid in her glass. "And you?"

"Just didn't want to be alone in my hotel room," Chloe told her. "I like to be around people."

"I guess that makes you good at your job."

"It certainly helps," Chloe agreed.

"So you aren't here looking for someone to take back to your hotel room?"

Chloe narrowed her eyes at her neighbor. Was she flirting? She looked vaguely familiar, which gave Chloe the impression she might be a public figure of some kind. And she was probably in the closet. Why else would she be in a gay bar, hiding her identity? "Not necessarily, no," Chloe answered her question. "I'm not usually a one-night stand kind of girl, but my job makes it hard to maintain relationships, so I've been known to indulge occasionally if I meet the right person."

The raven-haired woman held Chloe's gaze. "I'm not the right person."

"No?"

The woman shook her head, looking away. "I'm just here for a drink."

"That makes two of us, then."

ALSO BY RACHEL LACEY

Love in the City

Read Between the Lines

Vino and Veritas

Hideaway

Midnight in Manhattan Series

Don't Cry for Me

It's in Her Kiss

Come Away with Me

Almost Royal Series

If the Shoe Fits

Once Upon a Cowboy

Let Your Hair Down

Rock Star Duet

Unwritten

Encore

The Stranded Series

Crash and Burn

Lost in Paradise

The Risking It All Series

Rock with You

ABOUT THE AUTHOR

 Rachel Lacey is a contemporary romance author and semi-reformed travel junkie. She's been climbed by a monkey on a mountain in Japan, gone scuba diving on the Great Barrier Reef, and camped out overnight in New York City for a chance to be an extra in a movie. These days, the majority of her adventures take place on the pages of the books she writes. She lives in warm and sunny North Carolina with her family and a variety of rescue pets.

facebook.com/RachelLaceyAuthor

twitter.com/rachelslacey

instagram.com/rachelslacey

amazon.com/author/rachellacey

bookbub.com/authors/rachel-lacey